RULES OF CRIME

Books by L.J. Sellers

The Detective Jackson Series
The Sex Club
Secrets to Die For
Thrilled to Death
Passions of the Dead
Dying for Justice
Liars, Cheaters & Thieves
Rules of Crime

~~

The Suicide Effect
The Baby Thief
The Gauntlet Assassin

RULES OF CRIME

A DETECTIVE JACKSON MYSTERY

L.J. SELLERS

THOMAS & MERCER

Printed in the United States of America.

Published by Thomas & Mercer
P.O. Box 400818
Las Vegas, NV 89140

ISBN-13: 9781611098068
ISBN-10: 1611098068

Library of Congress Control Number: 2012917235

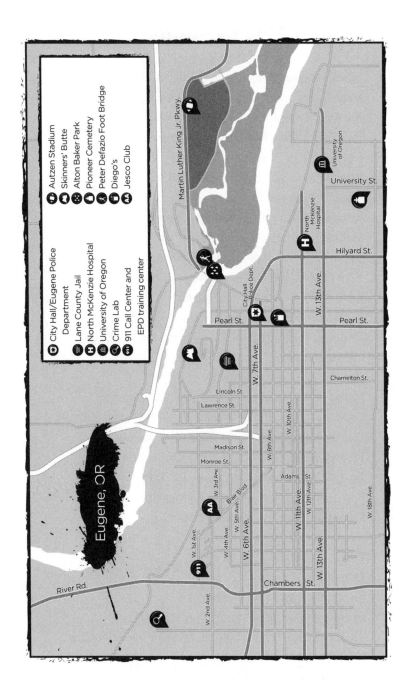

Eugene, OR

Legend:
- City Hall/Eugene Police Department
- Lane County Jail
- North McKenzie Hospital
- University of Oregon
- Crime Lab
- 911 Call Center and EPD training center

- Autzen Stadium
- Skinners' Butte
- Alton Baker Park
- Pioneer Cemetery
- Peter Defazio Foot Bridge
- Diego's
- Jesco Club

Martin Luther King Jr. Pkwy.

University of Oregon

University St.

North McKenzie Hospital

Hilyard St.

City Hall Police Dept.

W. 13th Ave.

Pearl St.   Pearl St.

Charnelton St.

W. 7th Ave.

Lincoln St.

Lawrence St.

W. 10th Ave.

Madison St.

W. 8th Ave.

Monroe St.

Adams St.

W. 3rd Ave.

Blair Blvd.

W. 11th Ave.

W. 12th Ave.

W. 18th Ave.

W. 5th Ave.

W. 1st Ave.

W. 4th Ave.

W. 6th Ave.

W. 13th Ave.

Chambers St.

River Rd.

W. 2nd Ave.

Cast of Characters

Wade Jackson: detective/violent crimes unit
Kera Kollmorgan: Jackson's girlfriend/nurse
Katie Jackson: Jackson's daughter
Jan: Katie's aunt/Jackson's ex-sister-in-law
Carla River: FBI agent
Rob Schakowski (Schak): detective/task force member
Lara Evans: detective/task force member
Michael Quince: detective/task force member
Denise Lammers: Jackson's supervisor/sergeant
Sophie Speranza: newspaper reporter
Rich Gunderson: medical examiner/attends crime scenes
Jasmine Parker: evidence technician
Joe Berloni: evidence technician
Rudolph Konrad: pathologist/performs autopsies
Victor Slonecker: district attorney
Jim Trang: assistant district attorney
Renee Jackson: Jackson's ex-wife/kidnap victim
Ivan Anderson: Renee's fiancé
Dakota Anderson: Ivan's daughter/TV reporter
Jacob Renaldi: Dakota's boyfriend/dog breeder
Daniel Talbot: investor/threatened Ivan Anderson
Gus Striker: ex-con/attends AA meetings with Renee
Dave Lambert: AA meeting leader
Noah Tremel: ex-gang member
Bartolo Diaz: ex-gang member
Lyla Murray: assault victim
Karen Murray: Lyla's mother
Brooke: Lyla's friend/reports her missing
Taylor Harris: Lyla's friend/last person to contact her
Ashley Harris: Taylor's sister
Rick Drummond: canine officer

RULES OF CRIME

CHAPTER 1

Saturday, January 7, 4:35 p.m.

Renee Jackson slipped out of the AA meeting a little early. She felt queasy and didn't want to talk to anyone after it adjourned. She shouldn't have come. The secret drinking had been going on for weeks and the meetings weren't helping. It was time to check herself into rehab, but she couldn't bear the thought of her daughter knowing she'd relapsed again.

Renee zipped her jacket against the cold, shuddering at the gray sky that seemed to swoop down and smother her. Christ, it was getting dark already.

Could she get away with one more shot of vodka without Ivan or anyone noticing? Probably. She kept a thermos in her car, along with a bottle of mouthwash. Her ex-husband, Wade, the detective, would know as soon as she spent five minutes with him. So far she'd managed to avoid him.

She waited for the traffic to pass, then trotted across the street to her car, pumps clicking on the asphalt. She'd parked in the alley next to the vegan restaurant, not wanting anyone to see her Acura RDX near the Jesco building. Not that anyone she knew would be in the Whiteaker neighborhood. If Eugene, Oregon, had a slum, this would be it.

As she entered the alley, two men stepped out from behind a large dumpster. Renee took in the details in a quick painful breath. Baggy jeans, heavy jackets, and tattooed necks. *Gang members.*

Her heart skipped a beat. Could she make it to her car, get in, and lock the door? Or should she turn and run? She froze, paralyzed with fear. Too late to dash to her car. Renee spun and started back toward the Jesco building. She wanted to run but was afraid to, feeling like she had a predatory animal behind her that would only be excited by the chase.

Then she saw Dave, the meeting leader, hurrying across the street toward her. Thank god. A car barreled past just as he stepped onto the sidewalk.

"Renee, I wanted to talk." He smiled but his tone was serious as he reached for her arm.

She glanced over her shoulder. The gang members turned and headed back down the alley. Had they ever been a threat? Was the alcohol making her paranoid already? It usually took years.

"I'm sorry, Dave, but I don't have time. That's why I left early."

"I know you're drinking, Renee. Can I do anything to help?"

It took every ounce of self-control she had not to burst into tears. God, she hated herself. "I've got it under control. Thanks, though."

She spun and trotted to her car, unlocking it with her clicker. Guilt made the sick feeling in her gut worse. Dave was a good guy, but she wasn't ready to talk about her drinking. Her fiancé, Ivan, was a casual drinker and she knew she had to make an impossible choice. Renee started the car and backed toward the street. In the growing darkness she heard the rumble of an engine. Was it the thugs' car? She peered down the alley, framed by thick shrubs on one side and the back side of the restaurant on the other. Headlights came on.

Renee glanced back at Blair Boulevard, saw no traffic, and gunned her car into the street. Out of the corner of her eye, she saw Dave head into the Jesco building. He glanced back at the revved sound of her car and Renee looked away. She raced to the first stoplight and grabbed the thermos of vodka from under her car seat. After a quick sip, she shoved the metal container back. Her chest warmed and her panic subsided.

An engine rumbled behind her. Definitely not a new-model car. The same sound she'd heard in the alley. She glanced in her rearview mirror. A red lowrider idled behind her. The driver wore a heavy dark jacket and had a shaved head. Why were they following her?

Renee jumped on the green light and sped through the intersection. To go home, she needed to turn right, cross downtown, and head south. She'd moved in with Ivan a month ago, giving up her apartment by the park to live in his plush, oversize home in the foothills. She wasn't ready to face him, but had no idea where she was headed. Was she ready to quit drinking? *Damn!* How had she let herself get into this mode again? Would the cycle ever stop?

Instinctively, she drove toward the university area.

A quick glance in the rearview mirror told her the lowrider was still back there, but not directly behind her anymore. She gave a little sigh of relief. They were just going in the same direction. It happened all the time.

She kept driving, not knowing where, not making conscious decisions. Ten minutes later she parked a half block from Serenity

Lane, an inpatient rehab center for drugs and alcohol that was tucked into a quiet residential area near the campus. The site of the building made her cringe. Renee reached for the thermos and took a long slow belt of vodka. She'd never make it through the door this sober. Grabbing her phone from the seat, she started to text Katie, but couldn't do it. Not yet. She'd call her daughter later, after she checked in.

Renee clutched her purse and stepped from the car. Would three times be the charm? Would this be her last inpatient stay? Fortunately, she ran her own publicity business now and didn't have to explain to any boss why she needed a month off. One foot in front of the other, she forced herself to start down the sidewalk, toward the building with the glass door she knew so well.

The lowrider was suddenly there, only five feet away on the street. In the twilight she felt, as much as saw, two guys burst from the car. Renee screamed and started to run. Her heel snapped and she stumbled. From behind, a thick hand slammed over her mouth and yanked sideways. She kicked wildly, panic driving her. She connected with a shin, and the man punched her in the neck. She choked on her cry and hot tears filled her eyes.

Another pair of arms wrapped around her torso and dragged her into the back of the car.

In six seconds, she'd disappeared off the sidewalk. Had anyone witnessed it? A student bicycling to class?

The car raced forward, away from the rehab building and student housing. Renee struggled, but the alcohol made her weak and the man shoved her to the floor. Strong, thick fingers dug into her flesh and quickly bound her hands and mouth with duct tape. A knife was suddenly in his hand and her heart missed a beat. She screamed into the duct tape but only made a gurgling sound. The man cut her purse strap from her shoulder, then rummaged through her pockets until he found her cell phone. He shoved her last little hope into his jacket pocket, then taped her ankles together and tied a blindfold around her head. *Oh god, what did they want with her?* Panic exploded in painful shards in her lungs and she couldn't think straight.

A few minutes later, the car stopped, and the men dragged her from the floor of the backseat and shoved her into the trunk. They slammed down the lid and left her alone in the small dark space, trussed like an animal on its way to slaughter.

Heart pounding, all she could think was, *I wish I'd finished the thermos.*

CHAPTER 2

Sunday, January 8, 11:48 a.m.

Wade Jackson stepped off the boat, relieved that the trip was over. He turned back and offered his hand to Kera as she climbed down after him, looking radiant. Her sun-kissed skin glowed and her bronze hair shimmered in the bright sunlight. The sight of her made him smile, despite the seasickness that had plagued him all morning. Their snorkeling adventure had been great at moments, but he was glad to move on to something else. A flash of guilt joined the nausea in his stomach. Kera loved every minute of their time in Maui, and he was trying to be a good vacation partner. But his mind was restless and he looked forward to an afternoon of getting caught up on the stack of hot-rod magazines he'd brought with him.

"Are you okay?" Kera asked, as they entered their hotel room twenty minutes later. "You're awfully quiet."

"I felt a little queasy the whole time we were out there," Jackson admitted. "But it's going away now."

"I'm sorry. We should have bought some Dramamine."

"Meds are for wussies." Jackson laughed. He took his share. "I'm fine. Hungry though."

His phone, which he'd left in the hotel room, rang for the first time in two days. A strange anticipation came over him. He'd missed the urgency and adrenaline that came with most of his calls. He looked at the screen. Why was his daughter calling him?

"It's Katie," he told Kera before answering.

"Dad, I'm sorry to bug you on your vacation, but Mom is missing."

The word *missing* triggered a wave of emotions: fear, anger, relief. "What do you mean by *missing*?"

"She didn't come home last night and she's not answering her cell phone."

Jackson had one thought: *Renee had started drinking again and landed in jail or in the hospital.* But he had to be diplomatic with his daughter. "Have you called her friends? Or possibly the hospital?"

"Ivan and I have called everyone. He even called the jail." Katie was on the verge of tears. "I know what you're thinking and you're probably right. But she's never disappeared before."

His daughter had a point. In all the years of marriage to Renee, despite her daily consumption of vodka, she'd never gone AWOL. She preferred to drink at home, where it was safe. "Don't worry, Katie. We'll find her. I'll call the department and put out an attempt-to-locate. And I'll get the next flight home." Jackson glanced at Kera, who was raptly listening to his end of the conversation. She looked worried but not upset.

"I'm so sorry, Dad. I hate ruining your vacation. You never take time off." His fifteen-year-old daughter burst into sobs and it tore his heart. Katie was mature beyond her years—from having an alcoholic mother and a workaholic father—and rarely cried. But her grief was not about his ruined trip to Hawaii. She was coming to terms with the fact that her mother had relapsed again, and possibly done herself irreparable harm.

"Let me talk to Ivan for a minute." Jackson felt surprisingly neutral about Renee's fiancé, even though she'd moved in with him after only a few months of dating.

Ivan Anderson came on the phone, sounding calmer than Katie but still with an edge to his voice. "Hello, Jackson. I've called the department about filing a missing-person report, but they said it was too soon."

"Twenty-four hours is the policy for adults, but I'll work around that and get patrol officers looking for her car." After twenty years in the department, he was a senior detective and carried a little clout. "She was in her car, correct?"

"Yes. She left the house around three yesterday afternoon to go shopping and never came home. I've called her friends, her sister, the hospitals, and the jail. I don't know what else to do."

"It sounds like you've covered it, but I need her license plate number. She was driving her Acura?"

"Yes. I'll be right back."

After a minute, Anderson came back with the information and Jackson jotted it down. He hesitated, then said, "I hate to ask this, but how has Renee been acting lately? Any sign that she's been drinking?"

"The other night she seemed a little slow to react to something and I wondered if she'd been drinking. But she has the Ativan prescription and it has that effect sometimes."

Memories of his ex-wife and her intoxicated behavior flooded Jackson's head. Renee tended to get horny and needy when she drank, but he couldn't ask Anderson about it. He couldn't even believe they were having this conversation and suspected his discomfort would get worse before Renee surfaced. "Sometimes when she first starts drinking again after a dry spell, she calls her mother. Have you talked to Betty?"

"No. Renee never talks about her mother."

"You should call her just to see if she's heard from Renee." Jackson started to look for his return ticket. "I have to call the airline and the department. With any luck, I'll be home tonight."

"Thanks, Jackson. Sorry to interrupt your vacation."

"It's okay." And it was. His brain was clicking and his adrenaline flowing. He'd missed the feeling. They said good-bye and hung up. Jackson turned to Kera, careful to hide his feelings. "I'm sorry about this, but I feel like I have to go back. Katie is distraught."

"Of course. I understand." The fine lines on her forehead scrunched up as she studied his face. "I think you're relieved. You were getting bored here, I could tell."

"No. It's been great to have so much time with you." He pulled Kera in for a hug.

She hugged him back, then lightly punched his arm. "Don't bullshit me, Wade. You're a workaholic, and you look engaged for the first time in days." Kera laughed, a melodic hearty sound that always made him smile. "Don't worry. I'm okay. We had three great days together, and getting this much sun in the middle of winter was a lifesaver. Make the calls." She smiled, shook her head, and started for the shower.

Three hours later, after securing some last-minute tickets by mentioning he was a detective investigating a missing person, they were on a flight to Eugene, Oregon.

CHAPTER 3

Monday, January 9, 6:01 a.m.

Jackson's cell phone beeped and he forced himself to get up. Staggering toward the bathroom, he nearly tripped on the suitcase he'd dumped on the floor when he got in around three that morning. He still wasn't used to this house after fifteen years in the previous one he'd shared with Renee. He'd grown up in this home, but the master bedroom had belonged to his parents, who'd been murdered in the living room on the other side of the wall. Thinking about it made him uneasy. Had moving in here with his brother been a mistake? It was temporary, he reminded himself. They planned to renovate, sell, and split the equity. But Derrick, now a long-haul truck driver, was never home. Jackson was glad for the privacy, but it meant he would be stuck with all the work.

In the shower he alternated between hot and cool water until he felt awake, then took his prednisone and dressed for work. The steroid was supposed to keep the fibrosis around his aorta from growing. He brewed a half pot of coffee, filled his tall travel mug, and headed out. He had to pick up Katie from Ivan's house and get her settled back in. He would make his daughter breakfast, reassure her that Renee would be found, then take her to school. With her mother missing, Katie might not want to go to classes, but staying home would just make her worry more.

Twenty minutes later he pulled into Ivan Anderson's driveway, looked up at the high-end home, and experienced a flash of envy. No wonder Renee had moved in with the guy. Would Katie get spoiled on her weekend stays and start to resent the modest older house they shared with his brother? He hoped not. His daughter wasn't materialistic compared to other kids her age, but she was going through a phase of rapid physical and mental change and it worried him.

He knocked on the door, self-conscious about arriving so early, but decided that Renee's fiancé probably hadn't slept much either.

Anderson responded almost immediately. He was shorter, thicker, and older than Jackson, but he dressed well and looked like he took good care of himself. "Thanks for coming." He gestured for Jackson to come in. "Katie said she'd be out in a minute. I know I'm not much comfort to her and she's anxious to go home."

"Anything new?" Jackson looked around the foyer—noting the marble floor and the one-of-a-kind chest of drawers—and realized how shabby his place was in comparison. He forced himself to stop thinking about it. He was never home anyway.

"No. Renee's mother hasn't heard from her and the police haven't called."

"I'll head to the department and fill out a report. Give me her credit-card and cell-phone information, so I can start making calls."

Anderson scowled. "What will that tell you?"

"We need to know if she's using the credit card and where. Same with the cell phone."

"You think she might have walked away from us on purpose?"

Jackson wanted to say, *If Renee is drinking, anything is possible.* But he chose to be diplomatic. "I have no idea. I just know that this is how we find people."

"Her cell phone is on my T-Mobile plan, and I'll see if I can find her credit-card statement."

As Anderson walked away, Jackson's daughter ran up the hall, her overnight bag bouncing against her side. In the last year, she'd grown four inches and lost her baby fat. And now with her hair pulled back, he missed the wild curls.

"Dad!" She threw herself into his arms with an intensity he hadn't seen since she was ten and got lost at the fair for a few minutes.

Jackson held Katie tight, his love for her threatening to overwhelm him. "It'll be okay. We'll find her." He almost said, *I promise*, then bit it back. Renee's disappearance baffled him and might not turn out well. After twenty-two years as a police officer, it was hard to be optimistic.

Anderson came into the room and his cell phone beeped somewhere inside his jacket pocket. Jackson and Katie both turned at the sound. *Let it be Renee*, Jackson prayed, *for Katie's sake.*

"It's a text," Anderson said, surprised. He clicked open the text, and his face went slack as he read. "Oh god. Someone has kidnapped Renee. He wants a hundred thousand dollars."

His daughter let out a yelp, then covered her mouth with her hand, while the news sucked the air out of Jackson's chest and left him speechless. It took a moment to process a response. He'd never handled a ransom kidnapping and didn't think his department had either. "Let me see the text."

"He wants the money in cash by three o'clock today or he'll start cutting off her fingers." Anderson's voice broke at the end, and his hand trembled as he passed Jackson the phone.

Katie burst into tears, and Jackson wanted to smack Anderson for saying that out loud. The guy was so stressed out he was oblivious that Katie was even there. He touched Katie's shoulder. "Please go wait in the car, sweetheart. There's no need for you to hear this."

"No! She's my mother." His daughter struggled to get control. "I'm not a little kid anymore. I have a right to know what's going on."

Jackson didn't want to waste time arguing. He read the brief text: *I have your girlfriend. I want $100,000 in cash today or I'll cut off her ring finger. You have until 3. Do not call the police or I'll kill her. Put the money in a backpack and wait for my instructions.*

Jackson forwarded the text to his own cell phone so he'd have a copy, then grabbed his notepad and jotted down the number the text came from. It was probably a cheap burner phone from Cricket, and the kidnapper—if he was smart—had thrown it away already.

"What does it say?" Katie asked. "Is Mom okay?"

"She's fine." Jackson tried not to visualize Renee tied up and terrified. The image came to him anyway. "We have to notify my sergeant and she'll contact the FBI. They have the resources to handle this."

"No!" Anderson grabbed his phone back. "I want to just give him the money and handle it ourselves."

For a moment, Jackson was tempted. It was the least risky course of action for Renee—and for Katie, who would be devastated if anything happened to her mother. But he couldn't do it. "Don't ask me to cover up a crime. I'm a police officer. "

"You're still on vacation," Katie pleaded. "Let's just do what he says and get Mom back."

Jackson hugged his daughter. "I'm sorry, honey. We have to do this right so we can catch the guy."

"I don't care about catching him. I just want Mom to be safe." She pulled away and wrapped her arms around herself.

Anderson said, "I'm not asking you to let him get away with it. I just want to pay the money and get Renee back. Then you can go after him."

Jackson sensed Anderson knew something he wasn't telling. "You said 'him' like you know who it is."

A long moment. "It might be a client of mine, Daniel Talbot. He lost a lot of money last year on a hedge fund I got him into and he sent me some hostile e-mails."

"We'll take this to my supervisor, get a warrant, and go arrest him."

"What about Renee? What if she's in a basement or storage unit?" Anderson lost control and choked up. "She could die while Talbot's in custody. We may never find her."

Jackson's chest tightened in a painful squeeze. "We have to get the FBI involved, set up a money drop, and follow him. It's the only way to catch the perp and get Renee back safely."

Anderson covered his face with his hands. "I can't let Renee die because of my financial mistake."

Jackson looked at his daughter and tried to sound confident. "Renee's not going to die." He caught Anderson's eye. "Don't say that again."

"Sorry."

Jackson turned to Katie. "Please call your aunt Jan. I think you should stay with her until this is over."

She started to protest, then stopped. "I can tell her about Mom, can't I?"

"Yes, since Jan is her sister. But please don't tell anyone else."

"What about Harlan?"

Katie's boyfriend had gone back to being just her good friend, and Jackson was relieved. "No. The fewer people who know, the safer your mother is." Jackson wasn't sure that was true, but it was how the department operated.

"I'm not going to school today."

Jackson didn't care about that. As long as Katie wasn't alone while he tried to get her mother back. "Call Aunt Jan." He turned to Anderson. "Let me see the e-mails Daniel Talbot sent you. We might as well print them as probable cause for a warrant."

Anderson headed down the hall and Jackson followed. On the way Anderson asked, "Why did he wait until this morning to contact me? He's had Renee since Saturday." Color had drained from his golf-tanned face.

"To make you worried and eager to part with the money." It was just a guess. Jackson wasn't a kidnapping expert, but he needed Anderson to stay calm.

They entered a large corner office with a wall of windows that had closed blinds. Anderson apparently had no use for the view. The stockbroker sat down at his computer and pulled up his e-mail on one of the monitors. After a quick search, he had two e-mails open and the printer rumbling. Jackson looked over Anderson's shoulder and read the text. It had no greeting and no signature, but the sender's address read *dtalbot@comcast.net*.

You call yourself a money manager? That Trenton hedge fund you suggested lost 26% of its value in the second quarter, but you said to hold. Now it's down another 18%. I've lost half my invest-ment. Eighty thousand. Gone! You'd better make good on this.—DT

The second e-mail simply said, *I'm filing a lawsuit and report-ing your firm to the Better Business Bureau. You're incompetent and shouldn't be allowed to give anyone financial advice.*

"What do you know about this guy?" Jackson reached for the printouts.

"Just that he owns a construction company. He was a new client with a chunk of cash and asked me to put him into something aggressive. That means high risk, which I explained."

"Did you meet him in person?"

"Yes, why?"

"What's he look like?"

"He's in his early fifties. He wore jeans and looked like he's spent a lot of time outdoors. You know, a tanned, lined face."

"Any reason to suspect he might be violent or unpredictable?"

"Not at the time."

"Has he filed a lawsuit?"

"No. He knows it's almost impossible to prove fraud or negligence in the market. It was just a bad trade."

"Let's get down to the department." Jackson moved toward the hall.

"Shouldn't I start liquidating the cash?"

"If you plan to pay."

"You don't think I should?"

"I can't advise you one way or another. Department policy. And I'm sure the FBI won't either." No one wanted the financial or emotional liability.

Back in the living room, Katie was seated on a couch, staring at her cell phone.

"Did you get a hold of Jan?" Jackson asked.

"Yeah, she's leaving work now. She'll meet us at her house." His usually playful daughter had never looked so serious. It crushed him to see it. He hated that he couldn't protect her from everything.

Jackson turned to Ivan. "I'll drop Katie off, then head into the department. I'll be in touch as soon as we have a plan. Do not contact Talbot."

Jackson bounded up the stairs from the underground parking lot and hurried to the area that housed the Violent Crimes detectives. Just seeing the group of crowded desks and wall-to-wall filing cabinets calmed him. This was his real home, the lifeblood that defined him and gave him purpose. Moving to the new department building next year wouldn't change that. The feeling wasn't about the physical space. It was the energy that pulsed through the people who worked here and their shared pursuit of making things right. Jackson clicked on his computer, dropped his carryall to the floor, and started toward Lammers' office.

Rob Schakowski, a longtime partner in the unit, looked up from his desk. "You're back early. The vacation was that good?" Schak started to say something else, then stopped, most likely from the look on Jackson's face.

"Renee's been kidnapped and I have to see Lammers."

"Holy crap."

Jackson wanted to say more, but it already felt like too much time had lapsed since the perp's contact. "I'll update you soon." Schak would probably get assigned to help him with the case.

His boss' door was closed so he knocked once and pushed it open.

Sergeant Denise Lammers stood by her window. At the sound, she spun, looking startled to see him. "What are you doing here? You're not supposed to be back until Thursday." She was Jackson's size—six feet, two hundred pounds—but on Lammers it looked bigger.

"My ex-wife has been kidnapped."

"For fuck's sake." She stared at him for a long moment, assessing the seriousness of his statement, then plopped into her chair. "What does the perp want?"

"A hundred grand. But I'm not the target. Renee's fiancé, Ivan Anderson, got the text."

"Where is he now?"

"Liquidating assets into cash."

"Let me get the FBI on the line and we'll do a conference call." Lammers gave Jackson an odd look. "We've got a new liaison over there. I met her last month but I'm not sure about her yet."

While they waited for the agent to pick up, Lammers asked, "How was your vacation? I mean, up until it was interrupted."

"Relaxing."

"Liar." Lammers gave him a knowing grin.

The FBI supervisor came on the line. "Agent River." Her voice was deep, smooth, and confident.

"Sergeant Lammers here with Detective Jackson. We have a kidnapping. Jackson's ex-wife, Renee Jackson." Lammers looked over at him for confirmation. Jackson nodded. When Renee had mentioned she was engaged, he'd hoped she would change her name when she got married. Now he just wanted her to survive.

"Kidnapped? As in, for ransom? Or simply abducted?"

"The perp demanded a hundred grand," Jackson said.

Agent River made a low whistling sound. "That's pretty steep for a police officer. This must be personal."

"I'm not the target," Jackson said. "Renee's fiancé, Ivan Anderson, got the text. He's a stockbroker and he thinks one of his disgruntled clients might want his money back."

"Is Anderson there with you?"

"No. He's rounding up the cash," Jackson said. "He intends to pay."

"How much time do we have?"

"Until three today. But he took her late Saturday afternoon."

"That's a little odd. Did you get proof of life?"

"No. Just a text."

"Not good. She may be dead already." They heard a shuffling noise, like someone moving into action. "I hope we have enough time. I'll get the tech guys and a mobile surveillance team down here from Portland and round up the local field agents who are available. We'll set up a command post at the target's house."

"Be discreet," Lammers said. "He may be watching the house to see if Anderson brings in law enforcement."

"Don't worry, we're not going in with a big FBI sign on the side of a van." Agent River tried for levity. When no one responded, she asked, "Who's the disgruntled client?"

"Daniel Talbot. I printed out some angry e-mails he sent Anderson recently."

"Fax those over to me, along with the text he sent. We'll get a surveillance team on Talbot as soon as we can."

"He owns Evergreen Construction," Jackson added.

"Good to know," River said. "Give me the target's address and we'll meet nearby in forty minutes."

"Ivan Anderson lives near the corner of Fortieth and Braeburn. We can confer in the parking lot of the Catholic church on Willamette."

"What's nearby? I'm still learning my way around Eugene."

"You'll pass a huge memorial park on the right."

"I'll see you in forty."

Lammers clicked off. "We'll let them take the lead, but I want you and Schak on the task force." His boss stood abruptly, as if she'd just remembered something. "I can't make the meeting with Agent River because I have cases to assign and I have to see the chief today."

"I'll keep you posted."

"We'll get her back, Jackson."

CHAPTER 4

Monday, January 9, 8:45 a.m.

Lara Evans stepped into Lammers' office and grinned at her boss. After the sergeant had made her a permanent member of the Violent Crimes Unit, Evans had stopped feeling intimidated. As the newest member, she got assigned all the weird grunt cases, so she didn't have much to lose. "Good morning."

"You can stop smiling. I've got another unconscious assault victim for you."

Evans sat, not worried yet. Her first solo case had involved a woman who'd come out of a coma after two years and claimed foul play. How bad could this one be?

"So far, we don't have a name. Someone dropped her off in front of the ER Saturday night without any clothes or ID." Lammers handed her a sheet of paper. "The hospital sent a report but there's not much to go on. Please head over to North McKenzie now. We need to identify her."

"Has anyone filed a matching missing-person report?"

"Not yet."

"I'm on it." Evans stood. "Was she sexually assaulted?"

"I don't know. They just said she had internal bleeding and required surgery."

"I'll do my best to get the bastard."

Evans grabbed her jacket and shoulder bag and headed for the parking lot under the building. Her bag was stuffed with tools for processing crime scenes, and she wondered how many she would get to use this time. She'd worked several homicides with her mentor, Wade Jackson, but she'd never been assigned the lead on a murder yet. Her last two assault cases had been homeless men attacked by other homeless men. Not her favorite. The witnesses were often incoherent and the attacks were usually provoked. This new case both intrigued and intimidated her. Starting with no ID and no witnesses would be challenging.

The drive out to the hospital took twenty minutes. That was one of the best things about Eugene and all its outlying communities. It was a real city, but you could still get almost anywhere by car, bus, or bicycle in less than half an hour. Evans also loved the cultural diversity—university students, Latinos, hippies, yuppies, outdoor enthusiasts, and environmentalists—Eugene had it all. A stimulating change of pace from bland, boring Fairbanks, Alaska, where she'd grown up. As a teenager, she'd tried to create her own excitement and it had landed her in trouble, including an overnight stay in jail. Her parents had kicked her out and she'd headed south and never looked back. She understood that on some level joining the police force was a way of keeping her own energy under control.

The victim was in the intensive care unit, so Evans stopped by the nursing station first. She caught the attention of a twenty-something woman in yellow scrubs. "I'm Detective Evans, Eugene Police. I'm here to investigate the assault victim with no ID."

"I'm happy to report that she's showing signs of waking this morning. We're optimistic."

"Tell me about her injuries."

"She has extensive bruising on her back, chest, and abdomen, as well as three cracked ribs and a head contusion. She also had internal bleeding in her peritoneal cavity, which Dr. Gau repaired. We think she was beaten with a stick or a bat. As long as the bleeding subsides, she should make a full recovery in time."

Evans made notes as quickly as she could, then looked up. "What time did she come into the ER?"

The nurse clicked a few computer keys. "She was admitted at eight thirty-six Saturday night. I'll take you to her room."

Evans followed the nurse past two open-door rooms with sleeping patients, both older women, tubes coming out of everywhere. She'd visited the hospital just weeks ago to question the homeless man who'd been stabbed and it wasn't any easier this time.

The nurse pushed open the next door, making no effort to be quiet. At first glance, the victim looked like a high-school girl, with smooth flawless cheeks and long black hair that stuck to her forehead with sweat. Thin clear oxygen tubes came out of her nostrils and her breath was shallow. As Evans stepped closer to take a picture, she realized the victim was probably closer to twenty.

The nurse flipped through the patient's chart, then said, "She was admitted wearing nothing but a pair of pink socks. She'd been left on the sidewalk in front of the ER entry."

"Did anyone see her being dumped?"

"I don't know. You'll have to talk to the ER staff."

"Was she sexually assaulted?"

"There was no sign of it."

"Did you do a rape kit?"

"Not without the patient's permission."

Evans wondered if she needed a subpoena to get a rape exam done on an unconscious woman. If there was semen in the victim's body, she needed the DNA to build a case. But first, she had to figure out who this woman was. Would someone be able to identify her from a photo with the ventilator mask on? She turned to the nurse. "Have you had calls from anyone looking for her?"

"Not that I know of."

"I need to take photos of her injuries, especially if she has bruising."

"She's bruised all right." The nurse closed the door, then came back to the bed and raised the victim's nightgown.

Ugly brownish-purple splotches dotted her breasts and stomach. What had he used to hit her? Evans had never seen anything like it. She quickly counted eight strikes, then moved in for close-up photos. If the victim didn't regain consciousness soon, Evans would get a lab technician in here with a high-powered camera to document the bruises. If she ever found the weapon, they might be able to match the patterns and use them in court.

"Does she have bruises on her back too?"

"Yes, but we can't roll her without a doctor's permission."

A small moan seeped out of the patient. They both snapped their heads to stare at the young woman. She opened her eyes and focused on Evans.

"What's your name?" Evans asked.

"Lyla."

"Last name?"

She looked blank, then her eyes rolled back in her head. As the beeping heart-rate monitor slowed, the nurse pushed Evans aside. An alarm filled the room and the nurse yelled, "She's coding."

The noise and adrenaline made Evans want to jump in and help with the rescue. She'd worked as a paramedic before joining the force, but this wasn't her territory now. She moved back as another nurse rushed into the room and began compressions. Soon after, a man with a crash cart rushed in. The three worked together as if they'd practiced, while Evans watched, thinking the scene played like a low-production movie.

After two shouts of "Clear," followed by shocks to Lyla's heart, the monitor began to beep steadily.

"She's probably bleeding internally again," the desk nurse said. "I'll page Dr. Gau, then let's take her to surgery."

Evans stayed against the wall as they wheeled the bed with the unconscious woman into the hall. Would Lyla survive? Evans worried that the next time she saw the victim would be at her autopsy. Who had beat her so viciously? Rage flooded her system. No matter what happened with Lyla, she would find the bastard who had done this and put him away. Evans left the now-empty room and headed downstairs to the emergency department.

The petite woman behind the desk looked too young to be a medical professional. Or maybe it was the diamond stud in her nose. Evans tried to keep her face impassive as she introduced herself. "What's your name and title?"

"Suri Gupta. I'm an intern."

"I need to know who was on duty Saturday night when the unidentified assault victim came in. And I'd like to see the records for her admittance."

"I was at the desk, covering a shift for someone." Suri's eyes lit up at the memory. "I've never seen anything like it."

"I need to ask some questions. Can you get someone to cover you for a few minutes?"

Suri looked over at the adjacent room, where only three patient-family clusters waited. The furnishings were so plush it could have been a vacation lodge foyer. *Maybe not the best use of patients' money*, Evans thought.

"It's not very busy," Suri said. "And Carson will be back from his break soon. What do you want to know?"

"Did you see who dropped off the victim?"

"No, but a woman in the waiting room did. Or at least she saw something."

"What's her name?"

The intern clicked her keyboard and scanned her monitor. "Claire Ferguson. Do you want her phone number? I made a point to ask for it."

Evans decided the intern was smarter than she looked. "Thank you." She dug her recorder out of her bag. "Take me through what happened Saturday night. Step by step, with as much detail as possible."

"I saw the woman from the waiting room, Claire, rush out the door. I was dealing with someone else and didn't think much of it until she came back in. She shouted that someone had dumped an unconscious naked girl on the sidewalk outside." Suri paused to put on lip gloss, and Evans willed her to focus.

The intern continued. "I called back to the central desk for a gurney, then ran outside. The patient was right next to the curb, lying on her back, and naked. I checked her vitals, then let the guys with the gurney load her up and take her in. After that, I had to return to the desk."

"What time did this happen?" Evans wanted confirmation.

The intern checked her log sheet. "Eight thirty-six p.m."

"Did she wake up or speak to anyone while she was in the ER?" Evans made notes as she talked.

"I don't think so."

"Anything else I should know?"

"She had excrement on her back and traces of soil on her chest."

It took a second to process the information. "She had shit and dirt on her skin?"

"Yes." The intern pressed her lips together, as if holding back a comment.

Disgust joined the rage that pulsed through Evans' veins. She'd heard of domestic violence cases that involved humiliation, occasionally torture, but they were rare. Most offenders just went after their partners with their fists. This bastard was especially sick.

"Did they save samples of the debris?"

"I doubt it. I'm sure they just wiped it all off. The patient's pulse was only forty-five and she had blood oozing out of her mouth. They were in lifesaving mode."

"Her name is Lyla, and they're in the same mode again right now."

In the car, Evans called the witness and left a message, asking for an immediate return call. What if Lyla died before she could identify her? The department hadn't had a Jane/John Doe homicide in years and she'd never handled a case like this. From a photo a witness had taken, she'd recently tracked down a perp who'd assaulted a homeless man, but this case was unique. At least she had a first name now.

As she drove to the department, her cell rang. Evans glanced at the phone on the seat beside her and saw that it was her boss. She touched her earpiece and answered. "Evans here. What have you got for me?"

"A young woman is here to report that her friend, Lyla Murray, is missing. You might want to come in and talk to her."

"That's our victim. I'm on my way."

"How is she?"

"She coded while I was in her room. They're operating on her again now."

"Damn. No statement?"

"Just a first name."

"Maybe the friend has information. She's waiting here in the lobby."

"I'll be there in twelve minutes."

Evans passed through the code-locked door into the small lobby. The black plastic chairs and stained, indoor-outdoor carpet made it look dingy, like a cheap motel. She couldn't wait for the department to move into the new building. A young woman paced back and forth, oblivious to her presence. The girl was tall and thin, with a protruding brow that gave her a wolfish look, but her bright-pink sweater made her look harmless.

Evans caught her attention. "Are you here about the missing person?"

"Yes. My friend, Lyla Murray." Her voice quivered. "She's not answering her phone and no one has seen her since Saturday night."

"Let's go back to my desk." Evans grabbed a missing-person sheet from the holder on the wall. Someday, nothing would be done on paper. Everything would go directly into digital files, and she looked forward to that day. She already took as many interview notes as she could on her iPad, but some conversations were brief and conducted standing up, so her process was still a messy mix.

Evans led the young woman down the L-shaped corridor to the Violent Crimes area, where the desks were crammed together amid filing cabinets and boxes of paperwork.

"What's your name?" Evans grabbed an extra chair and motioned the girl to sit, then clicked on her iPad.

"Brooke Hammond."

"And your relationship to the missing person?"

"She's my friend."

"Do you live together?"

"No. Well, sort of. We share a kitchen in a quad on campus."

"You're both University of Oregon students?"

"Yes. This is my second year, but Lyla's a freshman."

"Describe her to me."

"She's about five-six, with long black hair. She's pale and pretty and a little bit overweight."

Evans tried to come up with a gentle way to break the news and couldn't. "Lyla is in the hospital. She was assaulted and is undergoing a second surgery for internal bleeding."

Relief washed over Brooke's face. A moment later she practically shouted, "But I called the hospital yesterday and they didn't tell me anything."

"They have privacy rules."

Brooke bit her lip. "What do you mean *assaulted*? Was she raped?"

"We don't know. But she was beaten with something like a bat. Do you know who would do that to her?"

"No." The girl's eyes slid away.

"Who is Lyla's boyfriend?"

"She doesn't have a boyfriend."

"I think you know something. Why not tell me?" Evans didn't understand her need to protect the assailant. Unless it was a person in power. Evans had experienced her own degradation at the hands of a police officer when she was a teenager, so she knew what it was like to fear reporting someone. "Is it someone in authority?"

"I don't know."

"Did her father beat her?"

"Her father is dead and her mother doesn't live here."

"What is the mother's name? I need to contact her. Lyla may not make it."

Brooke's hand flew to her mouth. Evans had meant to startle her, hoping she'd take this seriously enough to report what she knew.

"You think she might die?"

"Her heart stopped and they had to shock her back to life. If they can't find the bleeding in time, yes, she could die."

Tears rolled down Brooke's face. "Her family is in Grants Pass, and I think her mother's name is Karen."

"Karen Murray?"

"Yes. I can probably find her contact information in Lyla's room if the manager will let me in."

"I'll head over there soon. First I want to know what you can tell me about Lyla. Did she have new friends in her life? Had she started using drugs?"

Brooke shook her head. "I don't know. We've only been quad-mates since late September and she doesn't talk about herself that much." She let out a little sob. "I should have asked more questions. I talk too much and Lyla let me. Now I realize I don't know much about her."

Evans wasn't moved by her guilt. She still thought Brooke knew something she wasn't telling. "Did she ever mention any men? Someone she might have been dating?"

"She likes a guy in her biology class but they're just friends."

"What's his name?"

"Josh Reynolds."

Evans remembered the shit and dirt on Lyla's skin. If a boy-friend hadn't done it, who had? And why? A startling thought came to mind. But it was the wrong time of year for hazings. "Does Lyla belong to a sorority or some university club?"

Again, Brooke looked away. "She mentioned a secret sorority once and said she might join. But I didn't hear anything else after that."

"What sorority?"

"I don't know. I don't think it's a traditional one. I think they're in a private house off campus."

Evans was intrigued. She'd attended a community college in Seattle and the idea of a sorority was alien to her. A secret sorority sounded like trouble. "What's its name?"

"I don't know."

"Do you know any of the members?"

"No." Brooke shifted in her chair. "I have to go. I have a chemistry test I can't miss." She stood and picked up her backpack. "I'll visit Lyla tonight at the hospital."

Disappointed, Evans extracted Brooke's address and cell phone number, then handed her a business card. "I'll walk you out."

Brooke stuffed the card in her back jeans pocket and followed without comment.

CHAPTER 5

Monday, January 9, 8:35 a.m.

After the conference call, Jackson sent a vague but reassuring text to his daughter, then called Ivan Anderson. He'd done a thorough background check on the man before he even let Katie stay over on a weekend with Renee and her new boyfriend, and Anderson had come up squeaky clean. But everyone had a private life and Jackson didn't really know the man. Didn't want to. His ex-wife had lost her overnight parent privileges the last time she'd started drinking again, then slowly earned them back after getting out of rehab. Jackson knew Katie was coming to the age where he could no longer control where she spent her time, and it terrified him. Yet it was also strangely liberating.

Anderson answered on the second ring. "What's happening?"

"We're meeting with FBI agents in half an hour in the parking lot of the Catholic church, near Thirty-Ninth and Willamette. Where are you now?"

"I'm in my office downtown. I've cashed out most of my stocks and the exchange is wiring the money. Normally, it would take longer, but I made some calls."

Jackson hated the thought of paying the perp, but he kept quiet. "I need Daniel Talbot's home and work addresses."

"Give me a second. The info is in my files somewhere."

Jackson keyed Talbot's name into the AIRS database while he waited. Two speeding tickets and a menacing complaint came up. Talbot's neighbors had filed a report, claiming Talbot had threatened them over a tree that straddled their property line. He'd denied the charge but let the neighbors trim the tree. The department hadn't pursued it, but now Talbot's threat seemed like part of a pattern.

Anderson came back on. "Talbot lives at 3355 Stoney Ridge Road and he owns Evergreen Construction, which has an office on East Amazon."

Jackson made Anderson repeat the addresses as he wrote them down. Talbot's home address matched what was in the database from 2002, so it seemed likely he still lived there. But if Talbot was the kidnapper, where would he keep his victim? As the owner of a construction company, he probably had access to empty and half-built houses around town, so the possibilities were numerous and daunting. Jackson felt a stab of guilt for thinking of Renee as *the victim*, but he had to stay objective or they'd kick him off the case. He was glad it wasn't Kera or Katie who'd been taken, and he felt guilty for thinking that too.

"What do you know about Talbot that can help us?" Jackson asked. "Where is he building houses?"

"You think Renee might be at a construction site?"

"Just speculating."

"I don't know. Can you get a list from his office?"

"We'll do that."

"What else can I do?"

"Think about who else might have taken her. We don't want to get locked into one suspect."

"I have no idea. I don't associate with criminals."

"Then we have to think about who Renee might have known or come into contact with recently." Jackson couldn't imagine his ex-wife crossing paths with thugs either…unless she was drinking. "Have you searched Renee's things?"

"For what?"

"Alcohol."

"Why would I? How could that be relevant?"

"Renee is unpredictable when she drinks. She may have met someone and bragged about your money. I'm just trying to make sense of this."

"I don't believe it."

Anderson didn't know her yet. "Send me a current picture of Renee. We may need it to show witnesses."

The file arrived a minute later and Jackson printed five color copies. He stuffed them in his carryall and grabbed his jacket, but left his coffee on the desk. Adrenaline had been building in his system since the ransom text had come in and he felt a little toxic. This would be a round-the-clock case and he likely wouldn't sleep much until it was over. He had to pace himself.

He stopped by Lammers' office to give her Daniel Talbot's information and she promised to have patrol units watch his locations until the FBI had people in place. Next Jackson updated Schak on the case and asked him to join the FBI meet-up. He left the building feeling better now that processes were in motion and Schak was on board.

Driving up Willamette, Jackson passed the huge grassy memorial park and thought about his murdered parents. Their ashes were interred in the Westhaven building, but he never visited. When he wanted to feel close to them he hiked Spencer Butte and gazed out at the city below, something they'd done as a family many times during his childhood. He'd wanted to spread their ashes on the butte, but his brother had insisted they put them in a vault where he could visit. Jackson didn't understand the notion, but it had been important to Derrick, so he'd let it go. Just as he'd let his brother stay in their parents' house instead of selling it. Some people had a harder time moving on.

He pulled into the church's parking lot, mostly empty on a Monday morning, and spotted Agent River's car immediately: a dark-gray sedan in the corner, far from the entrance to the three buildings. He parked next to her and climbed out. Another cold gray day that threatened snow. River got out too and they met behind the vehicles. She was tall for a woman, five-ten he guessed, and broad shouldered. Her eyes caught his attention: one was pool-water blue and the other a greenish brown. The difference was a little odd, but it didn't detract from her face, which was otherwise pleasant. Jackson couldn't guess her age.

"Good to meet you," he said, after introducing himself. "I hear you're new to Eugene."

"I transferred from the Portland bureau when Jensen retired."

"I look forward to working with you." Agent Jensen had been great to work with so Jackson was optimistic. On the other hand, Agent Fouts, who'd been with the Eugene bureau for decades, was a little crusty.

"Likewise." River offered her hand and Jackson was pleased by her strong grip. Big hands too. River continued, "Sergeant Lammers says you're her best detective, so I'm glad to have you on the task force. The fact that it's your ex-wife in captivity makes me a little nervous though."

"I left Renee two years ago and stopped being in love with her long before that. I can be objective and professional."

"Good. Do you have children together?"

"A daughter. She's fifteen."

"This must be hard for her."

"Yes."

Another gray sedan pulled in. Jackson was glad for the clump of trees that protected them from view of the street. Anyone noticing the group of dark sedans and people in matching dark suits would know law enforcement was up to something. He hoped the kidnapper wasn't patrolling the area. Anderson's home was a half mile away on the other side of the memorial park.

River introduced Agent Fouts, a slim silver-haired man with a moon-shaped scar on his left cheek.

"We've met." They shook hands anyway.

Jackson had worked with Fouts twice: once when a fanatic had bombed the Planned Parenthood clinic, and more recently when a group of Mexican drug runners had killed a man whose brother had stolen their meth.

Fouts' scar was new and Jackson was curious. It was easy to assume the agent had been hurt in the line of duty. But the scar in Jackson's own eyebrow was the result of a long-ago dog bite, a pathetic incident with no guts and no glory. Still, it had left him with a deep distrust of dogs.

"Our first cash-ransom hostage and it's your ex-wife." Fouts laughed. "I wish someone would take my ex-wives. Both of 'em."

Jackson wanted to respond with his own joke but words failed him. Renee was Katie's mother. Losing her would devastate his daughter. "I'm not the target. Her fiancé is."

"I heard. Is he going to pay?"

"He's getting the money together now."

Another blue Impala like Jackson's pulled in and they all watched Rob Schakowski climb from the car. Barrel shaped with a buzz cut, Schak looked more like an aging marine than a homicide detective, but he was sharp and had a bulldog-like tenacity. This time Jackson made the introductions.

"Where's Anderson?" Agent River looked around. "I need to get a pen register on his phone immediately."

"He's coming."

River looked at her watch. "It's eleven fifteen, so we have less than four hours until their cutoff. Fouts and I need to stay in the house with Anderson so we can be there for every communication. Agent Torres will be out here before the money-exchange deadline. We need to stall this for as long as we can. Once the tech van is here, they'll be able to triangulate any calls or texts off nearby towers."

"What's our part?" Jackson asked.

"Get Renee's cell info and have the company ping her phone. It may not be on her person but the kidnapper may still have it." River snapped her fingers. "We need to locate Renee's car too if we can. Both pieces of information will help us know where he abducted her from and where she might be now."

"I have an ATL on her car already," Jackson offered. "I told them to call you when they located it."

River gave him a quick look of appreciation. He understood that she was heading this investigation.

Anderson drove up just as someone came out of the church and walked over. Before the churchwoman could ask what they were doing, River showed her badge. "FBI. We'll be out of here in a few minutes."

The woman spun around without a word.

Anderson hurried over. "I don't have the money yet but it's coming. What's the plan?" His voice was wound a little tight.

River made more introductions. "We'll head up to your house to wait for his next communication. I'll ride in the back of your car with my head down in case he's watching the house. Fouts will park behind the house and come in the back. After that, one of us needs to be with you at all times."

"I have to return to the bank later to pick up the cash."

Agent River reached over and touched Anderson's arm. "I can't advise you whether to pay or not but we'll talk about some options later. Do you have other family members at home?"

"No. My daughter Dakota spends some weekends with me but she has her own place."

"How old is she?"

"Twenty-four."

"Where is she now? I'm a little concerned about her safety."

"She's at work and I haven't told her about Renee yet. She's a television reporter."

"If we don't grab the kidnapper at the money drop today, I'll assign someone to watch her."

"She'll hate that. She's so independent." Anderson rubbed his face. "I'm sure she's safe at work but once she leaves the station…" His voice trailed off.

Jackson was more worried Dakota would be tempted to break the story on live TV, but it didn't seem like the right time to share his distrust of newspeople.

River turned to him. "You can retrace Renee's steps just the way you would a missing person. If we find out where she disappeared from, it might give us information. Any questions?"

Schak suddenly spoke up. "Have you handled a kidnapping before?"

River gave him a crooked smile. "I've worked several child abductions but never a ransom demand. They're not very common." She held up a small spiral brochure and grinned. "But I have my handy guidance."

Jackson tried not to groan. The point person on Renee's kidnapping was reading off cue cards.

"Will we have more people in place for the money drop?" Schak shifted on his feet and glanced at Jackson.

"Yes. Agent Torres and Agent Gilson will join us soon. And we have the tech and surveillance teams coming down from Portland. Let's make sure we all have each other's phone numbers." River displayed hers for them to key into their devices. "And of course we'll use our radios when we're in proximity."

After a moment of quiet while they keyed in phone numbers, River said, "Let's go."

Jackson had mixed feelings about his role in the case. He wanted to stay with Anderson and be on the spot when the kidnapper's next demand came in. Yet sitting around waiting was not his strong suit and he was glad to have leads to track down.

As the FBI agents drove away, Jackson turned to Schak. "Renee's cell phone is with T-Mobile. Will you follow up on that while I try to retrace her steps on Saturday?"

"Will do."

Jackson sat in his car for a moment, trying to map a plan of action, and realized he needed more information. He called Anderson. "You said Renee went out shopping Saturday. Where did she go?"

"I think she mentioned Macy's, but I'm not sure. I don't really pay attention to those things."

"What was she wearing?"

"Why?"

"It could be important." Renee had certain clothes and shoes she always wore for high-end shopping. *Dressy but comfortable*, she'd explained.

"Jeans and a red sweater, I think."

"Thanks." Jackson hung up, knowing Renee had not gone out shopping Saturday afternoon. What had she been up to?

He started his car and headed for the liquor store at Twenty-Ninth and Willamette. If Renee had lied to her fiancé about where she was going, then alcohol was involved. Unless she'd taken up cheating too, but he didn't believe that. Renee was a good person...with a devastating disease.

CHAPTER 6

Jackson drove down Donald Street, worried about Eugene, where he'd lived his whole life. Once a small, peaceful, college town, it had grown rapidly since he'd joined the department two decades ago. Now unemployment, meth, and gang rivalries threatened citizens' safety, while jail beds lay empty for lack of funding. Still, there was nowhere else he wanted to live. An hour from the ocean and forty minutes from the mountains, it was ideal. He loved Eugene, with its lush, green-canopy streets, beautiful university, and lack of skyline. Except for the goofy retirement home at the base of the butte, Eugene didn't have any tall buildings. But it was big on trees and even the gas stations planted shrubs and flowers.

The state-run liquor store was tucked into a shopping center and took up less space than a two-car garage. The rows upon rows of colorful bottles made him uneasy. So much poison in such a small space. No one else was in the store, except the man behind the counter, who set down his reading device and looked up at Jackson. Gray haired with concave cheeks, the clerk looked headed for an early death.

"Detective Jackson, Eugene Police. I'd like to know if you've seen this woman." Jackson set a paper copy of Renee's photo out on the counter.

The clerk nodded. "Sure. She started coming in regularly about a month ago."

"When did you see her last?"

"Last week. Maybe Thursday. She always came in around noon. I figured she was on her lunch break." Concern pinched the man's face even further. "Is she okay?"

"I can't say." Jackson picked up the photo. Renee had been drinking again. That's all he needed to know here. Still, he asked, "Do you work Saturdays?"

"No. Melissa is here on the weekends."

"Will you give me her contact information?" Jackson wrote it down but realized the case would probably be resolved before he connected with the weekend clerk. He tapped the photo. "How often did she come in and how much did she buy?"

The clerk hesitated, but only for a second. "I saw her once or twice a week and she bought a fifth of Reyka vodka each time."

"Thanks." Jackson slid the photo back and left the store. Renee was still in the phase of moderating her consumption, telling herself it would be different this time.

Now what? During their marriage, Renee had done most of her drinking at home, with occasional nights out with friends. But if she was hiding the booze from her fiancé, Jackson didn't know how to predict her behavior. He started his car but sat for a minute, trying to get into his ex-wife's head. Saturday afternoon she'd told her fiancé and daughter she was going shopping, but she'd dressed in jeans, so she wasn't headed to Macy's. And she had been buying fifths from the liquor store, so she likely wouldn't have gone to a bar. What was on her mind?

Guilt and fear.

This was his ex-wife's second relapse after an expensive month in an inpatient facility. With a pending marriage to a wealthy man, who thought she was still sober, Renee had more to lose than ever. In a heartbeat, Jackson knew where she might have gone on Saturday. To an AA meeting, hoping for a miracle that would relieve her of her desire to drink. But which meeting? There were so many possibilities. The Jesco Club, where she first attempted sobriety when Katie was seven, had sentimental value. He would start his search there.

Before leaving the parking lot, Jackson checked his phone. No voice mail and no texts. When would the kidnapper text with instructions for the money drop? The deadline was only a few hours away. He drove toward downtown, crawling along Willamette in lunch-hour traffic. The Jesco Club was just west of the city center in the Whiteaker neighborhood. Once considered Eugene's slum, the neighborhood had experienced a revival in the past few years, with restaurants, breweries, and art shops opening and thriving. Still, the area held a hub of apartment buildings known as Heroin Alley, and many of Eugene's gang members called it home.

The two-story, boxy Jesco Club sat right off the sidewalk with little parking. Most of its attendees no longer had the privilege to drive, so parking wasn't an issue for them. Jackson pulled up against the curb and hoped for the best. His dark-blue city-issued sedan was more likely to be vandalized than ticketed.

Inside the building, Jackson heard a meeting in session somewhere in the back, but stepped over to the little office where the receptionist was on the phone. He knew the club was more than just a place for alcoholics to meet, but he didn't know what else went on there. While he waited for the receptionist, a thirty-something woman with Raggedy Ann red hair, to end her call, he tried to decide how much he could say. He also worried about how little she would tell him.

Finally, he had her attention. "I'm Detective Jackson, Eugene Police." He showed his badge, which he didn't often do. "A woman disappeared Saturday afternoon and she may be in great danger. Her sister thinks she attended a meeting here, right before she went missing. Was there an AA meeting Saturday afternoon? And were you here at the time?"

"Yes, at four o'clock." The receptionist nodded, her eyes lighting up.

Jackson pulled out Renee's photo and handed it to her. "Did you see this woman?" He purposely did not use Renee's name.

The receptionist pressed her lips together and glanced at a poster on the wall. "The meetings are anonymous. I'm not sure if I can say anything."

"Her life is in danger and I'm not asking you to tell me who she is. I just need to know if she was here."

The woman nodded.

"Did she stay for the whole meeting?"

"I was only here until five, but the meeting went beyond that. You should talk to Dave Lambert. He runs the Saturday group." She clicked her keyboard a few times, then jotted down contact information on a blue sticky note. "He works at Fred Meyer and you can probably catch him there now."

"Thanks."

On the sidewalk outside, Jackson stood and looked around, again trying to get inside his ex-wife's head. Where had she parked? Renee was impatient and would leave her car wherever it was most convenient, even if it meant paying a ticket later. She also tended to be late, which exacerbated the parking issue. He noticed the alley across the street. Had the kidnapper snatched her from this neighborhood? Their suspect, Daniel Talbot, was upper middle class, or he had been before the recession. This neighborhood was not a likely hangout for him unless he'd followed Renee here. Or sent someone to do the dirty legwork.

Where had Renee gone after the meeting? To Market of Choice to pick up something for dinner? And where the hell was her car?

Jackson checked his phone again. No messages. He found the number he'd recently keyed in and called it.

"Agent River here."

"It's Jackson. I've confirmed that Renee was at an AA meeting at the Jesco Club on Blair Street on Saturday afternoon. I hope to have more information soon."

"That's interesting. I don't know Eugene well yet, but the Whiteaker area has a reputation. Why would she go there?"

"The Jesco Club is respected in the treatment community and Renee had started drinking again."

"So Talbot could have followed her there. Or a desperate drunk could have grabbed her after the meeting, hoping to score a big payoff from her rich boyfriend."

"That's what I'm thinking. Or maybe Talbot hired someone to abduct her."

"Can you find out who else was at the meeting?"

"Probably not without a subpoena. I'm heading over to talk to the group's leader now."

"Keep me updated."

"Any word from the kidnapper?"

"Not yet, but Anderson is signaling me now."

CHAPTER 7

Monday, January 9, 12:55 p.m.

Anderson had just walked into the room, carrying two zippered bank bags. Agent Fouts had followed, then stepped outside to the patio. Anderson's mouth was open in distress. River clicked off her call, assuming he'd heard from the kidnapper.

Instead, he yelled, "What do you mean 'a desperate drunk could have grabbed her'? What was Renee doing in the Whiteaker area?"

"Jackson says she attended an AA meeting. You weren't aware of her, um, participation?"

"No." Anderson's face tightened and his eyes registered pain. "But I wish she had told me. I would have supported her."

"I'm sorry." River was reminded that no matter how much money people had, it didn't shield them from bad news or diminish the anguish of being human and caring for other imperfect people. "The good news is that we know where she was before she was abducted. It might help us locate her."

They were in Anderson's office and the space was larger than the living room in her new house. The vaulted wood ceiling, high-end French doors, and Persian area rug made River think a hundred grand to a kidnapper probably wouldn't devastate Anderson's finances. She respected him for being willing to pay the ransom.

The cell phone on Anderson's desk beeped and they both jerked in surprise. Anderson grabbed it. "Another text." He tapped the phone, then studied the message. "He wants the money now."

"What? It's only one o'clock." A surge of worry. "I thought we had two more hours." River grabbed the device and read the message: *Put the money in a plastic bag. Put the bag in a backpack. No tracking devices or she dies! Get in your car and start driving toward town. More instructions soon.*

Damn! She wasn't ready. The pen register that would record all numbers and calls on Anderson's phone was with the tech people, who weren't here yet. Portland to Eugene was nearly a two-hour drive, even at eighty miles an hour.

Live in the moment, River reminded herself. *This is the new reality.* She forced herself to look and sound calm. Inner peace would follow. "Let's do what he says. Do you have the cash?"

"Yes. But it wiped me out."

River didn't have a response. She opened the French doors and said, "Time to move, Fouts."

As she turned back, Anderson announced, "I'll get a backpack," and rushed into the hall.

River sat down on the couch, hit reply, and keyed in, *I need more time. I don't have all the money yet.* She had to stall as long as she could. A standard crisis-negotiation tactic.

Fouts rushed in, smelling like a cigarette butt. She showed him the ransom text rather than summarize.

"We have to use a tracking device." He handed the phone back to her.

"Of course. I brought one with me. We'll put it inside a bundle of cash in case the kidnapper transfers the money right away."

Anderson's phone beeped in her hand. A new text: *No more time. Get moving!*

River didn't bother to respond. She opened her laptop and clicked open fonefinder.net. She keyed the kidnapper's number into the search box and waited. It was a different Cricket phone. She'd done a similar search earlier with the number the perp used for the first contact. A call to the Cricket office revealed the service had been paid for in cash on Friday, then disconnected this morning, leaving her no way to trace the phone. The perp had obviously purchased several burner phones and was likely moving around, using different towers. They were dealing with someone smart and careful.

Using her own cell phone, she called the manager at Cricket again while keeping an eye on Anderson's device. "Agent River. I have another service that needs a ping immediately." She read the number slowly.

"This will take a minute. I'll get back to you as soon as we have it." The manager didn't ask any unnecessary questions. She'd discussed the kidnapping with him earlier and he'd promised to be available to her all day.

"I'm staying on the line until I get it."

"Okay. Excuse me for a second."

She heard talking in the background so she looked down at Anderson's phone. No communication. She stood and began to pace.

Anderson rushed into the room with a hiking backpack. "Will this work?"

She nodded and touched her earpiece to indicate she was on the phone. "Agent Fouts will help you pack it."

Anderson set the backpack on his desk, grabbed one of the bank bags, and started pulling out bundled stacks of cash. River had never seen so much money, let alone handled so casually. Early in her FBI career, when she'd been Carl instead of Carla, she'd worked a few drug busts that netted cash, but the largest take had been thirty thousand.

She watched Fouts place a palm-size tracker into the middle of a stack of hundreds and hoped he knew what he was doing.

The Cricket manager came back on the phone. "We sent the signal, now we're waiting for the bounce."

"Good. Can you find out if other phones were purchased at the same time as these two? And if they were, let's ping those numbers as well."

"I'll check."

River paced the room, which now felt smaller than she'd first thought. This was happening so fast. She'd never worked a ransom kidnapping before. What if she messed it up? Anxiety exploded in her chest, like little firecrackers going off, and she felt paralyzed. It was like being frozen in that moment right before your car plows into another one on an icy road. She took two long deep breaths and repeated her new mantra several times: *I can only do my best and control my part in this.* The thoughts calmed her and her body relaxed. She hadn't experienced a prolonged episode of anxiety since her operation and she hoped the worst of it was in her past— shed like the false male exterior she'd worn for nearly forty years.

She glanced over to see if anyone had noticed her bad moment. They were still bundling cash and stuffing it into the pack.

The Cricket manager's voice was suddenly in her ear. "We got a signal off a Sprint tower at 1810 Chambers."

"Thanks. Ping the number every five minutes and text me the tower locations."

She started to hang up, then remembered her other request. "Were there more phones bought with cash at the same time?"

"Yes, but they were all separate transactions. So the others may not be connected to this crime. I can't track them without a court order."

Damn. "I don't have time for that. This is going down."

"I'll do what I can with every number you get direct contact from."

"I'll be in touch."

Fouts was nearly finished packing the bag, so she called Jackson. "River here. We've had more contact. The money drop is happening now but we don't know where yet. Be ready to move into place at a moment's notice."

"I'm near downtown so I'll just park and wait."

"Good. Call Schakowski and alert him as well. I'll call Torres and Gilson. We'll be on the nonrepeater channel."

"I thought we had until three."

"This guy is smart. He uses a new phone for each contact. And he's not likely to tell us where to drop the money until the last minute."

"What about Daniel Talbot?" Jackson asked.

"We haven't located him yet. He doesn't seem to be at home or at his office but we're watching both."

"He could be our man."

"We'll know soon." River glanced over at Anderson and Fouts. They looked ready. "We're taking off now." She hung up, knowing Jackson wouldn't care. They didn't have time for polite formalities.

"I'll ride with Anderson again and keep low in case they're watching. Fouts, follow in your own car."

Pulse pounding, a cell phone in each hand, she led the way out of the house. Despite feeling rushed, this wasn't a worst-case scenario. The abductions she'd worked in Portland had involved children and she'd known the victims were likely being molested and/or killed while she and her team scurried around, doing what little they could do. They had moved with great expediency to catch the predator, but with little hope of saving the victims. In this situation, a woman's life was being bartered and they had a chance to save her. Getting it right was more important than catching the perp. The pressure was different from any she'd faced before.

Outside, she ran to Anderson's car and climbed into the backseat, where she'd have more room. She was glad he drove a luxury sedan instead of a Mini Cooper.

Anderson started the car but didn't put it in gear. Instead, he turned to face her. "Am I making a mistake paying the full ransom? Should we have filled the bottom of the pack with newspaper?"

She weighed her answer carefully. "This kidnapper is greedy and smart and we may not catch him. But he's probably not evil, and if you give him the money we'll probably get your girlfriend back."

"I hope you're right." His voice caught a little at the end.

CHAPTER 8

As they traveled down Willamette, a text came from the phone company manager: *We lost the signal. Service disconnected.* River had known it would happen but still felt disappointed. She didn't share the information with Anderson. Why worry him?

After a few minutes traveling downhill, the street curved sharply to the left and met up with Eugene's flatland grid. Anderson asked, "Once I hit the downtown area, what should I do?"

"Park and wait."

The instructions came five minutes later as they crossed Eighteenth: *Drive toward 7th and take a right.* It came from yet another number.

She read the directions out loud for Anderson and those on the radio, then texted the Cricket manager: *Ping 541.334.7281.*

As they waited at a four-way stop in the heart of downtown, she glanced out the window and saw a Ken Kesey statue in a small plaza. *One Flew over the Cuckoo's Nest* had always been her favorite movie, but she'd never read Kesey's novels. Now that she lived in his hometown, she might have to.

Anderson's phone beeped again with another text: *Leave the backpack under the sign on the bike path near where the two bridges meet.*

Bridges? That didn't sound good. River had crossed Ferry Street Bridge many times but didn't know Eugene well enough to visualize the drop spot. Into her mic, she said, "CR: Moving toward Ferry Street Bridge. The drop is near the path where the bridges meet." They used their initials for a certain level of discretion, even though other law enforcement could hear them.

Her agents copied back, then moments later, she heard from Jackson and Schak. She tapped Anderson's shoulder. "Do you know where the sign near the bike path is?"

"I think so. I bicycled through there with my daughter once." He glanced back at her. "You're not from Eugene?"

"I've only been here a few months. I worked the Portland office before this." *After growing up in San Diego.*

Anderson started to ask another question but she cut him off. "I have to get people in place."

River instructed her team members to cover the four corners of the bridge.

Jackson came back and said, "Someone needs to be on a bicycle. I'll try to get one of our bike squad officers over there ASAP."

"Copy." She liked his thinking and wished like hell they'd had more time.

"DF: What about the river?" Fouts asked.

"Can we get a team out there in a speed boat?"

"Probably not in time," Jackson said, "But I'll call the sheriff's office."

"Copy. Anyone have the eye?"

The responses were negative. No one had spotted the perp. Another wave of anxiety rolled over her. Converging bike paths. The muddy river high on its banks. A crafty perp on the move. This might not go well. *Whatever happens is meant to be.*

A text came in on her cell phone from the Cricket manager: *T-Mobile tower at 3022 Gateway.* The information surprised her. Why was the perp moving away from the drop spot? Unless there were two—one driving around sending texts, while the other got in place to pick up the money.

Anderson turned off Seventh and circled under the ramp to the bridge. He looked over his shoulder. "I'm going to park at EWEB."

She knew it was the utility company but had never been in this exact area. It was rather bleak and bounded by the river, train tracks, and overpasses.

She notified her team. "CR: Location is EWEB building. Target will soon deliver the package." To Anderson, she said, "Where is the sign from here?"

He pointed up the short incline to where Fourth Avenue met Coburg Road near the bridge.

"Take the handicapped space up front. We need to be able to see as much as possible." The universe would forgive her this once.

Anderson parked, then leaned his head against the wheel, breathing shallowly.

"You okay?"

"Yes." He sat up and turned to her. "What now?"

"We wait until everyone is in place."

After a minute, another text came: *Go! Or this is over and she loses a hand. Maybe a kidney.*

"Damn." She looked around. Were they watching?

"What is it?" Anderson's face looked ashen and sweat beaded on his forehead.

Was he about to have a heart attack? "You have to go now. Find the sign and leave the backpack. If someone approaches you or threatens you, lie on the ground and don't move." She hated having a civilian involved but they had no choice.

She spoke into her mic. "CR: The package is on the way."

Anderson slung the pack over his shoulder and climbed out of the car.

River rolled down her window, but stayed low. "It's going to be fine. He'll get the money and we'll follow him to Renee. If we lose him, he'll let her go anyway." She did her best to sound confident.

Anderson nodded and headed up the sidewalk, looking peculiar: an older man in a gray business suit with a red hiker's backpack.

River hoped Fouts and the others were moving into place. "Anyone have eyes on the bike-path sign?" She grabbed her binoculars from her briefcase and tried to spot it herself.

Fouts responded. "DF: I'm moving down the path on the other side. Bought a bike from a homeless guy."

That cheered her up, but it was brief. Torres and Gilson checked in to say they weren't yet in place at the other end of the bridge.

"Jackson here. I'm on the bridge, but the wrong side and I can't see the bench."

"The bastard picked the right spot." River hated the location. Impossible to reach by car, but with varying elevations and bike paths converging under the bridge.

"DF: On the bike path under the bridge and ready."

"Copy." Nerves jumping, River got out of the car and watched Anderson through the binoculars. He strode up to the short stone wall like a man with a purpose and sat down. He slid the backpack off and set it under the sign. After thirty seconds he stood, stretched, and walked back toward her.

"CR: Package is delivered."

The radio was silent as they all waited.

Suddenly, a dark figure darted out from behind a bush. Black jeans, black hoodie, slim build. The man grabbed the backpack and ran down the path into the curve under the bridge.

River's pulse escalated. "CR to DF, he's got the package and is coming your way."

"I've got eyes on him. He's off the path and headed through the shrubs to the water." Fouts sounded breathless. River heard the sound of metal slamming into concrete, then Fouts said, "I've lost visual."

Agent Torres' voice cut in. "He's under the bridge and I can't see him either."

Fouts was back. "He's in an inner tube and paddling with an oar."

Damn! The fool was on the river and she didn't hear any boat motors coming their way.

"Keep eyes on him." River ran up the sidewalk, signaling Anderson that she was headed for the bridge.

Fouts was in her ear. "He's crossing the river as he floats downstream."

"Where's he gonna come out? Let's get uniforms on the other side." Her voice was breathy from her run.

"Valley River Center. Maybe," Fouts said.

Agent Torres cut in. "I've got him in sight."

"Can you tell where he'll come out of the water?"

"No. He's not really in control."

A long minute of silence as her team watched the perp float away. River caught up to Jackson on the bridge and he pointed at the receding inner tube. "I wonder how far he's going. The river is pretty wild this time of year."

She picked up the perp in her binoculars. "He's gonna get away, isn't he?"

"Maybe not. Unless he's got a bike or a driver waiting for him on the other side."

River accepted the new reality. "As long as he lets Renee go unharmed, I'll consider this a success."

After a moment, Jackson said, "Yes."

A minute later, the tube snagged on something below the surface and flipped over. The perp went under and disappeared into the green swirling water.

CHAPTER 9

Monday, January 9, 11:45 a.m.

Evans popped in her earpiece, called the university's campus police, and asked to speak to Margaret Pearl, their liaison. While she waited for Margaret to come on the line, she hustled down to the break room and put her chicken-vegetable soup in the microwave. She really wanted a cheeseburger, but she'd gained a pound over the holidays with her colleagues bringing in all those baked goods, so she was sticking to healthy lunches for a while.

"Hi Lara. What can I do for you?"

It was nice to hear someone use her first name. Everyone in the Violent Crimes Unit called each other by last names. "I have an assault victim named Lyla Murray. She's in surgery and might not make it. I have to find out what happened to her. Do you have any reports that might help?"

"Let me look." A long pause. "What kind of assault?"

"A vicious beating. And her assailant rubbed dirt and shit on her and dumped her naked at the ER."

Margaret groaned softly. "That doesn't sound like domestic violence. I think they meant to degrade her."

"Have you heard of other incidents like this one?" Evans grabbed a paper towel and pulled her soup out of the microwave.

"Not really. Lyla's not mentioned in any of our incident reports either."

"What about a hazing? Her roommate mentioned a secret sorority Lyla was interested in."

"I've heard rumors about such clubs but this is the first mention of brutal violence."

"Do you have a name or location? Someone who might know more?"

"As a police officer, I'm not exactly students' first choice as a confidant."

"If you hear anything, let me know."

Evans took her soup to her desk and ate quickly, eager to get over to the victim's apartment. She had to contact Lyla's mother so she could make the three-hour drive from Grants Pass. Evans hoped Lyla would still be alive when her mother arrived. Leaving her bowl on her desk, she grabbed her shoulder bag and headed out.

Lyla's address was in a cluster of quads on Seventeenth Avenue, not far from the university. Evans knocked on the manager's door but got no response. Hearing music above her, she trotted upstairs and found the manager cleaning a filthy unit on the second floor. The pregnant young woman looked like she'd had better days—and better jobs.

Evans introduced herself, showed her badge, then asked for the woman's name.

"Tamara Jones. Is this about Kyle?" She hugged her baby-belly, clearly worried.

"It's about Lyla Murray from unit thirteen. She's unconscious in the hospital and I need to contact her mother. I'd like to access her apartment."

"That sucks. What happened?" The manager put down the toilet scrubber and pulled off her gloves. "I've got my master key and it's right down the way."

Evans followed her outside. "Lyla was assaulted. Do you know anyone who might want to hurt her?"

"I don't really know any of the tenants. This is just a job. But I've never had any trouble with Lyla."

The manager stopped three units down and unlocked a bright-orange door. "I probably should stay with you but I've got to get that pigsty ready for tomorrow. Let me know when you leave."

Relieved to be left alone, Evans moved quickly to the desk in the corner. As part of a quad, the apartment was only slightly larger than a bedroom. One interior door was open to a bath-room and the other led to a shared kitchen. Evans noted the room was exceptionally tidy, with a tucked-in bedspread and no clothes or clutter anywhere. And no signs of a struggle. The victim prob-ably hadn't been attacked here. Where were Lyla's clothes from the night of the assault? Unless she had been drunk or high, Lyla hadn't left the house naked. Evans pulled out her iPad and made a note reminding herself to check the hospital for the victim's drug and alcohol content.

She made a quick search for a cell phone, not expecting to find it. The device was most likely with Lyla's clothes or purse, which might have been tossed in the trash by now. The desk drawers held no surprises, except for a stash of chocolate-covered raisins that had turned gray. No address book. Did anyone under fifty use those anymore? She turned on Lyla's laptop and soon found Karen Murray in a contact file. Evans called the number and had to leave a message. She would have preferred to make personal contact but she couldn't delay the information. Lyla might not survive.

"This is Detective Evans with the Eugene Police Department. I'm sorry to inform you that your daughter, Lyla Murray, is in North McKenzie Hospital, undergoing surgery for internal bleeding. Her condition is serious. I'm investigating her assault and I'd like you to call me as soon as you can." She wanted to question Mrs. Murray about possible suspects, but being out of town, the mother might be the last to know if Lyla had a boyfriend.

Evans gave her number, then spent a few minutes glancing at Lyla's recent e-mails. One from a friend named Celia about studying together, one from Square Peg Concerts, and a newsletter from a nursing association. Had Lyla been studying to become a nurse? If so, this world needed her.

Evans shut off the laptop and wedged it into her shoulder bag, alongside her iPad. She would peruse it thoroughly later. She did a quick check of the bathroom and found no blood, drugs, or signs of struggle. Time to head out and check the neighbors. She needed to find out where Lyla had gone Saturday night.

After knocking on the adjacent doors and getting no answer, Evans trotted around the balcony and rapped on one of the opposite units. These two tenants shared a kitchen with Lyla and probably knew her. No one answered at the first door, but a sleepy-looking young man opened the second. Evans introduced herself and held up her badge. "Do you know Lyla Murray?"

"The chick on the other side?"

"Yes, the young woman in unit thirteen who shares your kitchen."

"Sure. Why?"

"Are you dating her?"

He made a face. "No. She's…" He stopped. "Not my type."

"Can I come in? I'd like to ask some questions."

"We can talk here." He stepped outside and closed the door behind him.

Evans wondered what he had to hide. Probably drugs. Or stolen goods. Could be anything. Right now it was not her concern. "When did you see Lyla last?"

"Uhh." He rubbed his already messy hair. "Saturday night. I saw her coming down the stairs as I was going up."

"What time was that?"

"I don't know. Maybe seven thirty."

"Did you talk to her?"

"We said hi, but that was it." He shivered and shifted on his bare feet.

His choice to stand outside in the cold. "How did she seem?"

"Like she might be in a hurry."

"What was she wearing?"

"I don't know." His eyes widened. "Why? Is she dead?"

"What makes you think she might be dead?"

"Cuz you're a cop and you're asking creepy questions." He looked concerned. "What happened to Lyla?"

"She's in the hospital. Someone assaulted her. What about her boyfriend?"

"I don't think she had one. I never heard anyone in her apartment, if you know what I mean." He blushed a little.

"Do you know anyone who might want to hurt her?"

"No. She's a nice girl."

Yet somebody nearly beat her to death. Evans handed the young man a business card. "Please call me if you think of anything that could help me find her attacker."

A few minutes later, as Evans climbed into her car, her phone rang.

"It's Margaret, in the campus PD office. Did you say Lyla was naked when they dumped her?"

"Except for a pair of pink socks."

"I have a report that someone turned in some clothes they found in the graveyard."

CHAPTER 10

Monday, January 9, 2:15 p.m.

Jackson climbed into his car, glad to be alone for a moment. The cash was lost, the perp was likely drowned, and they had no idea where Renee was. Maybe no one did now. What if they couldn't locate her? Would she starve to death, shackled in a basement somewhere? He slammed his hand against the steering wheel. They had to find her! He couldn't let Renee die that way. He was a cop. His daughter might never forgive him. He would never forgive himself.

The kidnapper may not be dead, he corrected, starting the car. The perp could be crawling out of the river right now or he might have hired a thug to collect the money. Agent River thought at least two perps were involved: one sending texts from a distant location while the other had waited near the river. She and Agent Fouts were headed back to Anderson's house, hoping to hear from the kidnapper again. Search and rescue teams were patrolling the river and its banks, looking for a body or a red backpack loaded with cash. In addition, FBI agents, uniformed officers, and county deputies were all involved in a massive manhunt for Daniel Talbot. Jackson would meet back up with the task force later that afternoon.

He put in his earpiece and drove past the restaurant toward the parking lot exit. For now, he would continue tracking Renee's movements the day she disappeared. He had to believe there was value in knowing where she'd been taken from or who had seen her last. Maybe a witness had seen her with the kidnapper. It felt strange to be on the perimeter of an investigation, just another grunt, instead of directing all the moving parts. But he was grateful to not bear that responsibility this time.

At the street he changed his mind, reparked, and called Katie. She had a right to know what was going on. She wasn't a little kid anymore and he couldn't protect her from the truth. His intestines twisted in turmoil. This would be the hardest conversation he'd ever had with her. He wanted to conduct it in person, to hug her as she processed what it all meant. But driving out to Renee's sister's house would cost him an hour—time that Renee might not be able to afford.

He pressed speed dial #1 and Katie cut in on the first ring. "Did you find her? Is Mom okay?"

Another jab to his gut. "We haven't located her yet but we will. I have to believe she's still fine."

"What happened with the ransom?" Panic crept into Katie's voice.

"Sweetheart, I'm sorry I'm not there to tell you in person, but I have leads to follow."

"What happened?"

"The kidnapper got into an inner tube and floated down the river with the cash."

"But he'll release Mom now, right? He'll call and tell you where she is?"

"We don't know." He drew in a breath. "The inner tube flipped over and the perp went into the water. Sheriff teams are looking for him now."

"Oh my god! If he drowns, what happens to Mom?"

"We think he had a partner. We believe we'll hear from the kidnappers again."

"But they didn't get the money! He said he'd cut off her finger." Katie burst into tears.

Jackson kicked himself for not driving over. "We tried to pay him. He knows that." *Did he?* Had the courier communicated with his partner about receiving the cash before he went under?

"What if Ivan doesn't have any more money? You have to find her!"

"I know, sweetheart. I will. I have leads to follow now. I love you." Jackson had to get off the phone. Katie's distress threatened to overwhelm him.

He drove west toward Fred Meyer, where Dave Lambert was a manager. The AA meeting leader might not be willing to share information but Jackson had to try.

In the store, he found Lambert in a tucked-away office at the end of a long corridor. Small, cramped, and windowless, the office made Jackson cringe. His witness was physically neutral, with sandy hair, beige clothes, and a bland, ageless face. Jackson introduced himself and noticed Lambert reacted with a slight look of alarm, which he immediately tried to hide.

"What's going on?" Lambert gestured for him to sit in an orange plastic chair.

"I'm looking for Renee Jackson. She attended an AA meeting at the Jesco Club Saturday afternoon, then was abducted shortly after."

"That's wild. And not what I expected to hear." Lambert was visibly relieved. "I spoke to Renee after the meeting. She seemed worried."

Jackson wanted to know what the store manager was worried about—and what he might be involved in—but he needed to stay focused on Renee. "What did she say?"

"Nothing, really. She just looked stressed."

"Did you see her get in her car?"

"Yes. She was parked across the street in the alley."

"Was she alone?"

"Yes."

"Did she talk to anyone at the meeting? Did one of the members seem particularly interested in her?"

Concern flashed in Lambert's eyes. "There is a guy who seems a little obsessed with her. I mean, he watches her a lot. I can see it from the front but Renee may not have been aware."

"I need his name."

"It's an anonymous meeting."

"Someone kidnapped Renee and threatened to kill her."

"Good grief." He clicked his pen in a rapid, nervous mode. "I only know what the guy tells us, and it may not be true."

"Tell me."

"He calls himself Striker."

A cool wave of fear washed over Jackson. "What do you know about him?"

"He used to be a logger but now he builds urban chicken coops." Lambert shook his head. "I shouldn't be telling you any of this. If you question him, please don't mention where you got the information. I'll lose my credibility with AA."

You could get sued too, Jackson thought, but didn't say. "What does he look like?"

"Big guy. Six-three and probably two hundred and fifty pounds. He has dark curly hair and a full beard."

Jackson made quick notes. "Any idea what he drives? Or where to find him?"

"I've seen him get into an old panel truck. It was black with tan sideboards."

"Thank you. I appreciate your cooperation."

"I hope you find her."

An image of Renee's dead body on the floor of a storage unit flashed in Jackson's brain. He pushed it away and stood to leave. "We will." He handed the manager a business card. "Please call me if you think of anything else."

In his car, he dialed Agent River. "It's Jackson. Any word from the kidnapper?"

"No. But we have a search warrant for Daniel Talbot's home. Two agents are headed over there now. You're welcome to join them."

"I can't. I have another possible lead. Renee was at an AA meeting Saturday afternoon from three to four. A man who attends the same meeting has shown an obsessive interest in Renee. He calls himself Striker."

"Run him through the database and we'll get someone on him."

"I'm heading to the department to do that now."

"Keep me posted."

Jackson thought about Evans and her little tablet with its internet access. She'd be sitting here scanning the databases now. He vowed to buy one before the day was over, even if the department wouldn't reimburse him. They couldn't afford to put computers in the detective cars either and it was a damn shame. To top it off, Lane County was losing its federal timber payments, and the sheriff's department had cut more jail beds and eliminated probation supervision for minor offenses. Gang members were moving to Eugene because it had become so soft on crime. Sometimes the lack of funding made him want to quit. What was the point of rounding up the bad guys if the system was just going to release them?

Driving across Ferry Street Bridge, Jackson was reminded of the search for the waterlogged courier. He called Sheriff Walters. "It's Jackson. Any word from the boat patrols or search-and-rescue teams?"

"Not yet. I'll call as soon as I hear."

"Thanks."

As he entered the Violent Crimes area, he ran into Schak. "What did you find out about Renee's phone?"

Jackson plopped down at his desk and Schak grabbed a nearby chair. "It hasn't been used since Saturday at three seventeen p.m. T-Mobile pinged it and got no signal. I think the kidnapper destroyed it when he grabbed her."

"We're dealing with someone smart." Jackson shook his head. "Except the final escape method. Getting on the river in the winter is always dangerous."

"Yep, but if he had made it ashore, he would've had a hundred grand and no eyes on him."

"Don't forget the tracker in the backpack."

"He could've found that in two minutes flat. Then thrown it on a passing car." Schak grinned, warming to the subject. "He may have been looking through the cash as he floated down the river. That tracker might be at the bottom of the Willamette."

"We'll know soon enough. We have a task force meeting at four thirty at Anderson's house."

"Anything I can do before we head out?"

"We need a list of Renee's calls and texts for the last week."

"I've already made the request, but it could take a day or so."

"Find out what you can about Dave Lambert. He's an AA leader and a manager at the West Eleventh Fred Meyer. Meanwhile, I'll be tracking down a guy who attended AA meetings with Renee and calls himself Striker."

"Sounds like a nickname for someone with insecurities."

"Lambert says Striker seemed obsessed with Renee."

"Your ex *is* kinda hot."

Jackson ignored the comment. After he'd kicked Renee out and filed for divorce, she'd gotten sober, lost fifteen pounds, and cut her hair. She looked better now than she had at any point during their marriage. But it didn't change anything for him. "Something about Lambert bothers me. He might be the one who's obsessed and purposely diverting me toward Striker."

"I'll see what I can dig up."

Jackson decided to start online. Sometimes websites had more current information than law enforcement databases. He googled *urban chicken coops Eugene Oregon* and found two local businesses, but neither was owned by someone named Striker. On a whim, he called Down to Earth, a local home and garden store, and asked to speak to the manager. After a brief conversation, he learned Striker had built a custom coop for the store's display and his first name was Gus. *No wonder the man went by Striker.* Jackson tried to get a phone number but the manager wouldn't say anything more. Eugene citizens were often like that. They tended to err on the side of protecting people until proven guilty. Even then, many people in his liberal hometown wanted to *fix* criminals rather than *punish* them. It made his job more difficult, but it also made him—and everyone in the department— better law enforcement officers.

Jackson clicked open the criminal-history database and keyed in *Gus Striker*. A list of arrests and convictions surfaced. Possession of meth, theft 1, unauthorized use of a vehicle, DUII, public intoxication, and several probation violations. But nothing for the last three years except a trespassing report.

Curious, Jackson read through it and learned Striker had been arrested at the home of a Molly Hansen. She'd called dispatch right before midnight to report seeing someone in her backyard. Patrol officers had found Striker hiding in a shed on her property. He'd claimed to be lost and drunk, pled guilty to trespassing, and paid a fine. Now Jackson wondered if there was more to it. Had Striker been stalking Molly Hansen?

Locating an address from Striker's last probation report, Jackson jotted it down, and shoved his notepad into his pocket. He started to get up, then had another paranoid thought. He opened Facebook and searched for the name Molly Hansen. He scrolled through about twenty until he found one in Eugene. When he opened her profile, he drew in a sharp breath.

Molly Hansen looked very much like his ex-wife, Renee.

CHAPTER 11

Monday, January 9, 1:35 p.m.

A damp, musty smell seeped out of the plastic bag as Evans removed the faded jeans. *Dirt*, she thought, *and a little moss.* Probably from the graveyard where the clothes had been found. Evans ignored the trace evidence, leaving it for the technicians, and dug into the pockets. She wanted Lyla's wallet or cell phone, or even a scrap of paper. She needed a solid lead.

"Why would she take her clothes off outside in January?"

Margaret, the campus police coordinator, scowled at the thought. "I'm sure it wasn't her idea."

Evans found nothing in the jeans, which had probably fit so tight there wasn't room for personal items. She pulled out the gray fleece jacket, shoved her gloved hand in a pocket, and it connected with a mobile phone. Tension flowed out of her shoulders. "I need to take all these to the lab."

Margaret nodded.

Evans shoved the jeans and jacket back in the bag, along with a green T-shirt that said *Go Ducks*. She would put everything in separate evidence bags once she got to her car. If she'd picked up the clothes at the actual crime scene, she would have processed them correctly from the beginning.

"What do you know about the person who turned in the clothes?"

"Nothing. The note just says they were found in the graveyard."

"That's a big area to cover."

"I know. I might be able to round up some volunteers to search."

"Thanks, but I think I'll request a canine and save a lot of time."

"Good idea." The campus officer looked relieved. "I'll keep asking about the sorority and let you know if I hear anything."

"Thanks."

Evans headed out, wondering if Lammers would approve the expense of the canine. The victim wasn't dead and the perp or perps were long gone. Finding the spot where Lyla had been attacked might prove to be completely useless. Or it could hold the key to solving this heinous assault. She had to try.

A cold wind stung her eyes as she hurried to her car, which was parked illegally across the street near the recreation center. The old redbrick buildings, surrounded by grassy commons, made Evans wish she'd gone to school here instead of at a modern community college in Seattle. The University of Oregon campus exuded an air of timeless knowledge as well as a sense of belonging. Evans didn't really have that with any place...or person. Eugene was growing on her after ten years, and her relationship with Ben kept getting better. But the only time she felt completely at home was when she was with Jackson. And she had to get over that.

In the car, she locked the doors out of habit, pulled her latex gloves back on, and activated Lyla's phone. A low-battery message came up immediately. *Damn.* She wanted to scroll through the text messages. Evans grabbed her phone charger, plugged it into the cigarette lighter, and tried it in Lyla's phone. Luckily, they both had newer smartphones and it fit. The battery icon began to flash.

While she waited for the phone to charge, a parking-ticket enforcer stopped next to her. Evans held up her badge and waved him on. *Jackass.* He knew she was a cop. Evans' stomach growled, and she realized the soup hadn't been enough lunch after her kickboxing workout that morning. She dug into her shoulder bag, hoping to find a half-eaten protein bar. No luck, but the survival bag had everything else. In addition to all the crime scene tools she carried—evidence bags, plastic gloves, cameras, and tweezers—she also kept band-aids, a tiny sewing kit, a utility knife, sunscreen, and a miniflashlight. Growing up with alcoholic parents in a backwoods cabin outside of Fairbanks, Alaska, had taught her to be prepared for anything. Surprises were the enemy. Six years as a patrol cop had reinforced that learning.

Leaving Lyla's phone plugged in, she clicked the text message icon and began to read. The last text, sent at 7:10 p.m. Saturday evening, had gone to *Mom* and said, *Too busy to talk now. I'll call you this weekend.* Evans' heart went out to the girl's mother, who was probably racing up the interstate now, frantic with worry that she'd never speak to her daughter again. You never knew what your last communication was with a loved one until it was too late.

Evans scrolled to the previous text, an incoming message from Josh: *Do you have notes from biology class today?*

Lyla's quadmate had mentioned Josh, but she'd said he and Lyla were just friends. Before that, someone named Taylor had texted: *Be there at 8.*

A shimmer of excitement traveled up Evans' neck. Taylor must have planned to meet Lyla in the graveyard. Who was Taylor? A guy or a girl? The assault on Lyla had been so violent, Evans was inclined to believe a male had committed it. She looked through the phone's contact list and found Taylor Harris, but with no picture and no details. Was Taylor a new friend or a casual acquaintance?

Evans' blood pulsed with possibilities, like a hound picking up the scent of prey. She played out a few scenarios. She could call Taylor and try to arrange a meeting, but if he was guilty or sensed danger, he might panic and hang up or simply not show. It made more sense to find Taylor Harris and confront him personally. If she could do it quickly.

Evans used her own phone and called Brooke Hammond, Lyla's friend who'd reported her missing. Brooke picked up right away and whispered, "Is this important? Is Lyla okay?"

"I haven't heard anything yet. Why are you whispering?"

"I'm in class but it hasn't started yet."

"I need to know who Taylor Harris is."

A hesitation. "I've heard her name but I don't really know her."

"Don't fuck with me." Evans rarely swore at citizens, but her adrenaline was pumping. "Lyla was supposed to meet Taylor Saturday night. So she probably knows what happened. I need to find her right now."

"I think she belongs to the sorority Lyla wanted to join." Brooke spoke so softly, Evans strained to hear.

"Where can I find Taylor?"

"She works at the campus daycare center."

"Where's that?"

"It's at Sixteenth and Moss."

"What does Taylor look like?"

"A cheerleader. Pretty and skinny, with long ash-blonde hair."

"Where is the sorority located?"

"I don't know. I have to go." Brooke hung up.

Evans was glad she hadn't left campus. Moss Street was only a few blocks away. Taylor Harris might be in class, or at home sleeping, or damn near anywhere, but it was worth checking.

Inside the daycare center, she was hit with the aroma of apple-sauce and baby wipes, while high-pitched little voices overrode her thoughts. Small children were a mystery to her, and Evans had never experienced a desire to breed. People told her she would eventually, but she was thirty-three and didn't see it happening.

A young man noticed her and came over, carrying a plump little boy. "How can I help you?"

"I'm looking for Taylor Harris. Is she here?" The irony of questioning an assault suspect in such a nurturing environment made Evans cringe a little.

"No. Why?" His tone seemed protective.

"I'm Detective Evans, Eugene Police. I'm investigating an assault and I need to speak with Taylor immediately."

"She's not here today."

"Do you know where she lives?"

"No." He looked away and shifted the toddler to his other side.

"I'd like to talk to your manager."

"She's not here."

Evans sensed the young man knew Taylor, maybe even had a crush on her. "Please put the child down and step outside with me."

For a long moment, he didn't move. "I really can't. There's only one other provider here—"

Evans cut him off, stepping forward as she spoke. "A young woman was beaten nearly to death. What do you know about that?"

"I'll be right back." He scurried over to the group of kids listening to a young woman read and set down the toddler.

Evans held the door open for him as he returned. He wasn't wearing a jacket and would soon be shivering in the January cold. *Good*, she thought, *that might expedite their conversation.* They stepped outside.

"What's your name?"

"Marco Salvia."

Evans made a show of writing it down. "Do you know Lyla Murray?"

"No. Is she the victim?"

"She's in critical condition and might die. If she does, this becomes a homicide investigation and Taylor Harris was one of the last people to communicate with Lyla. Tell me what you know."

"I don't know anything. I just work with Taylor and I haven't seen her since last week."

"Where were you Saturday night between seven and ten?"

"Drinking with friends at the Beer Stein."

A gust of wind came out of nowhere. Marco crossed his arms and tried not to shiver. Evans pretended not to notice the cold.

"Where does Taylor live?"

He looked around, then said, "I don't know the address, but it's a big white house on Potter Street. It's on the east side, right in the middle of the block. She lives there with a group of other students."

"A sorority?"

"I don't know. I just gave her a ride home once."

"What is Taylor like?"

"She's sweet and she's studying to be a teacher. I can't believe she had anything to do with an assault."

"Thanks for your help." She handed him a business card. "Let's keep this conversation to ourselves, but if you hear anything that might be useful, let me know."

Still hungry, Evans bought an egg roll from a street vendor and added another mile to the run she would do in the evening. She'd started the morning with a kickboxing workout, followed by push-ups and sit-ups. She liked to run at the end of the day to burn off stress and empty the garbage out of her mind after a day filled with liars, thieves, and assholes. She wished she had a hot cup of coffee too, but the vendor only sold green tea. She'd never been that desperate.

On the drive over to Potter Street, she munched on her egg roll and scanned through more of Lyla's texts whenever she had to stop for traffic. After a few minutes, the multitasking made her laugh out loud. Cops had to be the most distracted drivers on the road. She shoved Lyla's phone in her shoulder bag and turned on Potter Street.

A moment later, she saw the massive white house on the left. The Victorian home had been built a hundred years earlier, but even after decades of abuse by college students it was still stately and attractive. Someone had taken good care of it. Evans made a note to find out who the owner was. She guessed it was managed by a rental property company.

Scanning the street for a parking space, she finally left her car in a driveway down the street where no one was home. She was glad she didn't live or work in the campus area. Parking was a nightmare.

After several loud knocks and a three-minute wait, a young woman came to the door. Thin, with magenta streaks in her otherwise colorless hair, the student had sleepy eyes and a molasses-slow voice. "Who are you?"

"Detective Evans, Eugene Police. I need to see Taylor Harris immediately." Evans figured this wasn't Taylor because Brooke had said her suspect looked like a cheerleader.

"I don't think she's here."

"Where is she?"

"I don't know. I'm not her mother."

"Then I'd like to talk to you." Evans stepped into the house, forcing the girl to move back and let her in.

"What's this about?" The girl stood near the door, arms crossed.

"Let's sit down."

She sighed and moved to a couch, one of three in a long, cluttered living room with low-to-the-ground furniture.

"What's your name?"

"Kate Bertram."

Evans jotted it down. "Where were you Saturday night?"

"At a party. Why?"

"Lyla Murray was beaten nearly to death. Do you know her?"

The girl gasped and her hand flew to her mouth. "But she's okay?"

"Not yet. She could still die. How do you know her?"

"She's a friend of Taylor's. She's been here a few times to hang out."

"What's the name of this sorority?"

Kate blinked. "We're just friends who live together."

Liar. "Was Lyla going to move in here?"

"I think so."

"What's the criteria for being admitted?"

"It's up to Taylor. She picks our new roommates."

"What was your initiation like?"

Fear flashed in Kate's eyes and she glanced away. "There is no initiation."

"Bullshit. I saw your reaction when I mentioned it. Were you physically assaulted?"

"No."

"Did Taylor assault Lyla?"

"I doubt it."

"If you knew about the assault and didn't report it, you can be charged as an accessory to a crime." Evans leaned in. "Everyone in this house can be charged, and if Lyla dies, you could all go to jail."

Kate's breathing pattern was suddenly irregular and she jumped up. "I don't know anything about it."

A door banged shut at the back of the house and footsteps pounded upstairs. Evans jumped to her feet. "Is that Taylor?"

Kate was silent.

Evans strode toward the hallway, breaking into a jog as she reached the stairs. As she hit the second floor landing, she caught sight of a door closing at the end of the hall. She hurried past four other doors to the end room and knocked loudly. "Eugene Police. We need to talk."

No response.

Hot anger made her skin go clammy. Who did this girl think she was that she could beat her friend into a coma, then ignore a cop?

Evans pounded again and yelled, "Eugene Police. Open up!"

A loud thump came through the door, followed by scurrying sounds. Evans visualized Taylor trying to hide something. She grabbed the knob and shoved, but the door was locked. "Taylor! Open up! Eugene Police."

A window slammed open.

"Crap, she's gonna run."

CHAPTER 12

Monday, January 9, 3:27 p.m.

Jackson debated his next move. If this were a homicide, he'd simply round up Striker and bring him in for questioning. But Renee's life was still at stake and he couldn't do anything to jeopardize it. On the other hand, if Striker was the kidnapper and had drowned in the river, Renee could be locked in a shed on his property, abandoned and dehydrating…or hurting herself trying to get free. He pushed the awful image away and made a decision. With an hour before the task force meeting, he had just enough time to run out to Striker's place and take a look around. Jackson googled the location, left word with Schak, and headed to his car.

The last known address in Striker's file was on Bethel Drive, about a mile west of the Jesco Club. Jackson passed the railroad office and slowed down, watching for the numbers on the left. A couple of neglected homes stood near the road, but the house he wanted was in between the two shacks, down a fifty-foot driveway. The muddy little house sat under a giant oak tree, but no vehicle was present. Striker could still be home. With a DUI on his record and a predisposition toward alcohol, he might not have a driver's license.

Jackson climbed out, his hand automatically touching his Sig Sauer. He was always careful around suspects, but this neighborhood made him wary. Eugene's growing gang population congregated in cheap rentals, and the other dirt-poor residents here had nothing left to lose.

Train cars slammed together behind him and made him jump. How did people live here? Could you ever get used to the noise?

Glancing around, he noticed the property's boundaries: a laurel hedge on the right, a grassy strip on the left, and what looked like a beat-up wooden fence in the back. The corner of a green metal shed was visible behind the house. *Where did Striker build the chicken coops?* Jackson wondered. Was there a shop in back he couldn't see?

He stepped past an overflowing garbage bag and knocked on the door. A faint movement inside, then nothing. A moment later, a cat appeared in the window to the right. *Better than a dog*, he thought. He knocked again and waited a full minute. At this point he had no right to search the man's property, but Jackson couldn't make himself walk away. Renee could be captive here. *The mother of his child.*

He heard a voice near the backyard and told himself it had to be investigated.

Jackson strode around the corner and down the narrow path between the wood siding and the tall hedge. The green shed he'd spotted had a lock on it—no surprise—so he pounded on the door. No response from within. He pounded again, then moved to the back of the shed and put his ear against the cold metal.

No sign of life.

He turned to the rest of the yard. A makeshift carport filled most of the space. The grass under it had been trampled by work boots, and a table saw stood near the edge of the covered area. Two wooden birdhouses lay near the saw. Striker's shop. He was making do with the space he had. Jackson had a brief flash of respect for the man's effort to earn a living.

Then he imagined Renee tied up in a back bedroom of the house.

After a quick search of the perimeter, he tried the back door handle. The door pushed open. Jackson hesitated. If Renee were not his ex-wife, would he enter this home without a warrant? He had probable cause, he told himself. A woman was being held hostage and he was following a viable lead.

Jackson moved quickly through the small laundry room into the hallway. The overpowering stink of cigarettes and cat piss made his eyes water. He pushed open a bedroom door and called out softly, "Renee."

Right hand near his weapon, he stepped into the bedroom, which was spare and cold. He checked the closet, then backed out of the room. He was searching for a hostage. Anything else was illegal.

After a quick glance in the bathroom, he headed toward the small living room. It held only a beat-up recliner, a TV and a computer—both sitting on a brick-and-board shelf—and a large laminate table. On the table sat a row of plastic jars, an unopened pack of coffee filters, a Pyrex bowl, an eyedropper, and a funnel. Striker was starting a meth production business. Or had he decided it wasn't worth the hassle and moved directly into kidnapping for ransom? Was he a meth addict? The thought sickened Jackson. If so, Renee might already be dead.

Time to get a warrant. Jackson hurried for the back door, stopping in the kitchen to glance around. A photo taped to the refrigerator caught his eye. He stepped toward it and his heart skipped a beat. An image of Renee, sitting on a folding metal chair, wearing a red sweater and not smiling. The Jesco Club. *Striker was obsessed with Renee.* Had he also kidnapped her? Jackson leaned in close, resisting the urge to touch the picture. It had been printed on thick white paper rather than photo stock. He'd seen an old tower-style computer in the living room but no printer. Did Striker have more photos of Renee on his hard drive?

Jackson grabbed his camera from his carryall and snapped a picture of the refrigerator, then moved in closer for another shot. Could he take this photo to a judge and get a search warrant? Or would he just get himself in trouble?

A car pulled into the driveway, tires crunching on the gravel. Jackson spun toward the back door. He caught sight of the kitchen window, its blinds partially closed. He quickly pulled them open a little more, then bolted for the backyard. Camera still in hand, he zoomed in and took a photo of the refrigerator through the window. No one ever needed to know he'd been in the house.

Jackson grabbed his phone called for backup. In this neighborhood, a patrol unit would not be far away.

CHAPTER 13

Monday, January 9, 3:13 p.m.

Evans bolted down the stairs and made a left, running straight into a laundry room. She tried again. The old house had small rooms and short hallways, but she found the back door and charged into the yard. A young blonde woman opened a gate in the back fence and ran into an alley. Out of the corner of her eye, Evans spotted the giant oak tree next to the house, complete with hammered-in climbing boards. Taylor had clambered down like a pro.

Evans chased after her, glad she'd left her shoulder bag in the car. Adrenaline rushed into her veins. She could run faster and longer than anyone in the department, but Taylor was young and scared and knew the neighborhood better.

"I just want to talk!" Evans called out when she hit the alley.

Taylor was halfway to the cross street. Evans sprinted down the gravel alley, arms pumping and jacket flapping. Why had the girl run? She had to be guilty of something. Lyla's battered body flashed in Evans' mind. She leaped in the air and hurdled a giant puddle, landing with a thud on the uneven ground. As Taylor stopped at the street for a passing car, Evans closed the gap.

The young woman rushed across the road, heading for another alley, and Evans shouted again. Taylor kept moving, so Evans charged across the street after her. On the sidewalk, she lunged forward and grabbed Taylor by her long hair. The girl cried out and went down on one knee. Evans grabbed her cuffs from her jacket pocket and trussed her suspect before Taylor knew what was happening.

Evans took a moment to let her pounding heart settle, then pulled Taylor to her feet. "I just wanted to ask a few questions, but now we'll do that at the department."

"I want my lawyer."

Evans nodded. "All in good time."

She let Taylor sit in the tiny windowless interrogation room by herself for twenty minutes. Evans hoped to instill a little fear in the young woman, whom she suspected had never faced any significant hardship. Taylor's expensive clothes, confidence, and demand for a lawyer all indicated she'd grown up with money and was used to getting what she wanted. Evans repressed a tingle of resentment. If her suspect had assaulted another college student so savagely that she might die, then obviously the money and security in Taylor's life hadn't helped her become a good citizen. Evans had more respect for the homeless people who often shared what little they had with each other.

While she let Taylor simmer, she called the hospital to ask about Lyla.

"She's out of surgery but in a coma," the nurse said. "The doctors induced the coma to help her heal. The last bleed was in her brain."

Damn. Evans desperately wanted to talk to the victim. "Has her mother arrived?"

"Not yet."

"Has anyone else called to ask about her?"

"Yesterday afternoon, a woman called but didn't identify herself."

"Any way to track where that call came from?" She knew the answer before she asked.

"No. Sorry."

She made a quick trip to Full City Coffee across the plaza and would add another mile to her run that night to burn off the caffeine. She was trying to cut back, but this was turning into a long day and she needed to stay sharp. Her strategy for questioning Taylor would be more aggressive than usual, she decided. Normally she would try to empathize with suspects and make them believe she understood why they'd committed the crime. Sometimes a sympathetic ear was all it took to get a confession. But then, most criminals had once been victims, or at least they saw themselves that way.

Taylor would be different. She was confident and probably wouldn't care whether a cop understood her motivations. Her family could likely afford a good lawyer too. As much as Evans wanted to understand why the assault had happened, she wanted a conviction even more. She feared if Lyla died—and couldn't testify—no one would ever pay for the crime. There was no trace evidence and no witnesses. Evans remembered her plan to bring in a canine unit and turned down the hall to see her boss.

The door was open and the big woman was leaned back with her eyes closed.

"Sergeant Lammers."

Eyes popping open, Lammers lurched forward in her chair. "Yes? I was just resting my eyes. I'm reading this book that says you should, especially if you work on a computer all day."

"Sounds right." It was more personal information than her boss had ever offered. Evans stepped in and sat down. "I caught a break in the assault case. Someone found Lyla's clothes and phone in the campus graveyard and turned them in. I have a suspect in the interrogation room now, but I want to go out to the graveyard tomorrow with a canine unit and find the crime scene."

"You didn't talk to the person who found the clothes?"

"No. He dropped them off and didn't leave a name."

"And the victim won't give a statement?"

"She's in a coma."

"Let's wait and see what she has to say when she comes out of the coma. The canine search may be an unnecessary expense."

"What if Lyla doesn't recover and it becomes a homicide and I have to build a case without her?" Evans knew she sounded worked up and didn't care. "The more time that lapses, the less valuable the evidence is."

"Don't yell at me. I hate these budget cuts more than you do." Lammers ran her hands through her short hair. "For this kind of search, we need a scent-specific dog, and there's only one. I'll see if the officer is available tomorrow."

"Thanks."

Taylor's eyes had lost a little defiance by the time Evans wandered back into the closet-size room. She opened her coffee and let out the full aromatic scent but didn't offer Taylor anything.

Evans set out her recorder and stated both their names. "I'm documenting our conversation." The camera mounted in the wall was also running and she resisted looking at it.

"I still want to call my lawyer." Taylor rubbed her wrists where the handcuffs had been.

"I haven't arrested or charged you yet, so you're not entitled. But if you don't cooperate, I'm going to charge you with obstruction of justice for running from me and book you into the jail." Evans took a sip of coffee. "Have you ever been inside the jail?"

The young woman didn't answer.

Evans put Lyla's cell phone on the scarred wooden table. The space was small enough for Taylor to reach over and grab it. But she only stared.

"Saturday night, January seventh, you texted Lyla Murray and said—Evans picked up the phone and glanced at the message for effect—'Be there at eight.' That was about the time Lyla was brutally assaulted, then dumped at the hospital. She's still in critical condition. You understand how this looks for you?"

Taylor was silent.

"We have Lyla's clothes. If your DNA is on them, you'll do at least three years for this. If she dies, you could get life. Why don't you tell me what happened."

Taylor licked her lips. "I don't know what happened. Lyla was supposed to meet me at Pegasus Pizza, then we had plans to go to a party. She never showed."

"Did you talk to anyone at the restaurant?"

"Sure, but I don't know his name."

"What did you do when you left Pegasus?"

"Went to the party."

"What party and where?"

"At a house near Twentieth and Alder."

"Did anyone see you there?"

"Of course."

"I want their names and phone numbers." Evans tore a piece of paper from her notepad. "Write down the address of the house and everyone who saw you there, including their phone numbers."

Taylor's hand trembled as she complied.

Evans' gut feeling told her Taylor had not acted alone. But how to make her name her co-assailant? Evans had to move cautiously. "What's the name of your sorority?"

Taylor's head jerked up. "What are you talking about?"

"The house where you live with all the women. It's a nonsanctioned sorority. What do you call yourselves?"

"We're just roommates."

"That's not what I hear. And I plan to talk to every woman who lives there. While you're in jail." Evans reached for the list of names. "How long did it take you to become the alpha dog in the pack?"

Taylor snorted her contempt. "Because I'm a senior, I've lived there the longest. So what?"

"Some of the younger members will be scared and tell me everything. They won't protect you."

"You'd be surprised." The corners of her mouth turned up.

Evans kept her own face impassive even though Taylor had just admitted the household was a club with loyalty as a price for membership. "What do you give them in exchange for loyalty and deference?"

"We're just friends and roommates. We help each other with homework and class notes. You have the wrong idea." Taylor didn't meet her eyes.

"What does it take to be admitted into the house?"

"A deposit, like every other rental."

"Is the initiation always that violent?"

Taylor was silent.

"What was your hazing like? Are you still friends with the women who tormented you four years ago?"

"Of course." Taylor bit her lip, seeming to regret her words.

"So you admit the house hazes women who join?"

"No. I simply meant that I'm still friends with some room-mates who graduated."

Evans modified her tone to sound supportive. "I know you didn't commit the assault alone. Tell me who else was involved and I'll make sure you get a good plea deal."

"It's not an assault if someone consents to it."

Evans didn't know the legal grounds. This was a new situation for her. "So you admit you participated in Lyla's initiation? A consensual activity that involved striking her?"

"I was speaking hypothetically."

"What did you hit her with?"

"I'm done talking."

"What kind of car do you drive?"

Another surprised look.

"We have a witness from the hospital who saw the car that dropped off Lyla. If the description matches yours, the district attorney will press a judge to keep you in jail while you wait for a trial."

Taylor's eyes twitched. "I have a blue Mini Cooper that's been in the shop since Friday."

So Taylor hadn't been the driver, but Evans knew she'd participated. "I'll go check in with the lab and see what they found on Lyla's clothes."

Evans walked out, hoping Taylor would call her back to talk about a plea. Only silence followed.

CHAPTER 14

Monday, January 9, 3:15 p.m.

Renee's throat crackled as she swallowed and a second later her lower lip split open. She probed the wound with her tongue and tasted blood. Her stomach lurched and she fought the urge to vomit. Alcohol withdrawal always made her sweaty, nauseous, and dry, but now her thirst overwhelmed even the pain in her wrists and shoulders. They had restrained her hands together with duct tape, and even though the binding wasn't tight, the tape had irritated her skin after the first day. Or the second day. Renee felt a little confused, but she thought today was Monday, about forty-eight hours after being abducted. What did they want? If this was about money, why hadn't Ivan paid?

She stood, rising from the musty bed, and began to pace. Six steps across the small bedroom, turn, and six steps back. The movement was hypnotic, almost like meditation, and it kept her sane. As long as she was moving, she felt alive and could keep her mind calm. When she sat, doubt crept in and she feared she would never leave this room.

Black plastic covered the single window, so she had no idea where she was. But the crown molding at the top of the walls made her think she was in an old house. A closet-like bathroom was attached, thank god, even though the sink didn't work, so she concluded she was in a bedroom. The sounds she heard outside occasionally—a barking dog, a passing car in the distance— seemed to come from below. Renee thought she might be on the second floor. But what building? And where?

Not that it mattered much. She had tried and failed to free her hands, but there was nothing sharp to cut through the goddamn duct tape with. She felt helpless and enraged. Where the hell was her ex-husband, the lead detective, when she really needed him? Why could he solve everyone else's crimes and leave her to rot? Was he even looking for her?

He was in Hawaii with Kera, she remembered. The selfish shit. He could have at least taken Katie with him.

Images of her daughter flooded her mind and Renee tried not to cry. She loved Katie more than she'd ever been able to express. And her little girl had forgiven her over and over for being an irresponsible drunk. She was a crappy mother and had been a crappy wife. But she didn't deserve this. No one did. They hadn't even left her with a radio, and the silence was unbearable.

Renee pounded the door, desperate to try something. Her captor always wore a mask when he brought her food and water and zipped in and out of the room before she had a chance to try anything. Not that she could do much with her wrists taped. Clearly, Ivan hadn't paid the ransom and Wade wasn't coming to the rescue.

Renee fought the urge to sob, knowing it would only weaken her.

She slumped on the bed and envisioned her escape. Eventually, she'd break free of the ties and lie in wait for him. When he entered the room, she would stomp his ankle, then drive an elbow into his groin, like she'd learned in a self-defense class years ago. When the creep went down to his knees, she'd gouge his eye with her stiffened finger. What if she only managed to piss him off, and he knocked her out cold? So far, the men hadn't hurt her, except during the abduction, but that could change in an instant. What little she'd seen of her captors before they put her in the trunk frightened her. Young, dark-clothed men who stank of sweat and cigarettes. If this was only about ransom, they had no reason to keep her alive once they had the money.

But yet, they hadn't killed her. Maybe she should wait it out and not try anything foolish. Maybe Ivan had already paid and they just hadn't let her go yet. Renee got up and pounded again, but no one came.

A chill crept into her bones. What if something had gone wrong? Had she been abandoned and left to slowly starve?

CHAPTER 15

Monday, January 9, 4:25 p.m.

River's mind raced from one scenario to another as she waited for the rest of the task force to gather in Anderson's dining room. Fouts and Torres were there, and two surveillance agents from Portland had just arrived. The tech team was still in place down the road and two Eugene agents had just picked up Daniel Talbot. River nibbled on a bag of popcorn, knowing she needed some nourishment, but was too distracted to enjoy it. If the perp had acted alone and drowned in the river, they had to focus on finding the abductee. That meant getting Renee's photo all over the media. But if the guy who picked up the money had a partner, then the game was still on and the media exposure could lead to the victim's death. They would just have to wait a few hours and see if they heard from the kidnapper again.

As much as she tried to live in the moment, River hated waiting. She'd spent most of her life wanting to be someone else and waiting for the courage to make it happen. Then at thirty-seven she'd had a heart attack and vowed to change everything. Two years later, she was forty pounds lighter, nicotine free, and named Carla instead of Carl.

But that was only on her legal paperwork. She'd gone by River since she'd adopted the last name and liked it so well. Some agents in the Portland office had been supportive of the gender transition, but others had openly mocked her. And the higher-ups just wanted her gone.

Transferring to Eugene had given her the opportunity to start completely fresh—a new identity in a new place. Now if she could just find the nerve to leave the FBI. She loved her job. Rounding up lawbreakers and helping victims find closure had quieted the voice in her head that told her she was of inferior stock. Yet the bureau had sucked up most of her life, and now that she was free to be herself, she wanted more. She wanted to garden and travel and maybe find someone to share her life with. But was there another way to earn a decent living and pay her father's debt at the same time?

She heard cars in the driveway, and Agent Fouts got up and crossed to the front door. Moments later, Detectives Jackson and Schakowski followed him into the dining room. She knew how challenging it was for them to let another agency run an investigation on their home turf, and she appreciated their spirit of cooperation.

Jackson strode to a chair with an intense look in his eyes. He had something new, she could tell. River liked the confident way he moved and his rugged good looks. If she had normal hormones, he would be her type. But she would never get involved with anyone she worked with. She just hadn't figured out where else to meet men. River shook off the thought and started the meeting.

"Let's get up to date with leads, then we'll talk strategy." She glanced at her notebook. "Our agents found Daniel Talbot this afternoon at his cabin near Gold Lake. They're bringing him in for questioning now. There was no sign of Renee Jackson at the cabin, but some evidence to indicate Talbot had been at the cabin skiing for a few days. Still, he sent threats to Anderson and could have hired thugs to do the hands-on work, so he's still high priority." She looked down the table. "Jackson, what did you find out?"

"I have a suspect in custody. I had just enough time to bring him in and get over here."

Everyone in the room was suddenly more alert, ready to move. Startled, River blurted out, "Who is he? What does he say?"

"Gus Striker. He attended AA meetings at the Jesco Club with Renee. The group leader said he thought Striker was obsessed with Renee, so I went to Striker's place and looked around. Through the kitchen window, I saw that he had a picture of Renee on his refrigerator. He came home a few minutes later and refused to let me search his house, so I brought him to the department and left him in an interrogation room. An assistant DA is working on a search warrant for his house, his phone, and his car."

"What's your feel for him?"

"He's hiding something."

"Good work." She hesitated, knowing what she was about to say might piss off her fellow agents, but she believed in rewarding those who generated leads and ideas. "After the meeting, Jackson and I will interrogate Striker. Agent Fouts will stay here with Anderson in case the kidnapper texts again."

Fouts' eyes narrowed but he nodded.

"Anything else new?"

Schak spoke up. "Renee's cell phone hasn't been used since Saturday at three seventeen p.m. T-Mobile pinged it and got no signal. The kidnapper may have destroyed it when he grabbed her."

River added, "We don't have any new information on the burner phones the perps used this afternoon."

"You're saying perps," Jackson commented. "Are we confident there is more than one?"

"Not until we hear from him again. But I think so."

"How's Anderson holding up?" Jackson asked.

"He's doing okay. His daughter came over and that seemed to settle him down." Anderson had also been drinking Scotch since she told him his money went into the river. "They're both in his office. We'll confer with Anderson soon, but we need a strategy. How long do we wait to hear from the possible second perp before we go to the media to help locate Renee Jackson?"

"Two hours." Fouts sounded sure.

"What if the other perp is still out there, unsure of what to do next?" Jackson countered. "Rushing to the media could get Renee killed. We should at least interrogate both our suspects before we go public. Even meeting here is a risk if the perp is watching the house."

"I considered that," River said, worried but not defensive. "But we don't know if there is a second person. And if there is, he's likely guarding Renee and focused on what the hell happened to the money."

"Do you think he'll come back for more?" Jackson asked.

"I don't know." River shook her head. "This is new territory. We don't know for sure that the money is lost. The courier could have swum to safety."

A short silence.

River turned to Agent Torres, a stout young man who was prematurely gray. "Put together a media list and a generic statement that Renee Jackson is missing. Have everything ready to go. We'll start interrogations and see what happens."

"Did you say you have a suspect in custody?" A twenty-something woman burst through the archway. Dressed in a pale-green business jacket and skirt, Dakota Anderson was strawberry-blonde with dark roots, slender, and striking.

River envied her obvious sexuality. She also worried about the young woman's media connections. "We've brought two men in for questioning but we don't have anything solid."

Ivan Anderson followed her into the room, a drink in hand. "Dakota, it's best if you just let them do their job."

"But they should keep you informed." She spun protectively toward her father.

"They will." Anderson touched his daughter's shoulder. "Let me handle this."

"What about the ransom money?" Dakota spun toward River, her face tight with tension. "Was it recovered?"

"Not yet." River stared back. "Please don't repeat anything you hear about this case. Especially on the air. Renee's life is still at stake."

"I know that." Sounding defensive, the young woman spun again and strode from the room.

Anderson stayed, rocking a little on his feet, the combination of stress and alcohol weakening him. "What do we do now?"

"We'll question our two suspects. If we haven't heard from the kidnapper after that, we'll go to the media and ask the public to help us find Renee."

"What if he expects me to pay again?" Anderson squeezed his eyes closed. "I don't have access to more cash. I can borrow against my home equity, but that takes time."

"He may be desperate and willing to settle for less," River said. "But just hearing from him will be a good thing."

An engine revved in the driveway. River turned to the window and caught a glimpse of a small silver car as it sped down the slope. She was glad Anderson didn't have a houseful of young children, crying for their mother. But Renee did have a teenage daughter. River resisted the urge to ask Jackson how his child was doing. Not in front of everyone. She stood. "Let's get moving."

CHAPTER 16

Monday, January 9, 5:15 p.m.

He had arranged to meet Agent River at the department in an hour, so Jackson thought he had just enough time to stop and see his daughter. He felt like he'd been in nonstop motion for two days already and he really wanted to have a leisurely dinner with Kera. But she would have to wait. His girlfriend had broken up with him recently because he worked too much and canceled too many dates, so he worried about neglecting her. When she'd changed her mind and wanted to continue the relationship, he'd nearly wept with relief. Kera was a bright warm light in his otherwise dark and gritty world. Now here he was again, ignoring her while he worked a case. He put in his earpiece and pressed speed dial #2 as he drove off Anderson's property.

She didn't answer, so he assumed she was taking care of her baby grandson. He left a message: "Hey, Kera. Just checking in. We haven't located Renee yet but we have some leads.

I'll be working late of course." He wished he could tell her about the kidnapping but it was still nonpublic information. "I love you." He was getting more comfortable saying that. Kera said it with ease, but she'd been raised in a commune by a group of free-spirited people. His parents, on the other hand, had been Missouri Baptists who had hugged him often but rarely expressed verbal affection. He was doing his best to raise Katie to be more like Kera.

Renee's sister answered the door and Jackson was still surprised at how different they looked. Unlike Renee, Jan was ash blonde, well padded, and sober.

"Hey, Jan. Have I told you how grateful I am to have you in our lives?"

Jan just smiled. Another thing that set her and Renee apart. She waved him in. "Tell me you found her."

"Not yet, but we have a couple of leads."

"Okay. I'll keep praying."

"I've only got a few minutes. Where's Katie?"

"On the computer. She's distracting herself."

Jackson turned toward the family room but Katie came running. "Did you find her?"

He pulled her in for a hug. "Not yet, sweetheart, but we have a break in the case." Guilt and failure worked together to crush his heart. "I found a guy who seems obsessed with your mother. I'm on my way now to question him next."

Katie pulled back, eyes flashing. "Who is he? How did she meet him?"

Aware that Jan was standing by for information and that neither woman needed full disclosure, Jackson moderated his response. "Your mother was attending AA meetings and that was the last place she was seen."

A long silence while they digested what it really meant. Finally, Katie said, "So she was drinking again? But going to meetings. And some alcoholic pervert grabbed her?" His daughter's face compressed with anger, confusion, and hurt all at once.

"It looks that way. But she's not in the suspect's house and we still don't know if he made the ransom calls."

"What about Renee's phone?" Jan asked. "Have you tried to locate it electronically?"

"We sent a ping but the phone isn't responding."

"What about the guy with the money who went into the river?" Katie tugged at her braid.

"We haven't heard anything." Jackson felt overwhelmed. "Listen, both of you. What I tell you is strictly confidential and can't be repeated. At least until we go public with the abduction, which is our next move if we don't hear from the kidnapper again."

"We understand." Jan spoke for both of them. "Thanks for keeping us informed."

"It's the least I can do. And now I have to go. We have a suspect to interrogate."

"Have you had dinner? Can I make you a sandwich?"

"I don't have time to wait."

"It'll take five seconds." Jan trotted toward the kitchen.

Jackson hugged Katie again. "As long as I'm alive, I'll be here for you," he whispered.

"I know." She blinked back tears.

As he waited for Jan to bring the sandwich, his phone rang. It was Sheriff Walters. "We found a body in the river just north of Coburg. He's dressed in black like your perp who picked up the money."

Ignoring his daughter's pleading look, Jackson stepped outside. "Any ID on him?"

"Sorry, no. But he has a Westside Kings tattoo on his right shoulder."

"A gang member?" *What the hell was a banger doing mixed up in a kidnapping?* Jackson wondered. *Had Striker or Talbot paid him?*

"Or he used to be."

"Any trace of the backpack or the cash?"

"No."

"Where is the body?"

"On its way to the morgue."

"Thanks. Have Gunderson send me photos."

Katie stood in the doorway as Jan hurried past her with a brown paper bag. Jackson suspected it held more than a sandwich. A rush of love for the women who made his life bearable filled his chest. Unable to speak, he squeezed Jan's arm, waved at Katie, and bolted for the car.

Twenty minutes later, he pounded up the stairs from the underground parking lot, his belly full of roast beef on sourdough and his brain whirling with questions and scenarios. A gang member in a kidnapping for ransom was highly unusual. The thugs ran prostitutes, drugs, and burglary operations. If they abducted someone, they took him out to kill or beat him as a payback. Collecting ransom was too complex, too drawn out compared to the way bangers operated.

Jackson hurried toward the conference room, hoping not to run into anyone who wanted to discuss the case. He didn't have the time or patience. But Lammers stepped out of her office as he passed.

"Hey, Jackson. I could use an update."

He turned. "We have two suspects in custody for interrogation. Daniel Talbot, the construction company guy we talked about this morning, is with the feds. And Gus Striker, a lowlife from Renee's AA meeting, is here in the department."

"Any idea of Renee's status?"

"Not yet."

"I'm sorry. I wish I could offer more resources but the feds have more money."

"I know." Jackson nodded and turned away. He was already late.

Schak and Agent Rivers were in the conference room having a quiet conversation when Jackson walked in. Schak gave him a look that said, *Where have you been?*

"I'm glad you're here." River's tone was nonjudgmental. "We're ready to get started. Detective Schakowski will observe the interrogation. If we need to, we'll switch up after an hour or so."

"The sheriff called." Jackson didn't bother to sit. "They pulled a body out of the water that matches the description of the ransom courier. He's got no ID, but a crown tattoo indicates he's a member of the Westside Kings."

"Let's hope he's a hired thug," River commented. "Which means one of our suspects probably has connections to him. Let's hit that hard."

"The medical examiner will send us photos of the corpse. Maybe one of our vice detectives will recognize him."

"Is it possible your ex-wife was involved with drug running?"

Jackson shook his head. "No."

"We had a case a few years ago where gang members kidnapped a drug runner they thought had stolen some of their money. They demanded a ransom from his family."

Jackson fought to suppress his irritation. "It's a good thought, but Renee had no reason to get involved in that crap. She makes good money, her fiancé has even more, and she's never used drugs." *Except alcohol*, Jackson thought but didn't say.

"Let's go get some answers then."

* * *

Striker jumped up when they entered the interrogation room and River was glad he was cuffed. The suspect was six-three and built like a gorilla. On him though, the mass of black curly hair implied *crazy* rather than primitive. The dirty jeans and suspenders said *backwoods*.

"Sit down!" River yelled to get command of the situation.

"That bastard left me here for hours." Striker jerked his head toward Jackson. "I'll fucking sue you." He turned back to River. "I caught him in my backyard. I think he went in my house too. He can't do that without a warrant."

"Sit down!" River didn't know or care what Jackson had done. "You have a photo of a kidnapped woman on your refrigerator and no explanation for it. The FBI is going to crawl up your ass and stay there until this is resolved. Get used to it."

Resignation deflated his massive chest a size and Striker slumped into the chair. "I don't know where Renee is. I would never hurt her."

She glanced at Jackson. "Are we going to document this?" They both knew the camera was on.

"Always." He took out his pocket recorder.

"Good." She stated all their names for the protocol, then asked, "Why did you take Renee Jackson's picture?"

"Because she's pretty and I like to look at her." Striker looked up, defiant. "So what?"

"You're obsessed with her and I'm sure we'll find evidence of that when we search your house."

"I'm not obsessed. She's the only attractive woman at the Saturday meeting and I look at her. So what?"

"She's been kidnapped. And you're going to sit here until we find her, so you might as well tell us where she is and we'll try to cut you a deal."

"I have no idea."

"Where were you today?"

He blinked, trying to hide the panic in his eyes. "I drove out to Marcola to see a guy about a job."

"Who did you talk to?"

A quick pause. "Ted Striker. He's my brother."

"That's convenient." River rolled her eyes. "Give me his phone number."

Striker rattled it off. "He probably won't answer. He screens his calls."

River noticed the suspect's voice had tightened and he'd lost a little confidence. "Where were you Saturday afternoon around four?"

"At home." A pause. "Working."

"Can anybody verify that?"

"My ex-wife called to bitch about our kid so she knows I was home."

"It was a landline call?"

"No, my cell phone."

"Then I guess we don't really know where you were." River let a little mockery into her tone. "So far you have no alibi for the time of the kidnapping or for the time of the ransom demand." She turned to Jackson. "Let's go pick up a warrant and search his house. We need a little leverage for this conversation."

"There's no need to search my place," Striker pleaded. "You've got the wrong guy."

Jackson spoke up. "What are you hiding in there—if not Renee?"

"Nothin', man. I want a lawyer."

"Fine." River stood. "Let's go call yours."

Striker looked surprised. "I mean, a court-appointed one."

"That doesn't happen until you're charged with something."

"I haven't done anything."

River heard him think *yet*. She didn't actually hear the sound, because Striker didn't say it out loud, but he thought it so strongly the word popped into her mind. The phenomenon had happened enough times before that she trusted the communication to be real. "What are you *planning* to do?"

Striker flinched. "Nothin'!"

She smiled knowingly and shook her head. "You're a terrible liar. What are we going to find in your house?"

"I didn't kidnap Renee. I've never seen her outside of an AA meeting. You've got the wrong guy."

River wanted to confer with Jackson, who was being awfully quiet. "Excuse us for a moment."

They left Striker, cuffed and sweating, and stepped into the hall. "What do you think? You looked in his window. Should we take the time to search his place?"

"Renee isn't there." Jackson's eyes begged her not to ask questions. "But we should send someone out. Striker may have drugs or they might find his gang connections."

"We need to search his cell phone too. Does he have it in his possession?"

"No. I emptied his pockets when I left him in the interrogation room. His phone is in a bag at the front desk."

"I'm going to take a look at it before we let him go." River expected Jackson to object and he did.

"We have to wait for a warrant."

"You searched his house without permission, so don't get all self-righteous about this." She touched his arm. "Keep questioning him, while I go see who he's been chatting with on the phone."

* * *

Jackson headed back in, relieved that Agent River was taking the initiative. Morally, he felt no guilt. Police officers had been searching suspects' cell phones without warrants for years… until the courts recently ruled against it. But if a judge didn't eventually give them permission, nothing from the search would hold up in court. He slid back into his chair and mentally shut out the walls that were close enough to reach over and touch.

"When did you get involved with the Kings?"

Striker flinched. "What are you talking about?"

"We know you're cooking meth for them to sell on the streets."

"You son of—" Striker cut himself off.

He couldn't accuse Jackson of going into his house without indirectly admitting to having a meth lab.

"Who's your contact in the gang?"

"I don't know any gang members." Striker began to pop his knuckles.

"How does Renee fit into all this?"

"You've got the wrong guy."

Jackson decided to give him an out. "You know what I think happened? You grabbed Renee for your own purposes, planning to let her go unharmed. But the Kings got wind of it and pressured you to ask for a ransom. Did they take her from you or just threaten to turn you in?"

"I didn't touch Renee." Striker looked him right in the eye.

Jackson thought the gesture was overdone and he wasn't convinced. "Tell me where Renee is and I'll get you the best deal I can."

A funny smile crept over the suspect's face. "I just realized you and Renee have the same last name. Is she your wife?"

"No. Do you own any other property beside the house on Bethel Drive?"

"I don't own anything but some woodworking tools. And I'm not smart enough to plan a ransom."

Jackson was inclined to believe that.

He bought a Diet Pepsi from the vending machine and headed back to the conference room. A tug in his gut reminded him that he hadn't taken any naproxen since noon. But the prednisone he took every morning seemed to be working, and overall his pain level was decreasing. He had a CAT scan scheduled for later this week, and he hoped to see that the fibrosis had shrunk. Wishful thinking, he knew. Remission was rare for retroperitoneal fibrosis. The cloudy white growth usually came back and he knew he faced more surgeries down the road. *And an early death*, the voice of gloom always added.

Jackson shook it off and stepped into the room. Schak and River stood in front of the monitor, watching the last part of his session with Striker.

River turned. "I liked your empathy scenario, but he's not ready to trade information. We need more leverage."

"I'll call the assistant DA and see how the warrant is coming." Jackson dialed Trang, waited through seven rings, and almost hung up.

"Hey, Jackson. Glad you called." The ADA sounded a little breathless. "Judge Volcansek turned me down. She said having someone's picture is not illegal, and since Striker has no recent criminal history she won't authorize a search of his home or his car or his phone records."

"Crap. Can you take it to Judge Cranston?"

"I can't reach him. Sorry."

"Thanks. Send me the paperwork in case we come up with something else." Jackson clicked off and swore again.

"I take it that wasn't good news." River seemed quite calm. In fact, she'd been damn near serene throughout the whole afternoon, including the perp's dump into the river.

"What's the plan?" Schak turned off the monitor.

"You should head home," River said. "We'll let Striker go and one of our guys will follow him. If he has Renee locked up somewhere, he has to check on her eventually."

"You sure?" Schak scowled.

"Yes. I'll go over and check in with the Talbot interrogation, then head back out to Anderson's. The fact that we haven't heard from the kidnapper again means one of these guys is probably our ringleader."

Jackson desperately wanted that to be true, but either one might be willing to let Renee die rather than be followed and get caught releasing her. "I'll stay and update my notes." Jackson took a seat, unwilling to call it a day.

Schak clapped him on the shoulder. "You're a working fool and we love you for it."

"See you in the morning."

"Call me if anything breaks open." Schak directed the comment to Agent River.

"You got it."

After his partner left, Jackson closed the door and asked, "What did you get from the phone?"

"Nothing so far. No ransom texts, and all recent calls seem to involve clients, except for the one from his ex-wife." River sat down too. "But I have one number I haven't been able to trace. I sent it over to my lead tech guy."

As far as Jackson knew, the tech guys were still sitting in a van a block from Anderson's house.

River handed him a clear plastic bag containing Striker's wallet and phone. "Give me fifteen minutes, then let him go. An agent will pick up the tail outside and we'll see where he goes."

Jackson wanted to stay with Striker too. What if the suspect went straight to Renee? But Striker was just as likely to go home and stay there, meaning a long night in the car for whoever was tailing him. He glanced over while River was on the phone. She squeezed each finger on her left hand, then switched over and did the right fingers. It was slow, rhythmic, and probably soothing.

She noticed him watching her. "I got in the habit when I was a kid. My father made me nervous." She smiled, as though there was more to the story.

Jackson didn't think he should ask. "What did they say about Talbot?"

"He gave them nothing. And he has a pretty solid alibi for the time of the abduction. So we're going to let him go with a tail too." She stood. "I'm headed back to Anderson's house. You might as well go home."

Jackson looked at his watch: 8:11. It had been a long busy day and he could feel it in his bones. But with major cases, he often worked past midnight, slept on the couch in the *soft* interrogation room, and was back at his desk by five in the morning. This felt too early to call it quits. "I'll stay and try to dig up a connection between Striker and the Kings gang."

"Thanks, Jackson. I'm glad you're on the team."

CHAPTER 17

Monday, January 9, 8:15 p.m.

Driving out to Anderson's home, River missed a turn and had to circle back. She was still getting used to Eugene and its peculiar stop-and-start streets. But the lack of traffic, especially at night, made up for it. In San Diego, cars had been on the road until midnight. Even Portland, where she'd spent a chunk of her FBI career, was a real city with real nightlife. Except for a few bars in the small downtown area, Eugene shut down after eight o'clock, especially in the winter. Which was troublesome for a restless insomniac who didn't watch TV. The thought reminded her that she'd forgotten to contact the homeless shelter. She pulled off the road and called Eric, the director.

"It's River. I'm sorry, but I'm working late tonight and I can't come in."

"We'll miss you but you know I understand."

"Will you read to my group? We're on chapter three of *The Hunger Games.*"

"I'll try. When will you be back? The kids are always calmer after you've been here."

"Probably not for a few days. I'm working a tough case."

"I hope you solve it."

"Thanks." River hung up and let go of the guilt. She'd been volunteering in teenage homeless shelters for two decades and knew she'd done her part. Five years after her father went to prison, her mother had killed herself, and River—living as a male then—had ended up on the streets. She'd been homeless for her last two years of high school, until she'd finally contacted Joe Palmer, the FBI agent who headed the investigation into the murders her father had committed. Joe had given her his card during the investigation and said to call if she ever needed anything. One day, feeling sick, dirty, and hungry for a better life, she'd found the card in her wallet and made the call. It had changed her life, and later she'd vowed to never lose sight of teenagers in need.

Ivan Anderson's house was lit up like a Vegas hotel. Against the dark, quiet, upscale neighborhood, the brightness was jarring. *And unusual*, River thought. Agent Fouts was usually more of a sit-quietly-in-a-dark-corner kind of guy. Maybe the lights were Anderson's idea, a vigil of sorts for Renee.

River strode into the house after a brief knock and didn't see anyone. But the tech guys were still at their post down the road, and her team members were tailing their two suspects. Fouts and Anderson were in the study, watching TV. Her partner jumped up, while Anderson struggled to push himself off the couch.

"What's the update?" Fouts asked.

"We didn't get anywhere with the suspects, but we've got agents tailing both of them." She glanced at Anderson, whose eyes were glassy. "The sheriff's search team pulled a body out of the water downstream from the drop site. It's likely our perp, and he has a Westside Kings tattoo." She met Anderson's eyes. "Did Renee have any association with gang members?"

"Of course not." His words slurred like he'd had too much to drink.

River felt a flash of irritation. What if the kidnapper called and this idiot needed to function? "What about family friends or groups she belonged to? Did Renee do any volunteer work?"

"Her PR business takes up most of her time, and Renee's family here in Eugene consists of her sister and her daughter. None of them know any gang members."

River made a mental note to ask Jackson about his daughter's friends. "We're still hoping he had an accomplice."

"What about the cash? Did it turn up?" Anderson swayed as he talked.

"Not yet. The tracker went dead after the dump in the river."

"Oh christ. What do I do now?"

"We wait to see if he contacts you again and hope one of our suspects leads us to Renee."

"I need a drink." Anderson lurched toward the liquor cabinet.

For a second, River hesitated, then blurted out, "What if he calls and wants to try another exchange tonight? I need you to be coherent." She glanced at Fouts. Why had he let it go this far?

Anderson spun back, his face contorted. "I don't have anything to exchange. I cashed most of it out. What can I offer him tonight? My car? The keys to my cabin on the beach?"

"If he contacts you, decisions will need to be made."

"Christ, you're a nag."

Fouts tried to hide a smirk.

River turned away from them both. During a crisis, some people stepped outside their own limitations and performed heroically. Others medicated or wallowed in self-pity. Anderson disappointed her. No wonder his fiancée had started drinking again.

A jangle came from Anderson's phone. River pivoted back and watched, irritated, as Anderson looked for a place to set his drink. While the annoying ringtone filled the room, he fumbled with the device and finally clicked into his messages.

"It's a text from the kidnapper." Anderson choked back a sob.

Relief washed over her. The main perpetrator was still alive, which meant they had another opportunity to salvage the case and save Renee. "Let me see it." River strode over and reached for the phone.

The message read: *If you want your girlfriend back, start over. Have the cash ready again by noon tomorrow.*

"This is good news." River looked up. "It means Renee is probably still alive and we have another chance to apprehend or follow the kidnapper. But I want to demand proof of life." She wasn't really asking permission but she hoped Anderson wouldn't resist.

"What do you mean?" He'd pulled together a little and was trying to sound coherent.

"I want to see a time-stamped photo or hear her voice. We need to know for certain if she's alive."

"What if he says no?"

"We have to try."

"What should I say?"

"Let me send the text." River keyed in: *I want to talk to Renee. I need to know she's alive before I borrow more cash.*

While they waited for a response, Anderson put away the bottle of scotch and paced the room. River sat and took long slow breaths. This communication was critical. Even if Anderson didn't plan to pay another ransom, the kidnapper needed to think he would. The perp needed a reason to keep his captive alive.

When the phone beeped again, River clicked open the message: *She's fine. I'll send a photo soon. I still need a hundred grand so make it happen.*

She read the message out loud, then crossed her fingers. "Please let him send a photo. And please let it be from a smartphone."

"He seems too sharp to make such a mistake." Fouts shrugged. "It could happen though."

Her own phone rang and it was the tech team. "The last text bounced off a tower on Gateway Loop. But it's a throwaway phone with no GPS and we can't get a specific location."

"Find the owner if you can." River wasn't optimistic. All the other texts had come from untraceable phones bought with cash. She caught Anderson's eye. "We need to let him think you're going to pay again. If you want to actually pay and need more time, we'll negotiate for it. But if you don't plan to give him more money, then the sooner we set this up the better."

"It would take me a week to borrow another hundred thousand. I've spent most of my reserves in the last few years." Pain flashed across his face.

River wanted to know more about that situation but they had to respond to the kidnapper first. "Let's tell him you'll pay. This time we'll give him a bag filled with newspaper and we'll have more people in place ready to grab him."

Anderson nodded.

River keyed in, *I'll get as much cash together as I can. Where do you want to meet?*

A minute later, the text came back: *I'll let you know tomorrow.*

She typed back: *Send the photo.*

But Anderson's phone went silent.

CHAPTER 18

"Hey, Kera, I know it's late, but I'd like to stop by." Jackson left the message, disappointed she hadn't picked up. She was probably putting her baby grandson to sleep.

He clicked off his computer and headed out, feeling weird and guilty about going home while Renee was still missing. But this was the FBI's case and they had agents everywhere. There was nothing more he could do today. He'd found Striker and given the task force the best lead they had.

As he trotted down the stairs to the parking lot, Kera called back. "Of course you can. I'd love to see you." She paused. "I have a million questions but I'll wait until you get here."

He laughed. "You just don't want me on the phone while I'm driving."

"I like to see your face when you're talking. You're more expressive with me than you are with anyone else."

"Me and my face will be there soon." He was smiling as he hung up. He wished he'd told her she was the only person he didn't feel guarded with. Kera somehow made him want to tell her everything.

On the drive over, Agent River called to tell him about the new ransom demand.

"Did you get proof of life?" *Please let there be good news for his daughter.*

"Not yet. He said he'd send a photo, but we haven't received it."

"Is Anderson going to pay again?"

"He doesn't have the money and I don't want to leave Renee in the kidnapper's hands for a week while Anderson rounds it up. We'll have more agents in place for the next drop."

"I'd like to be there."

"Let's meet at Anderson's at nine tomorrow morning. The perp said noon but last time he jumped the gun."

"See you then."

Jackson pulled into Kera's driveway, remembering the first time he'd come here. She'd received a threatening letter after the Planned Parenthood clinic where she worked had been bombed. Moments after he arrived, she'd become deathly ill from ricin poison and he'd had to rush her to the hospital. Her courage in the face of numerous attacks had been one of the things that had drawn him to her.

He climbed out, feeling serene for the first time that day. The big house with the great view of the city lights always seemed to welcome him. Yet he hadn't taken Kera up on her invitation to move in. The birth of her grandson had changed everything. Then Kera had taken little Micah and her daughter-in-law into her home, and Jackson had decided he couldn't handle the chaos of living here.

Kera opened the door before he reached it and the sight of her gave him a jolt. A tall, athletic goddess. Sliding into her arms was like coming home. The tropical scent of her hair and her warm, velvety skin seemed to envelop him. She kissed him deeply and he wished they were back in Maui, just the two of them in a hotel room, with nothing to do but get naked.

"You're happy to see me," she whispered. "I like that."

"Are we by any chance alone?" He ran his hands down her back.

She let out a little moan. "No. Danette and the baby are both here."

Jackson pulled back. "Sorry we had to cut our vacation short."

"Me too. Come in."

Kera led him to the kitchen and made him a cup of decaf coffee and mint tea for herself. They headed for the family room, at the opposite end of the house, where Danette, the baby's mother, was watching TV.

"What's happening with Renee?" Kera asked.

"She was kidnapped." The three words didn't begin to explain all the crazy events of the day. Jackson tried to summarize without revealing anything that could be considered sensitive. "We had a ransom demand, but the perp drowned in the river and the money hasn't been recovered."

"Oh my god." Kera's hand flew to her mouth. "How will you find Renee?"

"He had an accomplice and we'll try another money drop tomorrow."

"How's Katie?" Kera frowned. "Where is she?"

"She's with Renee's sister. I think they're helping each other get through this."

"Of course. But you know she can come here any time."

Footsteps pounded down the hallway and Danette burst into the room. "Turn on the TV. You've got to hear this." She was wild-eyed and breathless. "It's about your ex-wife."

Jackson's pulse raced. Why hadn't anyone called him?

Kera jumped up, grabbed the remote, and clicked on the wall screen. "What channel?"

"KRSL with Dakota Anderson." Danette stared at Jackson. "She's talking about Renee's kidnapping."

The young strawberry-blonde woman sat behind the news desk, eyes blinking nervously. "Please contribute if you can. As I said, the kidnapper wants a hundred thousand dollars. My father paid the ransom, but the money was lost and he can't raise it again in time. The kidnapper will probably kill Renee without your help. Please bring any cash you can spare to the station. The FBI will collect it for the ransom. This is an opportunity—"

"What the hell?" Jackson bolted to his feet.

Dakota was still talking, but his own thoughts drowned her out. He had to call Agent River and they needed to get Dakota under control. He grabbed his phone and found the number in his call log. As he dialed, he glanced up at the TV. The station had cut away to a commercial.

"I've got to go." He kissed Kera on the forehead and rushed past Danette. The young woman looked so much like Kera it was eerie. Especially since she was her daughter-in-law.

As Jackson rushed out of the house, River answered. "What have you got?" Her voice was tight, as if she knew something was wrong.

"Dakota Anderson was just on the air asking viewers to bring in cash to help pay the ransom."

"Good glory." A long silence. "I never predicted that. I worried that her journalistic instincts would lead her to report the kidnapping but this is unprecedented."

Jackson climbed into his car. "I'm headed out to the station now. I'm worried she could become a target."

"I'll send an agent too."

Jackson didn't know what to think or ask next. "Should I call the station and ask them to retract her request?"

"I'll take care of it." Another silence while they both wondered about whether any viewers would bring in money. Finally, River said, "Although I suppose there's nothing wrong with letting a few Good Samaritans help out. We need some cash to cover the newspaper bundles we're going to use in tomorrow's rendezvous."

"It feels weird but I suppose we could leave it up to the TV station."

"I'll call and see what they say. I hope the kidnapper didn't catch her segment."

"She mentioned the FBI." Jackson started driving down the hill.

"Damn. But he has to know we're involved."

"He will now. What should I do with Dakota?"

"Detain her until an agent gets there. I'll have him bring her here and we'll keep her under house arrest."

"Will do." Jackson hung up. He hoped he didn't have to cuff the young woman in front of a station full of cameras. So much of police work looked bad on video, even when they did everything by the book. Restraining an innocent-looking person tended to stir up anger in fellow humans. It was physiological and he'd learned to ignore those reactions as a patrol officer, but it was never easy.

By the time he reached the TV station, the first good-hearted viewer was already in the lobby, trying to give a little stack of cash to a headset-wearing producer.

"We didn't authorize the newscaster to make that plea. It's best if you take your money and go back home."

"I want to help," the older woman insisted.

Jackson noted the producer didn't refer to Dakota by name. Distancing himself already? He strode over. "I'm Detective Jackson, Eugene Police. Where is Dakota Anderson?"

"We asked her to leave." The producer stepped away from the older woman. "We had to force her off the set."

"Where did she go?"

"I have no idea."

Crap. What now? Dakota hadn't committed a crime, so putting out an ATL for her seemed wrong. Was she in danger? If the kidnapper considered her a threat to collecting a ransom, she might be. But Dakota was clearly a wildcard, and who knew what she would do next. Jackson turned and walked toward the entrance, calling River on the way.

"Hey," the producer called out. "I need you to help me deal with this situation."

Jackson called over his shoulder. "An FBI agent is coming."

As he pushed out the double doors, River picked up. "What's happening?"

"Dakota left the station. I need her home address so I can check on her."

"Give me a minute."

The phone went quiet. Jackson watched as two cars pulled into the nearly empty lot. How much money would Dakota's plea raise? Would any big donors come through?

River came back on. "She lives at 2755 Crest, unit fifteen. Do you think she'll try another public stunt?"

"I don't know her. Ask her father. I'm heading over to her place now." Jackson started his car. "People are showing up here with money. The station could be bombarded when the bank opens in the morning."

"We'll get someone out there to handle it."

"Maybe we should use the cash as a reward for information about Renee's location."

"I like it. But we'll wait until we see if the perp tries for another money drop."

"I'll stay in contact."

The address proved to be a condo in the south hills, an upscale complex in a parklike setting. Jackson knocked on the door, but the unit was dark, and the corresponding space in the parking lot was empty. Jackson hoped the young newscaster had headed to her father's house. In his car, he called dispatch and put out an attempt-to-locate for Dakota Anderson, giving what few details he knew about her and her vehicle make and model. What else could he do to find her? How important was it?

Agent River hadn't seemed overly concerned with Dakota's safety, and Jackson decided she was probably right. With one kidnapper drowned and the other holding Renee, what was the likelihood of them staging another abduction? He was more concerned that Dakota would do something stupid and endanger Renee.

Exhausted, Jackson drove toward home, his thoughts turning to Katie and what her life would be like at Dakota's age. He dreaded the thought of his daughter leaving Eugene to attend college somewhere else…and possibly never moving back. Even more, he dreaded what she would go through emotionally if Renee were murdered. The death of a parent often derailed teenagers into self-destructive behavior. He'd started this case feeling optimistic they would find Renee alive and well, but ever since he'd seen her photo in Striker's kitchen, dread had settled in his stomach like a swallowed rock. What if he didn't find her? He hadn't let himself think about how he would feel if she died. Katie would not be the only one to grieve.

CHAPTER 19

Monday, January 9, 7:35 p.m.

Karen Murray looked so much like her daughter it startled Evans to see her sleeping in the chair. But Lyla was still in the hospital bed, with tubes in her nose and an IV in the back of her hand. Evans approached and cleared her throat, and the mother woke.

"Who are you?" She blinked and stood. Awake, her age was more apparent.

"Detective Evans, Eugene Police. I'm investigating Lyla's assault. Are you Karen Murray?"

"Yes." Worry jumped from her eyes and stress tightened her jaw. "Do you know who did this?"

"I have a good lead. But first, how is Lyla doing?"

She gave a small shake of her head. "Not good. They found bleeding in her brain as well as her left kidney, so they put her into a coma to help her heal."

"But she's stable?"

"Not really. One of her doctors tried to prepare me for the worst." Lyla's mother choked back tears. "Tell me what happened."

"I think some young women beat her as part of an initiation."

"No!" Karen's hand flew to her mouth. "Why?"

"I don't understand hazings either. I was hoping you could tell me something about the sorority she wanted to join." Evans grabbed the other chair and pulled it over.

"Sorority?" Mrs. Murray sat too. "I thought it was just a group of women who lived together."

Evans suppressed her disappointment. "What did Lyla tell you?"

"Just that she had applied to rent a room in a group house. She said it would be less money and more fun than the quad she was in."

"Did she discuss the application process?"

"No. I just assumed it was some paperwork. She asked to borrow five hundred dollars until she got her deposit back on the place she was in."

"Did you give it to her?"

"I sent it through PayPal. Is it important?"

"It might be later in court, to help establish Lyla's connection to the rental house."

"Who attacked her? Do you know their names?"

"Nothing is certain, but Taylor Harris, the house leader, texted your daughter and arranged to meet her right before she was assaulted. Taylor claims she and Lyla made plans to go to a party together and Lyla never showed up. But I'm just getting started."

"I heard my daughter mention that name."

"Anything specific?"

"No." She looked over at the bed. "The nurse said she had dirt and feces on her too." Karen Murray crossed her arms and began to rock. "Poor Lyla. She wanted so badly to belong. In high school she never once made the cheerleading team, and she lost the election for senior class vice president. I tried to build up her self-esteem, but after her father died in Afghanistan two years ago, she seemed lost."

"I'm sorry for your loss. And for your pain now." Evans vowed to put an end to the sorority's vicious practice, but it wouldn't change anything for this battered family.

"Please get the despicable women who hurt my baby girl."

"I will."

CHAPTER 20

River woke to the sound of a rooster crowing. After spending nearly her whole life in a city, she loved her new rural home. The big yard with room for a garden, the long stretches of quiet, a night sky lit only with stars. She sat up, noticed the floral wallpaper, and scowled. The entire home needed updating and she'd started taking bids from contractors. This case had put that process on hold.

A glance at the clock told her she was running a little late. She hadn't slept well, as usual—dreaming in spurts about rescuing a woman from a burning building, a familiar nightmare. Her shrink said it was about rescuing herself. River hurried into the bathroom and stripped for a shower. The sight of her small breasts always caught her by surprise. As did her lumpy, androgynous shape. She took pleasure in her new body only because she was no longer trapped in the old one.

She dressed in slacks and a turtleneck, scrambled eggs for breakfast, and tucked a breakfast bar in her shoulder bag. She'd vowed to start eating healthier soon. Maybe after this case. She opened her laptop and skimmed through the sender addresses in her personal e-mail. Two were from teenagers she counseled at the homeless shelter.

She responded to the kids, then grabbed a stack of envelopes from the breakfast bar. She'd brought the mail home from the department without looking through it. Typically, the personal mail she received at work was from victims who wrote to express gratitude or to ask for help with accessing services.

One return address made her chest tighten: *San Quentin State Prison*. A letter from a convict she'd put away? The name in the center of the envelope made her heart skip a beat: *Carl Barstow-River*.

This will be bad, she told herself, *don't even open it*. It was either from her father or possibly someone connected to one of his victims. As a teenager, she'd changed her last name from Barstow to River, feeling like the new identity would carry her away from her past and give her some peace. And it mostly had. But her father had learned of her name change—most likely from her aunt who stayed in touch with both of them—and once someone who knew her connection to Gabriel Barstow had contacted her through the bureau.

River tore open the envelope, which had been forwarded by the Portland FBI office. She hoped it was from her father and not a victim's relative. Thirteen women had died, all mothers. The anguish in the lives of their families was never far from her heart, even now. The man who'd contacted her years ago wanted to know why Gabriel Barstow had chosen his wife. As though she might have some insight. But her father had never confided his motives to his interrogators, and River's years in the bureau had not brought her closer to understanding. Serial killers were inexplicable.

River glanced at the signature: *Your father.* For a second she was relieved, then instantly worried again. He hadn't written in years, after decades of silence from her. What was this about? Was the old man finally going to be given the death sentence he deserved?

Her hands shook as she started to read the letter.

Dear Carl

Sorry son, but you are in danger. I wanted to be a good inmate but I made some enemies. Darien Ozlo gets out soon and he said he would hurt you to get even with me. He knows you're the only person I care about and I was stupid to talk about you being an FBI. I hope it's just talk, but you'd better watch out.

And come see me before I die.—Your father, GB

Good glory. Just when she thought she'd found a little peace.

River dropped the letter, momentarily overwhelmed by the double fuck-you life had given her. She'd been born in the wrong body to a despicable man. Were those things connected? More than one psychiatrist had tried to convince her they weren't.

Her phone rang as she pushed back from the table. She didn't recognize the number and was grateful it wasn't a personal call. She pulled in a breath and cleared her mind. "This is River."

"Jackie Matthews, Eugene Police. We've located the vehicle you're searching for in the kidnapping case. It's near the corner of Seventeenth and Patterson. An officer is with the car now."

"Thank you. I'll be right there."

River made a quick call to check on Ivan Anderson. "Have you heard from the kidnapper?"

"No. And I haven't heard from my daughter either. She's not home and she's not answering her phone."

"Could she be at a friend's?"

"I called her boyfriend and he hasn't seen her or heard from her either." Anderson was suddenly distressed. "What if she's been kidnapped too? I thought you were going to send an agent to the TV station to protect her. What happened?"

"The producer made Dakota leave the building. She was gone when we got there."

"They fired her?" A new level of panic.

"I don't know." *Why was Dakota's job important at this moment?* "What about a girlfriend she might go stay with?"

"She has some friends from college, but I don't really keep track of them."

"Can you find her friends' phone numbers and make some calls?" River kept her voice light. "We'll put out an alert for her and her car, but there's no point in panicking. Most likely she's with a friend. If the kidnapper has her, he'll tell us when he calls." She clicked off before he could unload on her again.

Had she failed to protect Dakota Anderson?

Every decision is correct in that moment. The mantra echoed in her head. Years of inner conflict in dealing with her own androgyny and her father's violent legacy had led River to adopt just enough Buddhism to keep herself sane.

She was glad she hadn't stayed over at Anderson's house. His drunken anger would have been hard to overcome. She and Agent Fouts had flipped a coin to see who had to stay with the target, and Fouts had lost as usual. She felt a little guilty, since he had a wife at home, but being a single person, she'd spent her whole life accommodating others who had spouses and children. Now that she'd shed her false skin, she wanted to live her life to the fullest. River grabbed her coat and strapped on her Glock, mindful that peaceful thoughts could only protect her soul, not her body.

Renee Jackson's red Acura had been left unlocked about ten blocks from the University of Oregon.

"It's a miracle it wasn't stolen." The patrol officer looked around at the older homes occupied mostly by students.

"Let's get some tape around this whole area," River said. "Who knows what evidence the technicians will find." She rummaged through the car's glove box while she called Anderson again.

"River here. Any idea why your fiancée would be parked on the corner of Seventeenth and Patterson?"

A slight pause. "Serenity Lane is nearby. It's an alcohol treatment center. She might have left the AA meeting and driven there to check herself in."

"Only she never made it that far."

"Can you find out for sure? What if she's in treatment and the kidnapper is conning us?"

How would the perp know? River thought it was a strange idea. "We may need a subpoena to get that information but I'll try."

River hung up and pulled out the registration. *Renee Marie Jackson, 230 Cheshire Street.* That wasn't Anderson's address. She'd been led to believe Renee lived with him. Were he and his fiancée on the outs? Was there a layer of deception and fraud going on here?

Further rummaging turned up a flashlight, an AA chapter book with meetings listed, and a half-empty package of Junior Mints. *About as useful as a grocery list*, River thought. She climbed out of the car to search under the front seats and found a thermos. One sniff of the contents told her it was alcohol, probably vodka.

She stood and turned to the officer. "Where's Serenity Lane?"

"Right around the corner." He pointed to the left.

River walked over, strode into the treatment center, and showed her badge to the middle-aged woman behind the desk. "Agent River. Renee Jackson is missing. Her car is parked nearby, but we've also had a ransom demand. I need one simple piece of information: Is she here in the building?"

Not this time. The receptionist's unspoken words popped into River's head. The thought was soft and hesitant, but unmistakable. Out loud, the woman said, "I'm sorry but I can't divulge client information."

"That's okay." River smiled and walked away. She had what she needed. Renee had not made it to check in. She'd been grabbed right outside her car. River called her office and asked for evidence technicians.

"One of our techs is out in the field, but I'll see what I can do."

"Thanks."

Knowing it would take the evidence people at least an hour to arrive, River spent a few minutes searching the street and sidewalk for blood spatters or dropped personal items. The area was mostly clean, netting only a wad of gum and a bus transfer ticket. She bagged both, almost hesitant to send them to the crime lab at Quantico, then hurried back to the victim's vehicle. She might as well check the backseat and pop the trunk if she could.

In the otherwise clean car with a deep black interior it stood out immediately. A single white glove lay in the middle of the seat.

CHAPTER 21

Tuesday, January 10, 5:46 a.m.

The grumble of an engine woke Jackson from a sound sleep. *Who was in his driveway?* He jumped from bed, pulled on pants, and grabbed his weapon. If Katie had been home, the Sig Sauer would have been locked in a fingerprint-activated case, but he'd left the gun on the nightstand this time.

The front door opened as he rounded the hall corner. His weapon came up, then dropped immediately.

"Jesus, Wade. Someday you're gonna kill me."

His brother, Derrick, looked haggard after three weeks on the road in a long-haul truck. But women found his cobalt eyes, wide jaw, and shaggy blond hair appealing even on his worst days. Kera thought he and Derrick looked alike, except for Jackson's dark eyes and cropped hair, but she was humoring him. His older brother had always been bigger, better looking, and a lot more trouble. Jackson had tried to compensate by always doing the right thing.

"Sorry. I wasn't expecting you this early." He tucked his gun in the back of his pants and gave Derrick a high five. "Good to see you." After an eleven-year falling out, they weren't up to hugging yet. They might never be.

"I always make good time when my days off are coming up." Derrick tossed his duffel bag on the floor and stepped into the kitchen. "Join me for some coffee? I'll brew."

"Sure. I'll be right back."

Jackson hurried to put on a shirt and leave his weapon on the nightstand. Back in the kitchen he made toast to soak up their coffee.

"What's new here?" Derrick asked, taking his cup to the small kitchen table.

"Renee has been kidnapped and held for ransom."

"What the fuck?" His brother spewed coffee.

Jackson reached for a paper towel. "Her fiancé is a stockbroker and apparently has some money, but it still surprises me that she was targeted."

"Is she okay? Have you talked to her or seen a video?"

"We don't have proof of life yet, and the first ransom attempt went badly. It's not looking good."

"Where's Katie?"

"With her aunt Jan. I'm working the case with the FBI, so it's a good place for Katie to be."

"What a freaky thing for Katie. What can I do? I'll be here for a few days if she wants to come home."

"Thanks. I'll let her know." Jackson sipped his coffee, still surprised to be sharing a house, even part-time, with his older brother. He liked it though, since Derrick was gone most of the time. Kera still wanted him to move in with her, but he wasn't ready to take on her entourage. So this arrangement was good for now.

"I met a woman I really like." Derrick grinned. "I know, I've said that before, but this one's special. I think it could get serious."

"Where does she live?"

"Fresno."

Jackson chewed his toast and pondered the implications. Would Derrick move away or want to sell the house?

"Will you help me build a trike this summer?" Derrick asked, out of the blue. "Every time I see yours sitting in the garage, I think I have to have one, so we can go out riding together."

"Let's do it." Jackson was pleased. He loved his three-wheeled motorcycle. Katie, who'd helped him build it, no longer had time for weekend rides with him. She'd moved into a new phase and was feeling popular at school and attractive to boys. "I'd like to use a different Volkswagen rear end this time."

"Whatever you say. I'll just be the helper."

"Start looking online for old VWs." Jackson stood and gulped the last of his coffee. "I have to shower and get to work. This case is a round-the-clock operation."

"I won't see you much while I'm here this week?"

Jackson shook his head. "Sorry. Bad timing."

"We were supposed to remodel the bathroom. For starters."

"We will."

A little later, Jackson hurried to his car, cursing the cold and early-morning darkness. His phone rang.

"Jackson, it's Sergeant Lammers. I'm sorry to report that Dakota Anderson was found dead at Wayne Morse Park this morning. I need you to take this case. It could be related to the kidnapping."

He stopped in his tracks. "Murdered?"

"I don't know. Dispatch said the woman who called it in was nearly hysterical." Lammers sounded upset too. "I'll send Schak and Quince. Evans is pretty deep into an assault case, so she's not available."

"The park is on Crest?" Jackson had never had a reason to visit the area. What was Lammers not telling him?

"Near Twenty-Fifth."

"Have you told Agent River?"

"I'll call her next." Lammers cleared her throat. "I'm scheduling a joint task force meeting this afternoon at four. I need to get up to speed on these cases. As soon as the media gets wind of Dakota's death, we have to make a public statement."

"Good luck with that." Jackson had no intention of dealing with the press. He hung up, his mind reeling. Dakota had gone on TV asking for help with her father's ransom situation, then was killed in a dog park hours later. It couldn't be a coincidence, but on the surface, the connection was mystifying.

He had suspected Dakota was in danger, yet he'd failed to bring her in and keep her safe. How many minutes had he missed her by? If he had left Kera's immediately and called Agent River on the way over, he might have arrived at the TV station in time to steer Dakota in a different direction. He mentally kicked himself for his hesitation. Yet he realized Dakota was willing to do whatever it took to get her way. And arresting her for her own good had never been a real legal option. Now the only way to make this right was to find her killer.

In the car, another icy thought squeezed his heart. If the perp had killed Dakota, had he already killed Renee too?

The park was near the intersection of two newly paved winding streets in the south hills. Calling it a park was an exaggeration. There was a small covered area for humans, but it was mostly grassy acres with a narrow creek in the middle, where people let their dogs off their leashes to run and get muddy. The acreage, surrounding tree grove, and historic house had been owned by the late senator Wayne Morse, whose family had donated the land to the city. Now it was open to the dog-loving public.

Early Tuesday morning, only a few cars were in the parking lot. The owners had probably been questioned by the officers, who had beaten Jackson to the scene, then blocked the entrance with their patrol cars. He parked in an empty driveway across the street and sat for a moment. *Why dogs? Why him?* A Rottweiler had bitten him above the eye as a young man, leaving an ugly scar and a deep distrust.

He pulled on his overcoat and stepped out. The cold stung his face but he heard no barking. Soft fog hung over the area as he crossed to the park. A patrol officer strode to meet him in the parking lot.

"What have we got?" Jackson pulled out his notepad.

"A dead young woman who looks like she was mauled by a dog." The officer shuddered a little. "I didn't even get close and it nearly made me sick."

Dread filled Jackson's torso like liquid lead. *Should he turn this case over to someone else?* "Do we have any witnesses?"

"Just the woman who found her. She's in her car with her dog." The officer nodded toward a yellow Volkswagen bug. "She was hysterical but she may have calmed down enough to answer questions now."

"Any other people or dogs in the park this morning?"

"An older couple with two little terriers. I questioned them but they didn't see anyone else in the park, nor did they see the body. So I sent them home. They live right down the street if you want to talk to them again."

Jackson started to say something but the officer added, "I wanted to get all the dogs secure and out of the park while we investigate."

"Thank you." Which dog had mauled the victim? Not likely a couple of terriers with their owners in tow. "Did you take pictures of the terriers?"

"I did." The officer patted a camera in his pocket. "I also took some with my phone and sent them to the crime lab."

"Good work. The evidence techs should be here soon. Where's the body?"

The officer pointed northeast, to a cluster of trees in the far corner of the fenced area. Wishing he'd worn his boots, Jackson took off down the sawdust path, then trudged through the tall grass to reach the crime scene.

The body lay on a sloped bank leading down to the creek, her feet nearly touching the water's edge. What was left of her face was not recognizable and her throat had been torn open as if by an angry bear. Dakota wore the same skirt and pale-green blazer she'd had on at work the night before. One sleeve had been shredded and the arm underneath was torn open with deep bite marks. Blood had seeped into the collar and shoulders, blending with the green to look like spilled chocolate.

Distress pumped through Jackson's veins and he fought the urge to look away. *Please let someone else take this case.* If the dog factor wasn't bad enough, processing the bodies of young female victims had become overwhelmingly difficult. His thoughts always turned to Katie and he started to visualize his own daughter in similar circumstances. Thinking of her being mauled by a dog enraged him and made his heart pound. Jackson took three deep breaths and tasted the iron in the blood that had flowed everywhere. Bile rose in his throat, and he popped a piece of mint gum in his mouth.

How had this happened? Was it a tragic accident? If Dakota hadn't been connected to the other case, it would be easy to think she'd come here to visit and been killed by a loose dog. It had never happened in the park before, or even in Eugene, but lots of children across the country are attacked and killed by dogs.

Jackson looked over at a second patrol officer, standing rigidly nearby, his ghost-white face expressionless as he guarded the body. "Where's her ID? How do we know this is Dakota Anderson?"

The patrol officer held out a small silver purse. "I wore gloves when I opened it. Her driver's license is in there."

"Is there a cell phone?"

"Yes."

"Good news." Jackson pulled on gloves and reached for the purse. He did a cursory search, finding only a wallet, cell phone, keys, thumb drive, and lipstick. Nothing unexpected. He put the keys in his jacket pocket, thinking her car was likely in the parking lot and they would need to search it. He tucked the purse into an evidence bag and slipped it into his carryall. The cell phone and thumb drive begged to be explored, but he needed to examine the body before the medical examiner showed up and took over the scene.

After snapping a dozen pictures from various angles, he took a moment to scan the area around the corpse, looking for anything the dog's owner or the victim might have dropped. Nothing popped out. But the grass and clover mix was six inches tall, and without crawling around and manually searching every square inch, he probably wouldn't find anything. He would leave that task to the evidence technicians. A sense of urgency compelled him to move quickly into questioning suspects.

Jackson knelt next to the body, not even sure what to look for. This attacker wasn't human and he'd never dealt with anything like it. Out of habit, he picked up the victim's hands and looked for defense wounds. They were remarkably untouched. On her right hand was a ring with bands of turquoise mixed with another stone that was a translucent white. Opal popped into his head, but he wasn't sure. As he was about to let go, he noticed a faded blue mark on the top of her wrist. It looked like it might be part of a stamp, like the kind you get after you've paid to enter an event. He took several close-up photos. As much as he wanted to know where she'd been and when, the time it would take to track down the information seemed daunting with his limited manpower.

Jackson shifted his attention to Dakota's feet, noting that she had on black pumps, likely the same shoes she'd worn to work the night before. She hadn't changed her clothes before coming to the park in the middle of the night. Small bits of grass stuck to the edge of the soles, and the instep held a little smear of what looked like dog poop. Had she been brought here against her will? If not, why had she come?

Dark nylons obscured her legs but surprisingly little debris clung to the fabric. Jackson scanned all her clothing but didn't see any stray hairs or lint. The overcast sky and the shade of a nearby tree darkened the scene. He stood to grab a flashlight and saw Michael Quince jogging across the grass.

"What have we got?" Quince called out. The younger detective looked grim, but his face was handsome even when he wasn't smiling. He'd joined the Violent Crimes Unit after several years in vice and sex crimes and he had a broad range of contacts and informants.

"Dakota Anderson. She's the daughter of Ivan Anderson, the ransom target in Renee's kidnapping."

"What the hell?" Quince stared at the body. "She was attacked by a dog?"

"It looks that way." Jackson dug though his carryall for a flashlight and evidence bags. "I need you to talk to the woman in the yellow Volkswagen. She found the body."

"Then what? Look for more witnesses?"

"Yes."

"Do we have a time frame?"

"We know it happened after Dakota left the station at ten thirty last night and before eight this morning when she was found. But no time of death."

Jackson turned back to his task, shining the beam back and forth across her skirt. The flashlight illuminated a cluster of tiny caramel-colored seeds clinging to the hemline. He scooped them into an evidence bag, worried that they might dislodge at any moment. If Dakota had picked them up somewhere besides the park, the evidence could help trace her movements or implicate her killer.

He examined her jacket, focusing on the shredded sleeve. He flashed on an image of a Doberman pinscher sinking its teeth into Dakota's arm to bring her down. Revulsion turned somersaults in his stomach. Could he look at her face and neck? Jackson braced for it, telling himself this was just a training exercise with fake wounds and blood.

Her throat had been ripped open, exposing a mangled esophagus and carotid artery. She'd bled profusely and the blood had pooled and thickened in her open wound. Above her jawline, her once-pretty face had been torn open in a series of long gaping wounds. Most of her nose was gone and one eye had been torn from its socket. Jackson had to look away. He wasn't a canine expert and there was nothing he could learn by staring at these wounds.

Springing to his feet, he gulped in cold wet air to fight the nausea. He hoped Anderson wouldn't feel compelled to see his daughter's body. No father should ever have to see this. I'll get the bastard, he promised the slain young woman. We'll put the dog down, and if the owner let this happen, we'll put him away too.

"It's heinous, isn't it?" The patrol officer hadn't moved.

"The worst I've seen." Jackson stepped back.

"Do you think someone sicced the dog on her?" Anger tightened the officer's voice.

"I don't know." The ugly thought had hovered at the edge of his mind too.

The rumble of engines in the parking lot made Jackson turn. The medical examiner's white station wagon had pulled in, followed by a white crime lab van. He hoped Jasmine Parker was driving it. She was the best technician in the department and this case would be challenging. The pathologist might not even rule it a homicide.

While he waited for the death specialists, he bent down and searched the pockets of Dakota's jacket. She carried a small tube of strawberry lip gloss in one and a Visa credit card in the other, and he bagged them both.

"Hey, Jackson. Give me some room to work." Rich Gunderson's voice was friendly and bossy at the same time.

Jackson stepped away from the body, watching Gunderson unload his heavy bags of equipment. The ME turned and called, "Bring the lights" to Jasmine Parker, the tall, slender Asian woman following him. She turned and headed back to the van.

"Good god, she's been mauled." Gunderson's jaw dropped, then snapped back. "I've only attended one other fatal dog attack, a toddler killed by the family's pit bull, but it was nothing like this." He squatted next to Dakota. "Maybe I'm glad this will be my last case. I've seen enough death and destruction."

"You're quitting?" Jackson was stunned.

"I'll be laid off next month if the county doesn't find a couple million dollars fast. The federal timber payments are not coming through."

"Who'll handle death investigations? The pathologist?"

"No one will. But I can't talk about it now. Give me some time with the body."

Jackson watched as the ME pulled down Dakota's skirt and plunged a temperature probe into the white flesh of her hip. "It dipped below freezing last night," Gunderson said, not looking up, while he waited for a reading.

Jackson resisted the urge to ask questions.

"She's at 82.6 and in full rigor mortis." The ME looked at his watch. "Considering how it frigid it still is, I'd say she's been cooling for eight or nine hours, so she likely died around one o'clock this morning. Give or take thirty minutes on either side."

Dakota had left the TV studio at 10:30 p.m. What had she done in between? Hopefully, her cell phone would tell him.

Schak walked up with Parker, carrying a large tripod light. Jackson noticed Schak moved less comfortably and had gained back some of the weight he'd lost after his heart attack.

"What do we know?" Schak asked, as he set up the light.

"She was killed by a dog at one this morning. No witnesses, so far."

"Jesus." Schak clasped his hands over his head.

"Don't assume it was a dog just because we're in a dog-run park," Gunderson corrected. "It could have been a cougar or coyote."

"Those wounds don't look like claw marks," Jackson said.

"No they don't, but I'm not an animal expert and neither are you. We'll have to call someone in to assist with the autopsy." He looked back over his shoulder. "Do you two have other areas to investigate?" Gunderson was always a little grumpy, but his pending layoff was making him downright testy.

Jackson handed Dakota's keys to Schak. "These are the victim's. I need you to find out if she has a car in the parking lot."

"Will do."

Jackson looked around to see if he could determine Dakota's route to get here. She had probably followed the same dirt trail he had to reach the fork in the path. Had the charging dog—or animal—driven her off the path and toward the creek? Or had she headed for the tree?

Jackson walked slowly toward the tree, scanning the ground for anything. Halfway there, he spotted a glint of silver. Squatting to reach for it, both knees popped and he was again reminded that his life was getting shorter by the minute. His fingers looped through a necklace and he lifted it out of the grass. The silver chain held a pendant made of turquoise and opal, matching the ring on Dakota's finger. Not seeing any blood, he bagged the necklace and kept scanning and walking toward the tree.

The grass here was shorter and thinner. A section near the base of the tree was slightly matted down, as if someone had lain there recently. How long did grass stay bent over? The area was six feet long and several feet wide, as if more than one person had stretched out. Jackson snapped several photos, then knelt and took several more. He did a quick visual search and didn't see anything unusual. Parker and her crew would search it inch by inch, staying all day if they needed to. Eager to hear what Gunderson had to say, Jackson pushed up, his knees popping again. He was glad his coworkers hadn't heard. Schak would have given him shit about it.

When Jackson reached the body, Gunderson looked up. "There's no livor mortis on her front side."

"So she died right here?"

"Most likely. Unless she was transported immediately and left on her back the whole time."

"What else?"

"I scraped under her nails but I don't think we'll find any tissue."

Dread and guilt filled Jackson's gut. This case file could easily join the boxes of others that were never solved.

CHAPTER 22

Tuesday, January 10, 8:42 a.m.

At the streetlight, River glanced at her watch. She hoped to still make it to Anderson's by nine, despite stopping to examine Renee Jackson's vehicle, which would soon be on its way to the Eugene crime lab to be dusted for prints. She wasn't optimistic about finding any that were useful. The perps had likely grabbed Renee while she walked to the treatment center. For now, the white glove was in an evidence bag in her briefcase. She needed to ask Anderson about it. Instinct and experience told her it wasn't just a stray piece of clothing. Who wore white gloves in January?

As she accelerated, her phone rang. *Eugene Police Department.* "This is River."

"It's Sergeant Lammers. We have a development with the kidnapping case."

Her heart skipped a little. "What's happening?"

"Dakota Anderson was found dead this morning in the dog run area at Wayne Morse Park. I sent Jackson and Schakowski to investigate."

"Dead how?"

"Possibly mauled by a dog. The dispatcher could hardly understand the woman who called it in."

"Good glory." River couldn't make the new development fit the kidnapping for ransom, yet it couldn't be a coincidence. "Poor Ivan Anderson. This will devastate him. Does Jackson want me to tell Anderson about his daughter?"

"You might as well. Find out what you can about Dakota too."

"Of course."

"Any word from the kidnapper?"

"Not this morning."

"Let's all meet this afternoon at four and see if these incidents are even connected," Lammers said.

"Let's use our conference room. It's bigger."

"Okay. Keep me posted in the meantime." The sergeant clicked off.

River smiled at the abruptness. She respected Lammers, but the woman didn't have an ounce of charm in her entire Shrek-size body. Working your way up through a male-dominated, gun-toting organization could do that to you.

River kept driving south toward Anderson's.

A landscaping truck sat in the wide driveway and a crew member stepped out of the passenger's side. River tensed and shut off her car. As she reached for the weapon under her jacket, the short dark man turned and stared. Who the hell was he? Most people didn't have landscaping work done in January. Was it the kidnapper's crew? More gang members?

She stepped out of her car, fingers still on the holstered weapon. "Put your hands in the air. Now!"

The man went wide-eyed and froze. Slowly his hands went up. River walked toward him. "Who are you?"

"Manuel Gutierrez. I'm legal."

As River processed the information, the driver's-side door flew open and the other man bolted across the side lawn. Ignoring the impulse to give chase, she touched her headset radio and spoke to the tech guys in the van down the street. "CR here. A Hispanic man is running your way. Grab him if you can."

Ivan Anderson charged through the front double doors. "What's going on?"

"Do you know this guy?" River hollered across the wide lawn.

"He's my landscaper. I forgot to call and cancel their monthly service." Anderson was in the same clothes from the night before, with disheveled hair and puffy eyes.

She holstered her Glock and gestured to Manuel. "Get in the truck and leave please."

Without a word, he ran for the driver's side and backed out.

River spoke to the tech van again. "Forget the runner. He's a landscaper." The guy was probably an illegal immigrant but she didn't care. People were all strangers in a strange land.

She moved toward Anderson. "Have you heard from the kidnapper this morning?"

"No. And I haven't heard from Dakota either. I think they took her too." Anderson shook with silent sobs.

River squeezed his shoulder. "Let's go inside."

Once they were in the house, Anderson got control and offered her coffee. She declined but followed him to the kitchen. Caffeine made her jumpy and light-headed, a bad combination for someone with a gun. "Just water, please. Where's Agent Fouts?"

"Taking a shower."

"Sit down with me. We have to talk about something." She didn't have much experience breaking this kind of news and she braced herself for his emotions.

He spun around from the counter. "What have you heard?"

"We have some news about Dakota. It's not good."

"Did he threaten her? Does he want more money?"

"Please sit."

"No, dammit. Just tell me."

"She was found dead in a park this morning. Possibly killed by a dog."

"What?" Anderson blinked rapidly.

"I'm so sorry. I know this is horrible for you. But that's all I know right now."

Anderson lurched for the kitchen sink and threw up. A scotch-and-sour vomit smell permeated the kitchen.

River waited while he splashed water on his face and cleaned up, sobbing intermittently. She recited peaceful mantras in her head to keep his emotions at bay.

"I don't understand," he cried, finally collapsing in a chair. "Why would a dog attack her? Does this have anything to do with Renee's kidnapping?"

"We don't know yet but we'll find out. Detectives Jackson and Schakowski are at the scene now looking into it."

"I can't believe Renee and Dakota are both gone." Anderson shook his head, his face sagging with grief. "I've had two wives die on me already. How much is a man supposed to take?"

The two dead wives were news to River. A dark suspicion wormed into her brain, and she knew she had to ask some probing questions soon. "I believe Renee is still alive. Don't give up hope. I need your help to get her back."

"What am I supposed to do?" His anguish was so raw, it made River's skin hurt.

"Stay strong, tell me what you can about your daughter, and do what the kidnapper says when he calls." *And stay sober*, she mentally added. But she didn't have the heart to say it out loud. If she were facing his situation, she might stay medicated too.

"Tell you *what* about Dakota?" Wariness overcame his grief for a moment.

"Everything. Who her friends are. The name of her boyfriend. Who she might have met in the dog park."

"What's the point?" Anderson gestured with both hands. "Daniel Talbot is behind all this. He wants to hurt me."

"Dakota's death may not be related. Or if it is, it could lead us to Renee. What's her boyfriend's name?"

"Jacob Renaldi. But they just started dating."

River opened her laptop and started taking notes. "Does he have a dog?"

"I don't know."

"Where did she meet him?"

"I don't know that either." He stood, but his shoulders were hunched over in pain. "Oh wait. I think she said they met at a friend's birthday party."

"What friend?"

"Maybe Jacob's boss."

"What does Jacob do for a living?"

"Construction, I think."

"Who else might want to hurt Dakota? Was she having problems with anyone?"

A new wave of tears rolled down Anderson's face. "She was well respected, but Dakota did suffer from depression and could be difficult."

River noted he'd said *well respected* but not *well liked*. It was time to ask. "You said you lost two wives? How did they die? Was that the reason for your daughter's depression?"

"Yes. Adrian died of liver cancer when Dakota was ten and it was devastating to both of us. Dakota stopped communicating for a while." He paused to steady himself.

River's suspicion faded as she thought of her own mother's suicide and the aftermath for her. Like being kicked out of a boat, in the dark ocean, without a life jacket. She had fully expected to drown, had even wanted to for a while, but somehow she'd drifted ashore.

Anderson picked up his backstory. "Then I married Sable when Dakota was thirteen. After a rough couple of years, Dakota bonded to her stepmother and they became very close. Then Dakota's first year at the university, Sable died in a freak skiing accident. My daughter dropped out of school and started drinking and spending money to numb her pain. But she rebounded, made it through college, and got a great job at the TV station. She seemed happy lately."

"Was there someone new in her life?"

"Just Jacob."

"Has she ever received any threats? From viewers or maybe a stalker?" River remembered the letter from prison. How long before she faced her own threat?

"Not that I know of."

River was starting to think his daughter's death from a dog attack might be just another freak accident…with very bad timing. "Why would Dakota go to Wayne Morse Park late at night?"

He shook his head. "I know it's not far from here, but I've never been there and Dakota never mentioned it."

"How long have you lived in Eugene?"

"Only a few years. Dakota came here to attend the University of Oregon and I eventually moved to be closer to her."

Anderson's phone jingled while he was talking. He fumbled through his pockets to find it, then stared at the screen. "It's a text from an unknown number."

"Why don't I read it?"

Anderson took a deep breath and touched the screen. After a moment, a bitter smile. "It's the kidnapper. Renee's life has been discounted today."

River reached for the phone and read the message: *Put 20 Gs in backpack. Cash. Get on #36 bus at noon and wait for instrux. No cops or Renee dies.*

She noted the missing *a* in front of backpack and the abbreviated *instrux*. Was this text by the same person? Out loud, she said, "With Dakota dead, for whatever reason, we need proof of life."

Anderson didn't answer, so River keyed in: *Have Renee call or I'm not paying again. I need to know she's alive.*

They sat in silence, the minutes ticking by on the kitchen clock. After a six-minute eternity, Anderson's phone rang, a different sound from the text alert. It was the same number. River handed the phone to Anderson, who said a timid hello.

Lips pressed tightly together, he listened for a moment, the relief obvious on his face. "I love you too, Renee. I'll see you soon." He clicked off. "She's alive." The sobs he'd been holding back burst out and River walked away, giving him a moment. Anderson had lost his daughter but knowing his fiancée was still alive might help get him through.

She met Fouts in the hall, hair still wet from his shower. "Good morning. Did you have a rough night with Anderson?"

"Not really. He got drunk and passed out early. Then I watched three episodes of *Mad Men* on his TiVo and slept like a rock in a nice guest bed. It was far better than being at home with the wife and dog both snoring."

With Fouts, she could never tell if he was being sarcastic or serious. She thought he cultivated misdirection to keep people from getting to know him. Law enforcement people were often like that.

"What's new?" he asked.

"A lot." She briefed him on Dakota's death as they walked back to the kitchen.

"That's weird. Most dogs won't attack an adult unless commanded to, even the aggressive breeds."

"So you think it was murder?"

"Considering the kidnapping. Yes."

River sat at the kitchen table and Fouts poured himself coffee. Anderson stood, staring at the window. She continued her update. "The kidnapper called a few minutes ago. We have to be ready for a noon exchange. The instructions are for Anderson to get on the number thirty-six bus. You and I will be on it too, sitting near the doors."

"I'll be the runner. I may be coming up on fifty but I'm still fast."

"Can you ride a bike? We need to be prepared for everything."

"Remember? I bought a bike from the homeless guy during the first money drop." Fouts patted his skinny quads. "Hell, I used to ride to the coast and back on weekends for fun."

River rolled her eyes, and Anderson turned to them. "Eugene buses have racks on the front that carry a couple of bikes."

"Perfect." River turned to Fouts. "Get down to the bus station and let them know we'll be on board and we expect cooperation. We'll map the route of the bus and have Eugene patrol units in the area." She turned back to Anderson. "We'll stay on him this time until he leads us to Renee."

Anderson nodded, his eyes vacant.

"Are you up for another exchange? Can you do this?"

"What choice do I have?"

"We can have an agent stand in for you. If the kidnapper is sending couriers to pick up the cash, they might not know what you look like."

"I'll do it. It's better than sitting here worrying and thinking about Dakota."

"Good. Do you want to give him real cash or mostly newspaper?"

"I just lost my daughter. I can't take any chances with my fiancée." Anderson closed his eyes for a moment. "My business partner will probably loan me the money."

"He may not have to." She called Torres for an update, then told Anderson, "The TV station has collected over twelve thousand since Dakota made her plea last night. An agent has the money and will be here soon. One donor gave five thousand, all in hundred-dollar bills."

Anderson let out a strangled cry. "I haven't taken money from anyone since I was twenty."

"After we find Renee, we'll arrest the perp and you can give the money to charity."

He nodded. "I'll get the other eight grand now."

CHAPTER 23

Tuesday, January 10, 8:42 a.m.

Evans pulled into the crime lab and waited at the automatic gate. The brick building with no windows on the first floor and no signs at all looked like a secret drug-testing facility. She flashed her badge at the camera and the gate opened. Moments like this still gave her a thrill that she'd been allowed into the department and trusted with important business. As a teenager in Alaska, she'd been a troublemaker, mostly out of boredom, and her life could have turned out very differently. When she'd boarded the ferry for Seattle, she had only hoped to escape her fate of early motherhood, poverty, and alcoholism. Ending up a police detective was beyond anything she'd imagined.

Inside the building she logged the evidence into the computer, then put Lyla's clothes into a locker that opened on the other side into the crime lab. She remembered the canine search she wanted to do and grabbed the T-shirt back out before heading upstairs. Jasmine Parker wasn't in her office, so she trotted down to Joe Berloni's workspace.

Joe glanced over, his crooked nose and massive upper body making him look like a boxer. "Hey, Lara."

"I have a strange request."

"Good. I like strange."

"I need you to go out to North McKenzie with your high-powered camera and take pictures of bruises."

"That's not all that strange."

"The victim is in a coma. I need scrapings from under her fingernails and DNA samples taken too."

"Give me an hour." He clicked something on his computer, then turned back. "The new hospital, I assume?"

"Yep. By the way, where's Parker?"

"She got called out to a crime scene. A woman was found dead at Wayne Morse Park."

"A homicide?"

"Mauled by a dog or some wild animal."

"Gruesome." Evans wondered who'd been assigned the case. "Do they have an ID?"

"I'm not sure. Ask Jackson. Parker said he was the lead."

The information surprised her. Jackson was working his ex-wife's kidnapping with the FBI. Why would Lammers assign him an accidental death? Something big had to be going on and she wanted to be on the task force.

"You'd better get going or I won't finish this in an hour." Joe waved her away.

"Lyla Murray is in the ICU. Room seven."

"Got it. Go."

On her drive to the courthouse, Evans flashed back to her interrogation of Taylor Harris and the young woman's you-can't-touch-me attitude. Where did that come from? Either her parents were rich or they had spoiled her or both. After questioning, Evans had booked Taylor into the county jail for obstruction of justice and asked that she be held overnight if possible. With only 130 beds open, the deputies had to let almost everyone but killers and pedophiles go, then crossed their fingers and hoped the guilty showed up in court. It infuriated Eugene cops, but the county ran the jail and the county was broke. If Taylor's parents or friends posted bail—a likely scenario—she had probably been released. Evans had to work quickly to get a warrant signed and conduct a search.

She pulled out her phone and called Lammers. "Evans here. Did you find a canine unit to work the cemetery with me?"

"I just got the call-back. Officer Drummond and his dog can meet you this afternoon. Give him a call."

"Thanks. So who's the victim at Wayne Morse Park?"

"Dakota Anderson, the daughter of Ivan Anderson, the target of the ransom kidnapping."

"She was mauled by an animal?"

"So it seems."

"That's bizarre. Is Jackson on both cases?"

"Yes. And they need more boots on the ground. How close are you to nailing a suspect in the assault case?"

"I have one. Taylor Harris, a potential roommate. I think it was a hazing gone too far and other sorority sisters may have participated in the attack."

"A hazing? For fuck's sake. What the hell is wrong with people? Why would an intelligent person let someone else beat them?"

The outburst surprised Evans. Lammers rarely commented on people's behavior because she always expected the worst.

"I think Lyla was away from home for the first time and wanted a local family." Evans was winging it, trying to understand the behavior. It wasn't something she would have ever subjected herself to. When someone hit her, she fought back. It was in her DNA. She'd once taken down a sergeant after he'd assaulted her.

"Can we prosecute her?" Lammers wanted to know.

"I hope to. Joe Berloni will go out to the hospital to take high-res images of Lyla's injuries, and I'm on my way to get a search warrant for Taylor's house, phone, and car. If I find the weapon, maybe Joe can match it to her bruises."

"The victim is still unconscious?"

"She had a second surgery and they put her in a medical coma to help her heal."

"We need to resolve this with or without her help. I want someone to do time for the assault. I hate that hazing shit."

"I'm on it."

Judge Marlee Volcansek looked annoyed to see her. "I have to be in court in five minutes. Can this wait until my break at noon?" She was pretty for an older woman and Evans noticed her face looked tight, as if she'd had some work done.

"No. I need to search now before the suspect hides the weapon or ditches her cell phone."

"What's the case?" The judge sat back down at her desk.

Evans remained standing, hoping it would be quick. She summarized the case details, then added, "I want to search Taylor Harris' room, car, and phone. She lives in a house on campus with a group of other women." Evans set the paperwork on Volcansek's desk and the judge skimmed through it.

"Have you questioned Taylor Harris?"

"Yes."

"And?"

Crap. The judge was going to give her a hard time about this. "She denies meeting with Lyla Murray, the victim. But so far,

Taylor's alibi doesn't hold up." Evans hadn't been able to reach any of the contacts her suspect had given her, so that was a bit of a stretch.

"Do you have any evidence linking her to the assault?" The judge gestured impatiently with her hands.

"Not yet. That's what I hope to find."

Volcansek sighed. "I don't think I can sign this."

Evans wasn't giving up. "I believe the beating was a hazing. When I said that to Taylor, she claimed that if a person consented to a hazing, then it wasn't an assault. Her statement is in the warrant."

The judge's face stayed impassive but her eyes sparked with anger. "I'll let you search her car and her room for the weapon, but not the rest of the house she resides in. And not her phone. That's too invasive of her personal life, based on how little you have. You don't want to compromise her trial."

Evans started to argue, then changed her mind. She could come back for the phone search after she found the weapon…or any other evidence. "Thank you."

The sun broke through the clouds just as she reached the big house on Potter Street. In the glaring winter light, the home looked less stately than it had before. The paint was old, the siding curved in places, and moss covered the left side of the roof where it was shaded by a tall fir tree. There was still no place to park. Evans circled the block and finally left her car in the driveway, blocking the Subaru that was sitting there. She remembered Taylor saying she drove a Mini Cooper and that it was in the shop.

Evans knocked on the door and a different young woman answered. "What's up?"

"Detective Lara Evans. I need to see Taylor Harris."

"I don't think she's here."

"That's okay, I have a search warrant for her room." She held out the paperwork.

The girl's eyes went wide. "What am I supposed to do?"

"Come with me upstairs. I'd like to ask you some questions while I search."

"Me? Why?" She stepped back and tightened her bathrobe.

"Because I'm trying to solve a vicious assault. Come with me." Evans strode through the kitchen, catching sight of another young woman slipping out the back door. She had shoulder-length red hair, so she knew it wasn't Taylor. Eventually, she'd question everyone in this house, but finding a solid piece of evidence would give her the leverage she needed to get one of the members to confess or rat on her sisters.

She jogged up the stairs at the back of the house, glancing over her shoulder to see if bathrobe girl was following. "What's your name?" she called out.

"Caitlyn Steinbach. Can I get dressed first?"

"No."

Evans stopped at Taylor's room and knocked. She announced herself, knocked again, then tried the doorknob. Locked. She looked back at Caitlyn. "Is there a set of master keys?"

"Taylor has them."

Evans dug through her bag for a set of lock picks and got to work. It was faster than taking the door off the hinges and she didn't want to call the SWAT unit to bash the door in.

"I'm calling the house's owner," Caitlyn announced.

"Good. I need to talk to him too." The day before, Evans had called the company that managed most of the campus rentals, but they no longer had this house on their roster. But they had in the past, and they'd given her the owner's contact information. She'd tried and failed to reach him.

The lock gave. Evans pushed open the door and turned back to Caitlyn. "Go get dressed, then come stand in the hall again." She needed a few minutes to concentrate.

Clothes were piled on the end of the bed and textbooks were stacked next to a cluttered desk. A large mirror filled one wall, making the room seem bigger. Evans headed straight for the eight-foot closet with folding doors. The space was crammed with clothes, shoes, and sports equipment. Evans pulled on latex gloves and began filling a large plastic bag with potential weapons to take to the lab. Two tennis rackets, a softball bat, and a hockey stick. Technically, she was only supposed to search for the weapon, but that gave her license to look at everything. She lifted piles of sweaters on the top shelf and peeked in shoes boxes but didn't find anything of interest.

Evans dropped to her knees and looked under the bed, pushing things around as she searched. A sleeping bag, a tent, and a suitcase. Nothing that could be used to strike and bruise. Her bet was on the baseball bat. As she stood, Caitlyn called from the hallway, "I'm back."

Evans glanced over. "Where were you Saturday night?"

"Performing at a dance recital. Why?"

That would be easy enough to check. "What's the name of this sorority?"

"We're not a sorority."

"How long have you lived here?" Evans opened a drawer and dug through T-shirts as she talked.

"Two and a half years."

"What does it take to get in?"

"An invitation from Taylor or one of the others."

"What others?" Evans pulled open another drawer.

"House leaders who used to live here."

"Who invited you?"

"Ashley Harris. Taylor's older sister."

"What was your initiation like?" Evans looked over to watch her face.

"I can't tell you." Caitlyn looked nervous.

"Why not?"

"It's against the rules."

Evans stepped toward her and locked eyes. "Taylor is about to go to prison for assault. I don't think you should be worried about getting kicked out of the house. If you were there in the cemetery on Saturday night when Lyla was beaten, I suggest you tell me now before Taylor blames you. The first one to talk gets the best deal."

Caitlyn's eyes filled with unshed tears. "Is Lyla all right?"

"She's in a coma and she's lost a lot of blood. Tell me what you know."

The girl bit her fingernails. "I didn't know it was like that now. I got paddled but I survived."

"Why would you let someone do that to you?"

Caitlyn made a scoffing sound. "An hour or so of pain and humiliation in exchange for knowing that I'll have a steady place to live and popular friends who'll have my back? It was an easy choice."

Evans reached for her recorder, preparing to take a statement. Footsteps thudded in the hallway and a thirty-something man stepped between her and Caitlyn.

"I'm Austin Hartwell, owner of this property. Can I ask what you're doing?" At six-four, he was nearly a foot taller than her, but his blue eyes and sweet smile kept him from being intimidating.

"Detective Lara Evans, Eugene Police. I'm conducting a search." She pulled out the warrant again and showed him.

Hartwell barely glanced at it. "You should have called me first."

"I left you a message last night."

"Sorry. I'm a busy man."

"What do you do?" Evans jotted down his name.

"I own and manage several businesses. Why?"

"Do you meet and interview the women who rent rooms here?"

"Other than dealing with one main tenant, no. I let the house leader handle the individual rentals."

"Did you know the women accepted to live here are initiated with a violent hazing?"

He pulled back in surprise. "I had no idea. Is Taylor involved? Is that why you're searching her room?"

Evans ignored his questions. "Do you know Lyla Murray?"

"No. Is she a tenant?"

"I believe she was about to become one, but now she's in the hospital."

"I'm sorry to hear that." Hartwell glanced at his watch. "How much longer will you be here? I was on my way to a meeting."

"Maybe another hour. I still need to get a statement from Caitlyn but you don't need to stay."

"Let me know if I can help in any way."

Behind him, Caitlyn ran down the hall.

"Hey," Evans called out. "I'm not done with you."

Caitlyn kept moving.

CHAPTER 24

Tuesday, January 10, 10:52 a.m.

Jackson climbed into his car and started the engine, relieved to be out of the cold. He felt guilty that Quince was going door-to-door and Schak was searching Dakota's vehicle, both in the cold, while he sat in his car with the heat on, perusing Dakota's cell phone. Outdoor homicides in the winter were a bitch and they'd had several already this season. It was even worse for Parker, who would be outside most of the day.

The phone's icon for missed calls was flagged, so Jackson looked at the log first. Her father, Ivan Anderson, had called at 8:05 that morning, and someone named Jacob Renaldi had called at 8:47. Jackson punched #1 and hoped her voice mail didn't require a password. A canned message gave him some options, then Ivan Anderson's frantic voice said, "Dakota, I'm worried sick. Please call me. I appreciate what you tried to do for me and Renee last night, so don't think I'm upset. Just call me."

Jackson waited through another annoying list of voice mail options, then a male voice came on. "It's Jacob. I'm sorry about last night. Will I see you today? Call me."

Who was Jacob Renaldi and what was he sorry about? The name and number went into Jackson's notebook. If Renaldi was the boyfriend, it would save Jackson some digging around. He clicked open an icon for text messages and began reading. Renaldi had texted this morning with the same message, right after calling. He had also been the last person to text the night before at 10:48 p.m. Jackson opened their conversation and read:

Dakota: Can I come over? I think I just lost my job.

Jacob: Sure. What happened?

Dakota: Tell you then.

Jackson called the department on his own phone and asked a desk officer to find an address for Jacob Renaldi and get back to him as quickly as possible. Renaldi was likely the last person to see Dakota alive. While Jackson waited, he scrolled through a few more texts. Most were from women with names like Brittany, Katrina, and Ashley. They used abbreviations that often weren't obvious to him, but mostly the texts were about getting together or gossip about another woman.

The desk officer called back with information: "Jacob Renaldi lives at 40855 Bailey Hill Road. He has no priors, except a minor-in-possession charge for alcohol when he was twenty. Anything else I can get you?"

"Repeat the address, please." Jackson checked his note and made a correction. "Thanks."

He clicked off and hurried across the street to the park.

Schak had his head in the trunk of Dakota's silver Honda, so Jackson stood next to him, waiting. Finally, Schak stood and turned. "Nothing interesting. A set of golf clubs in the trunk and a shopping bag with some shoes in the backseat. No blood, no drugs, no dog hair."

"A gas receipt or fast-food container?" Jackson wanted to know where Dakota had been between the time she left the station and was killed in the park.

Schak shook his head. "I took photos of the stuff in the trunk and I'll let it go to the crime lab with the car."

"Makes sense."

They heard footsteps and looked over to see Quince jogging toward them.

"Anything useful?" Jackson asked.

"Not a damn thing from the neighbors. And no one was in the park's historic house, so I'll have to check back and see if it was open to the public last night. Which I doubt."

"What now?" Schak rubbed his head again. "We've never had a case where the suspect was a dog."

"I need to update Agent River and she can tell Dakota's father." Jackson had a pang of guilt for passing that gut-wrenching task to someone else, but he was also relieved. "Then we need to find Jacob Renaldi. According to Dakota's text messages, she went to see him last night after she left the TV station. I have a home address but see if you can find out where he works."

"Anything for me right now?" Quince asked.

Jackson handed him Dakota's phone. "Start calling everyone on her list. Find out who owns a dog."

They each climbed into their car to get out of the cold, but sat there working their devices. Their jobs hadn't become easier in the digital age, but the way they investigated had been simplified. Jackson pulled out his new computer tablet, got online, and went straight to Facebook. New technology had once intimidated him but now he appreciated it. If his city-issued Impala had been properly equipped, the little tablet wouldn't be necessary. But this was Eugene, with the most underfunded police force of any city of its size. After watching Evans make quick productive searches with her tablet, and sitting in his car yesterday wishing he had one, he'd stopped and bought one last night. Even his doctor used the device now. Which reminded him that he had a CAT scan scheduled soon and he needed to check his calendar.

Jacob Renaldi's profile photo showed a close-up of an attractive man with a shaved head. A knowing smile played on the man's mouth and Jackson distrusted him already. His Facebook page was lean and no-nonsense, as if it had just been posted, but the information section mentioned that Renaldi owned a business called Security First. Jackson googled it but found no Eugene connections.

A moment later, Schak trotted over with his awkward short-legged gait. "I can't find anything on Renaldi."

"Ever heard of Security First? Renaldi's Facebook page says he owns it."

Schak shook his head.

Jackson clicked off his tablet. "Let's go check his home address."

His phone rang; he saw that it was River, and braced himself for bad news. "Jackson here. What's happening?"

"Another money drop is going down. We've got it handled but I thought you'd want to know."

"Did you hear from Renee? Is she alive?"

"Yes. Anderson spoke to her."

"Thank god." The knot in his stomach loosened a little, but the need to be in two places still tore at him. "I'd like to participate, but we need to question Jacob Renaldi. He could be a suspect or witness in Dakota's death."

"Go pick him up. We'll be fine."

"I'll send Detective Quince to assist. Where do you need him?"

"At the city bus station."

"Will you break the news about Dakota to Anderson for me?"

"I did. He's taking it hard."

"What father wouldn't?"

Jackson drove out Eighteenth Street, pushing the speed limit, with Schak following. They turned left at Churchill High School and started the slow climb up and across the hillside. New housing had been built at the Bertelsen junction but several lots in the little subdivision were vacant. The recession still had a grip on his community and the housing market had been slow to recover. Jackson hadn't been out to this area since he and Renee had visited a nearby business to look at koi when they'd considered putting in a pond years ago. He passed a little market and slowed, figuring Renaldi's place had to be along here somewhere. He spotted the address on a small sign and turned into a gravel driveway that led uphill into a grove of oak and fir trees. The driveway curved at the top and opened into a parking area in front of a newly constructed home. Jackson spotted buildings behind the house and a series of metal fences.

As he climbed from the car, he heard the barking.

Dogs. Lots of them. A jolt went up his spine and he grabbed for his weapon. Renaldi was either a breeder or a boarder and it was starting to look like he knew exactly what had happened to his girlfriend the night before. Jackson reached back in and grabbed his taser, thinking he might need it for Renaldi. If a dog came at him, he'd simply put a bullet in it.

He watched the side yards for low fast movement and waited until Schak was at his side. There was nobody he'd rather be in a tight situation with.

"Sounds like this could be our man." Schak had his taser in hand too.

"But what is Renaldi's connection to Anderson and Renee?"

"Maybe there isn't one." Schak shrugged. "It might be just a tragic case of bad timing."

Jackson had been thinking the same thing. "Ready?"

"You know I am."

They strode up the cement walk, eyes darting to the paths leading to the kennels behind the house. The barking grew louder with each step.

Five feet from the front porch, the door flew open and Renaldi yelled, "You need an appointment!"

"No we don't!" Schak called back.

"Detectives Jackson and Schakowski, Eugene Police." Jackson noticed the dog standing silently behind Renaldi's right side. Its head was level with the suspect's belt and its hungry eyes were trained on Jackson. What the fuck kind of dog was it?

"Step out here but leave the dog in the house."

"No. She stays with me."

Jackson visualized Dakota's shredded face and rage flared in his veins. "That thing is no match for two armed police officers. Do it a favor and step outside."

"What is this about?" Renaldi hadn't budged.

"Dakota Anderson is dead, and we'd like to ask some questions."

Renaldi's shoulders flinched but his expression didn't change. "Dakota's dead? How?"

"We'll ask the questions." Jackson suddenly became aware of how private the property was, an ideal location for keeping someone hostage. "We'd like to search for a missing woman as well."

"There's no one here but me and the dogs, and you're not searching without a warrant."

Jackson weighed the situation. They had no real reason to believe Renee was here. They might get a warrant to examine the dogs in connection with Dakota's death, but he couldn't justify barging in to look for Renee. Not yet.

"Then you're coming with us." Jackson raised his voice just enough to be intimidating.

Schak stepped forward, taser held out.

"Keep your hands in front and come out of the house." Jackson moved forward with his taser drawn as well, and his other hand on his gun.

Neither had to make good on the threat. Renaldi cursed under his breath, held his face in his hands for a moment, then gave the dog a command. He stepped outside and locked the door, then moved slowly down the steps toward them.

Jackson said, "Turn around and put your hands behind your back."

"There's no need to cuff me. I'll come peacefully and tell you what I can."

"Give me the knife you're carrying." Jackson instinctively knew he was that kind of guy.

Renaldi passed him a large fold-lock hunting knife. "I want it back."

"You'll get it. Climb into the backseat and sit in the middle. I'll lock you in for the ride downtown."

Once Renaldi was in the car, Schak asked, "What about the dogs?"

"We need a court order to take impressions of all their teeth. We'll leave 'em here and come back with a county vet and animal control specialist."

"Did you see the size of that monster? I think it's a mastiff, maybe mixed with something else, like a rottweiler."

Jackson repressed a shudder. "I dread searching this place."

CHAPTER 25

"Do we have a plan?" Schak stopped outside the interrogation room where Renaldi had been waiting for ten minutes.

"As much as I want him to tell us about Dakota's death, whether it was homicide or criminal negligence, we can't forget Renee. She's still alive and this jackass might know where she is." Jackson gulped his coffee, hoping the jolt of energy would hit him soon. It was too early to feel tired. "I'll question Renaldi about Dakota, then I want you to jump in with a question about Renee every once in a while. See if we can catch him off guard."

"Do we have any leverage?"

"Just the dog connection and the phone text arranging to meeting Dakota. As far as we know, he's the last person to see her alive."

"So we act like we know he's guilty, offer him a plea?"

"Yes. And hopefully search his place while he's here in custody."

Jim Trang, the assistant DA, was working on a warrant for the property and subpoenas for the dogs' forensics. Now that two detectives had been laid off, they took whatever help was offered by the DA's office or even from volunteers.

Jackson nodded. "Let's do this."

Schak went in first, knowing Jackson needed to sit near the door. Even so, the closet-size room squeezed him, like he had a rubber band around his chest.

Jackson pulled out his recorder, clicked it on, and identified all the participants. A recessed video camera was also in use but he preferred not to point that out. He met Renaldi's eyes. "How well do you know Dakota Anderson?"

"We've been dating a few months."

"Were you lovers?"

"Of course."

Jackson didn't understand why smart young women with college degrees slept with dog-owning thugs with shaved heads and tattoos. He prayed his daughter would never succumb to the bad-boy attraction. "Did you see Dakota last night?" He almost hoped Renaldi would lie and give them some leverage.

"Yes. She came over after she left work."

"What time was that?"

"Around ten thirty."

"What happened then?"

"We had sex and she left an hour later."

Jackson made note of the times. "Why did she leave?"

Renaldi closed his eyes. "Will you tell me what happened to her?"

"I think you know. Why don't *you* tell me?"

"I have no idea. Dakota was upset about her job and the whole kidnapping thing. She wanted to drink and talk but I needed to get some sleep so I could get up early for work. So I asked her to leave."

"What do you do for a living?"

"I breed protection dogs and do part-time construction work. We finished drywalling a house this morning."

Jackson needed to know more about both, but the mention of construction bothered him. "Which company?"

"Evergreen."

A shiver ran up his spine. "So you know Daniel Talbot."

"He owns the company, but I don't see him much."

Jackson took a moment to process the information. Daniel Talbot had been their primary suspect. He'd lost money because of Ivan Anderson and had sent threatening e-mail. What if Renaldi's relationship with Dakota was all part of his boss' retaliation plan?

In the silence, Schak jumped in. "When was the last time you saw Renee Jackson?"

"Who?"

Schak slammed the table. "Don't bullshit me. You know Ivan Anderson's fiancée."

"Not really. Dakota told me she was kidnapped, but I didn't pay attention to her name."

"When did you meet Renee?"

"I didn't. Dakota never brought me home to her family. We don't have that kind of relationship." A little smirk in his expression. "I did meet her dad once accidentally."

Jackson resisted the urge to smack him. "How did you meet Dakota?"

"At a friend's party."

Jackson was making connections. "Was it your boss, Daniel Talbot?"

"Yeah, why?"

"Did you know how Talbot felt about Ivan Anderson?"

Renaldi shrugged. "I knew he was pissed off and bitter."

"But you dated Anderson's daughter anyway. How did Talbot feel about that?"

A quick jerk of his head. "He didn't know."

"I think he did. I think he asked you to start dating Dakota to pump her for information."

"No." Renaldi scowled. "Dakota came on to me. And except for that party, I don't really see Daniel Talbot. I work for Darrell Jarvis, the contractor."

Schak jumped back in. "We think you helped Talbot kidnap Renee. Tell us where she is and we'll cut you a deal."

"This is crazy. My girlfriend is dead and you won't tell me how." Renaldi shoved his chair back and stood. "And you think I kidnapped her father's girlfriend, a woman I didn't even know."

Before he finished, Jackson and Schak were both on their feet. "Sit down!" they yelled in unison.

Renaldi took a series of rapid breaths and pressed his thumbs to his temples. After a moment, he sat. "How did she die? Why are you questioning me?"

Jackson was torn. He'd hoped the suspect would reveal crime-specific information, but that hadn't happened. If Renaldi wasn't involved, the man had a right to know how his girlfriend had died. Finally, Jackson said, "She was mauled by a dog, or dogs, in Wayne Morse Park."

"Oh god." Renaldi squeezed his eyes shut again. "It wasn't my dog. I would never—" He broke off and balled his hands into fists. "Dakota and I were mostly friends. Fuck buddies. But I cared about her. She was kinda messed up but that's what made her special. I had nothing to do with her death. I've never been in that park."

"What do you mean by messed up?"

"Her mother and her stepmother both died, so she had issues."

"Like what?"

"She was a shopaholic. Like she was trying to fill some void inside her. I think sex was like that for her too."

"You're saying Dakota had multiple partners?"

"We both did."

Schak cut in. "Were you screwing her father's fiancée, Renee?"

"No."

"Did you help your boss kidnap her?"

"No."

Jackson took back the questioning. "Do you know where Talbot might hold her for ransom?"

Renaldi cocked his head. "He has a skiing cabin up at Gold Lake."

"We've been there. What about a construction site?"

"Seems unlikely. They're all in development." Something registered in his eyes.

Jackson said, "You thought of a place. Where?"

Renaldi nodded. "It's an underground safe room in a house we're building on Skyridge. The work on the main house has stopped for the winter because the owners are worried about mold, but the underground room is mostly finished."

"Address?" Jackson knew better than to feel hopeful. Renaldi was just trying to shift the focus off himself.

"It's near the top of Skyridge on the left, but it may not even have an address yet."

"If we find her there, we'll have a lot more questions for you."

Schak stood, walked around the table, and squatted next to Renaldi. "We know you put the dog on Dakota. It's only a matter of getting teeth impressions and DNA. Once they match any of it to her wounds, you're going down. So tell us your version. Did Dakota find out you grabbed Renee Jackson? Did you have to silence her?"

Renaldi blinked like a man in a dust storm. "I breed and sell protection animals, so there are aggressive dogs out there that are closely related to mine. DNA could be misleading."

"We'll leave that to the experts." Jackson had no idea if they could get a match with canine teeth or DNA that would hold up in court. He'd never handled anything like it. "Where were you last night between midnight and two a.m.?"

"I was at home, sleeping. I told you. I had to work this morning."

"Can anyone verify that you were home?"

"No." Renaldi's tone relayed his irritation. Or was it fear?

"Where did you work?"

"At a new house on Monroe Street, near Twenty-Eighth. We finished the drywall and knocked off early."

"Who's your supervisor?"

"Darrell Jarvis. Like I said."

"What's his phone number?"

Renaldi rattled it off. "You're wasting your time."

Jackson jotted down the number, not even sure he would make the call. They needed to find the dog. Or maybe the crime techs would get lucky and find something Renaldi had left at the scene. "I'd like a list of customers who've bought dogs from you."

"I can't do that. They have a right to privacy."

"A judge may not agree." Jackson felt restless and eager to escape the tiny room. "Why not cooperate with us? Don't you want to know what happened to Dakota?"

"Yes, but I can't let you ruin my business."

"Why do you train your dogs to attack and kill?"

"I train some to protect." He emphasized the word *protect.* "I don't have the time or desire to work with them all. Most of my customers hire a trainer for their specific needs after they've bought the dog."

"But you have dogs on your property that will kill on command."

"Just Tesla, my own protection dog."

"When was the last time you commanded her to attack?"

Renaldi shifted in his seat. "Tesla has never hurt anyone."

Frustrated with the lack of a breakthrough, Jackson struggled for a new line of questioning. "How did Dakota feel about your dogs?"

"She liked Tesla but was never around any of the animals out back."

"Do you have other animals besides dogs?"

"No. Why would I?"

"Let's take a break. Would you like a soda?"

"Just water. I don't poison my body with sugar and chemicals."

Good for you, Jackson thought, getting up.

Out in the hall, he turned to Schak. "Will you call Trang and see if he has a warrant yet? I'd like to keep Renaldi in custody until we search his place. He has to be involved in Dakota's death somehow."

CHAPTER 26

Tuesday, January 10, 11:42 a.m.

Twenty thousand dollars was such a small pile of money, River thought, as she handed the backpack to Anderson. She'd bundled the cash into rubber bands back at the house, and the two stacks of bills would have fit into the average purse. Instead they were in the bottom of a small backpack as directed.

Why had the kidnapper offered to take so much less the second time? River wondered. Was he worried about getting stiffed if he asked for the whole hundred grand again? Or was he just in a hurry and not willing to wait for Anderson to beg or borrow the rest?

Anderson gripped the strap like a drowning man. Her heart went out to him. Hours earlier he'd learned of his daughter's death and now he was going out again, hoping to save his fiancée. The past few days had probably robbed him of five or ten years of his life. "Are you sure you want to do this?" she asked. "We have no idea what he'll want you to do next."

"I have to."

"Is your radio on?"

Anderson touched his earpiece and nodded.

River looked over at Agent Fouts and the group of three men standing by. Except for Detective Quince, they wore casual clothes, jeans and sweatshirts or zippered sports jackets. River was sporting a maroon velour tracksuit, something she referred to as *street clothes* for undercover work, but that she happily wore at home. She suspected they still wouldn't quite blend with the bus-riding crowd in Eugene, which tended to be a mix of blue-collar workers, students, homeless people, and drug dealers. For the moment, they were in a parking lot near the downtown bus station. The new four-story brick library loomed nearby and the transit station across the street took up an entire city block. Both entities seemed overbuilt for the size of the town, but after living in San Diego and Portland, Eugene felt rather Podunky. River checked her watch: 11:50.

"It's time. Fouts, go first and take the front of the bus. Anderson, follow in a few minutes and sit somewhere in the middle. I'll get on at the last minute and head to the back. Quince, Torres, and Gilson, fan out around the station in your cars." She didn't really need to repeat the information. They'd been over it thoroughly but she was being careful. After the last failed effort, losing both the money and the courier, she couldn't afford to botch this one too. The bureau was looking for a reason to fire her. She no longer fit their profile. But dumping her after her operation would have been politically ugly, so they were waiting for an opportunity. The universe had gifted them with this potentially high-profile train wreck. No one had ever expected her to handle anything like a ransom kidnapping after she'd relocated to Eugene. A made-to-order FUBAR scenario.

"I still can't believe the transit people actually wanted us to do this without our weapons," Fouts complained again. "This town is so fucking politically correct, it's surprising they even have a jail."

"We don't," Detective Quince said. "It's run by the county." He grinned, climbed into his car, and headed for the Chase bank on the other side of Eleventh Avenue.

Fouts moved quickly to the station, a lean man with a muscular, caffeine-fueled walk. After a minute Anderson followed, head down and legs heavy. River hurried along the block and approached the idling bus from the other side.

In addition to the three cars they had in the proximity, two more agents were parked along the bus route and several Eugene police officers were on standby in the area as well. River would have liked more agents on the scene, but she had tag teams watching her suspects, Striker and Talbot, round the clock.

She ran the possible scenarios in her head again. The kidnapper could text Anderson and order him to throw the money out the bus door when it opened, then grab it from the sidewalk and run or bike away. Or he might already be on the bus and grab it as he passed by to exit. Or he might order Anderson to get off the bus and onto a bicycle. Or worse yet, onto another bus. The thought made her clench her hands. An unexpected change of direction would put Anderson out of their communication reach and give the kidnapper the best chance of escaping. If they followed Anderson onto another bus, the kidnapper would likely see them and call off the drop. Either way, it might put Renee's life at risk.

River took a cleansing breath and reminded herself that she would make peace with any outcome. Ultimately, she was not in control.

She jostled through a crowd of unloading passengers from another bus and scurried aboard the number 36 bus moments before the driver pulled the door closed. She flashed her badge as if it were a monthly pass. Fouts sat directly behind the driver, looking like an uptight accountant in his elbow-patch jacket and narrow glasses. Anderson sat near the middle, wearing jeans and a gray sweatshirt with UO lettering on the back. After her sleep-less night, River probably looked like a housewife who had taken one too many Valium and forgot where she parked her car.

The bus rolled forward and threw her into a seat in the back. She hadn't been on public transportation since college. The stench of the idling engine was overpowering. Was this a mis-take? Should she have followed in her car? No, she was here now and it was the right move. Staying with the target was key.

They exited the station onto Tenth Avenue, then turned on Willamette. After a few blocks, Anderson's voice was suddenly in her ear, whispering, "He just texted and said to get off the bus, run down Thirteenth, and catch the number twenty-eight."

"Do what he says. Fouts will stay with you. I'll hang back in case he reverses direction." They couldn't both follow him to another bus without it being obvious. If the kidnapper was watching Anderson, a careless move on their part could be fatal to Renee.

River spoke into her radio. "CR to Quince: Follow the num-ber twenty-eight bus on Thirteenth." He was the closest. The oth-ers had moved farther down the bus line toward Eighteenth, and still others were waiting farther west.

"Copy that."

The number 36 bus had stopped and Fouts trotted down the steps, ahead of Anderson who was still making his way to the front. River exited out the rear door just in time to see a cyclist whiz by and crash into Fouts, knocking him down. The cyclist went down too, swearing as he lost contact with his bike.

Was he part of the courier's escape plan? River ran toward the two men on the ground, as Anderson took off down the side street as instructed.

"Fouts, are you okay?"

"Yes and no."

The bus pulled away from the curb with their bicycle still mounted on the front rack.

Damn.

She looked over as the 28 bus rolled up on Thirteenth Avenue. The doors popped open and Anderson climbed aboard.

Damn. Someone had to stay with the target. She spoke into the radio: "This is CR: DF is down. Following target on bicycle."

River cursed under her breath, grabbed the bike that had crashed into Fouts, and mounted the two-wheeled contraption.

Fouts tried to stand and cried out in pain. From the ground, the cyclist yelled, "What the fuck?"

"FBI. You'll get it back."

River pushed off, asking the universe to keep her safe. She hadn't ridden anything but a stationary exercise bike since grade school. All her years in the field had never required her to pedal anywhere. She'd clung to the back of a motorcycle once during a brief high-speed chase, but most fieldwork involved sitting in cars, asking questions, and occasionally following on foot.

River started pedaling down the bike lane. Cars whizzed past her and she couldn't believe people rode next to traffic like this all the time. *Please let Quince or Torres pick the tail.* She was in no shape to keep up with the bus. Yet she gave it her all, sucking wind and pumping until her legs ached. Which took about two minutes.

On the radio, Quince said, "I've got eyes on the number twenty-eight."

"Copy."

The bus couldn't move any faster than the traffic on Thirteenth and had to stop once for a red light, so she managed to keep it in sight. As they neared the university, she realized what the kidnapper probably had in mind. Being the only agent on a bicycle, it would be all up to her.

Anderson's fuzzy voice whispered in her earpiece. "He just texted. I'm getting off the bus and walking left." Or at least that's what she thought he said.

River was sucking in too much oxygen to respond. The driver pulled over at the next bus stop and Anderson exited. She stood and pushed hard, hoping to make the light. Cars honked as she crossed in front of them and she swerved hard to keep from hitting a pedestrian. The young woman turned and cursed at her. River kept pedaling, watching Anderson as closely as she could, while still keeping one eye on the road in front of her. *Good glory. How did people do this every day?*

Anderson walked past a group of connected shops and said something, but she couldn't understand. There was too much traffic and noise.

Another cyclist passed her. River scanned ahead and saw that the sidewalks on the next block were filled with young college students. They were near the edge of campus now. As Anderson approached Alder Street, he slipped the backpack from his shoulder and carried it by his side.

Oh no.

A young man on a bicycle came out of nowhere, grabbed the backpack, and raced toward the college. No! The courier had the money and was a block and a half away. River pushed harder, but her thighs burned and her throat closed up like a dry vacuum. She tried to focus on the courier details. Oversize dark jacket and dark knit cap. She couldn't see his pants well enough to know what they were. As she approached the cross street where Thirteenth Avenue dead-ended into the campus, Quince yelled into the radio, "Stay with him! I'll park and follow."

She did her best, but the campus was swarming with students and she had to slow down to weave around them. She saw the courier make a sudden right onto a path between two buildings. She followed the turn but couldn't spot the guy in the puffy black jacket. Had he ditched the bike and run into one of the huge brick buildings? Students swarmed around her, some looking her up and down like she was an alien specimen.

River kept moving but she knew she'd lost him.

CHAPTER 27

Tuesday, January 10, 3:52 p.m.

Jackson and Schak crossed the street to the federal building, jumped through the security hoops, and took the elevator to the third floor.

"I hope this goes quickly," Jackson commented as they approached the conference room. "We still need to search Dakota's condo and get into all her electronic files."

"Renaldi's place comes first, if we get the warrant."

"I'm not holding my breath. Who knows how long it will take the county to authorize an animal-control specialist to get out there. This funding crisis is crippling us."

"And the scumbags are laughing it up."

They entered the meeting and took seats at the long table. River and four other agents were already there, looking impatient. Detective Quince was seated at the end.

River stood. "Let's get started. We still have a missing woman out there who may be in worse danger than ever." She looked at

Jackson. "The money drop didn't go well. The kidnapper had Anderson make two bus changes, then grabbed the backpack and disappeared into a sea of students on campus. We had a GPS unit in the cash, but he ditched the backpack and the tracker in a bathroom on campus."

The news was a body blow and Jackson tried not to flinch. "What about Renee?"

"We're hoping he'll let her go now that he has the money, but we can't assume that."

Jackson knew it was just as likely the kidnapper would kill Renee, or order his thugs to, just to eliminate a possible witness. An image of his grief-stricken daughter flashed in his mind. The damage that losing her mother could do. "Have we heard from the agents tailing our suspects?"

River looked at the agent across from Jackson. "What's the report?"

"Daniel Talbot spent the day at Talbot and Finch Accounting on Twentieth and Willamette and is still there now. Gus Striker was home most of the day, then left just after three p.m. and drove to Lucky Numbers, a tavern on Highway 99. He's still inside."

River added, "Our tech team says the messages to Anderson's phone bounced off a tower at Eighteenth and Chambers, which means Talbot could have been sending them from his office, while a courier picked up the money."

"Striker sounds like he's out of the running." Jackson was relieved he'd never have to explain entering the man's house without a warrant.

River moved toward a large whiteboard where she'd listed Talbot at the top on one side. "Are we down to one suspect?"

"We have Jacob Renaldi too." Jackson looked at his notes. "He's Dakota Anderson's boyfriend and the last known person to see her alive. He also works for Evergreen Construction, which is owned by Talbot. I think they may have worked together on the kidnapping."

River absorbed the information like water after a marathon. "Fascinating. What else do we know about him?"

"He breeds *protection* dogs, so we think he knows what happened to Dakota."

"Do we have him in custody?" River talked over her shoulder as she wrote the information on the board.

"He's in an interrogation room at the department."

"Excellent. I'd like to question him later. What's your take?"

"He's hard to read, impassive one minute and semi-distressed the next. You can watch the video."

"We need to get teeth imprints from his dogs."

"An assistant DA is working on the subpoena and we have a call in to county animal control."

Agent Torres made a grunting sound. "They'll have to tranquilize the dogs. How many are there?"

Jackson was embarrassed that he didn't know. "We're not sure. Renaldi wouldn't let us look around and he didn't want to talk about the dogs."

"What else have we got?" River glanced over at her agents.

Agent Gilson reported, "We started searching Talbot's construction properties today, but were interrupted by the second money drop."

"Did you search the Skyridge home with the underground safe room?" Jackson asked. "Renaldi mentioned it as a possibility of where Talbot might hide her."

"Not yet, but we will right after the meeting."

"A safe room?" River stared at him. "When did you learn this?"

"Moments ago during Renaldi's interrogation."

"What did he say about Renee?"

"He claims he never met her."

River made a note on the board. "Any witnesses from the crime scene at the dog park? Anything unusual?"

"No witnesses yet," Jackson said. "But about twenty feet from the body the grass was pressed down in a large oval, as if two people might have lain there."

River kept writing on the board, her marker making a squeaking noise. Jackson wished they were working from his department. He liked to look at the case board early in the morning when his brain was fresh.

River summed it up: "So Renaldi and Dakota may have had a rendezvous in the park before the dog killed her?"

"Maybe. We'll know more after I hear from the crime scene techs."

Schak spoke up. "This may be minor, but Renaldi mentioned that Dakota was a shopaholic."

"She lost a mother to cancer and stepmother in an accident," River said, her voice quiet. "Which probably explains that. My instinct is to think she was killed because she broadcast information about the kidnapping on live TV."

"Or found out that her boyfriend was part of it," Schak suggested. "Maybe she confronted Renaldi and he killed her to keep her silent."

The earlier mention of Dakota's vehicle made Jackson ask. "Did you find anything in Renee's car?"

"Oddly enough, I did." River had a puzzled look in her eye. "There was a white glove on the backseat, but no matching glove or other clothes were in the car. Jackson, you know Renee. Does she wear white gloves?"

"Not that I've ever seen, but was it a woman's glove?"

"Not necessarily." River walked to her briefcase, pulled out a clear evidence bag, and handed it to Jackson. "What do you think?"

The glove was made of thin suede, like a driving glove, and it seemed an average size, larger than most women's hands but too small for many men. "The kidnapper could have dropped it." He had no other explanation.

A moment of silence as they all churned it over.

"A calling card?" Agent Fouts tentatively suggested.

"Seems unlikely in a cash-motivated kidnapping." River wrote it on the board anyway, then turned back. "Just before the meeting, we learned that the first perp to pick up the money was identified as Noah Tremel, a member of the Westside Kings. The courier today was wearing a dark, down- or polyester-filled jacket and dark knit cap. Gang clothing. We either have a local gang trying to cash in big or the kidnapper hired a few gang members to help him abduct Renee and fetch the money. We all need to go to our street sources and see what they know."

Jackson thought of his informant. Loki had once been loosely connected to the Westside gang through his brother. He would call him after the meeting.

Schak cleared his throat. "If Renaldi is one of the kidnappers and we have him in custody, then he can't let Renee go."

A longer silence this time.

"But if we let him go," River argued, "he can get rid of the attack dog before we get impressions of its teeth. And Talbot is probably the main perp. He has the beef with Anderson." She looked around for disagreement. "Let's keep Renaldi in custody until we can process his dogs."

"What's our next step?" Agent Fouts asked.

"Hit the streets and talk to CIs and the Westside Kings. Somebody out there knows something. I'll question Tremel's direct associates, and Quince, who's investigated local gangs, will join me." She looked at Jackson. "Can you do anything to expedite the warrant for Renaldi's property?"

"I'll try." Jackson was itching to search Dakota's apartment, but finding Renee had to be the priority. "The media has known about the kidnapping since Dakota's broadcast last night. When do we ask for the public's help in finding Renee?"

"We give the kidnapper—or Renee—another hour to contact us. If not, we'll get her photo on the late news tonight."

"I'd like to get it into tomorrow morning's paper as well, if it's not too late." Jackson thought of Sophie.

"I'll let you handle that."

"Should we release the news of Dakota's death?"

"Yes, but not how she died. We have to keep something back for now."

"Of course."

When it was time, Jackson would contact Sophie Speranza, a reporter for the *Willamette News*. She'd left him two messages today, and knowing her, she'd leave him two more again tomorrow. She'd once nearly ruined his career with an ill-timed front-page photo, and he'd resented her for it. But since then she'd given him critical pieces of information that led to breakthroughs in his cases. He'd come to respect her tenacity and investigative skills, but she was still a pesky reporter.

River was still talking. "You need to stay focused on Dakota's death. It could lead us to Renee."

Jackson knew what he needed to do, he just didn't have legal permission yet. He'd always been a by-the-book officer, but waiting for paperwork while his family was at stake didn't seem right.

CHAPTER 28

Tuesday, January 10, 2:47 p.m.

Evans finally found a place to park in front of McArthur Court, a century-old auditorium that was no longer used for university basketball. Directly across the street was the Pioneer Cemetery, which took up about four square blocks and in places was thick with trees. The cemetery had been there first, and the university had tried and failed several times to condemn the property and build on the land. But unearthing the dead was not politically popular, so the graveyard remained.

She looked around for Officer Drummond's vehicle and didn't see it. *Damn.* She hoped the dog handler wouldn't be too late. Her date with Ben Stricklyn, an Internal Affairs detective, was at six and she wanted time to go home and shower first. If things went well, they'd end up at her place for a sexual romp, so she wanted to freshen up. Afterward, Ben would go home to his teenage sons and she would probably go back to work, then out for a run. Their relationship, which was usually confined to weekends, was fun and satisfying but neither felt any pressure to push it along. She'd only met his boys once and they had been polite but not overly warm. They were also old enough to be on their own. She'd left her parents—and Alaska—right after graduating from high school and didn't understand why young people stayed so long at home now. Didn't they value privacy and independence?

Evans trotted up the old stone steps to the cemetery and looked around. Rick Drummond was coming toward her with his dog, a scent-trained black Lab. The rest of the canines in the department were German shepherds, which were better for adrenaline-based search and apprehension.

"Hey, Drummond. Thanks for making time for this."

"No problem. This is what we do." He reached down and touched the dog's head. "This is Trigger."

"Hey, Trigger." Evans didn't know what else to say. She glanced at Drummond. "Lyla lived on Seventeenth, so she probably entered the cemetery from the southwest corner. I think if we start there, it will narrow the search."

"Sounds good."

They walked along the perimeter trail to the far corner, and Drummond said, "I heard the victim was badly beaten. Is she going to survive?"

"The doctors are optimistic but she's still in a medically induced coma."

"Barbaric." He shook his head. "We'll find the spot. What have you got for scent?"

"The victim's T-shirt." Evans reached for the evidence bag and handed him the green material. The lab hadn't checked it for evidence and it felt wrong to expose it to contamination. What else could she do? She needed to examine and photograph the crime scene, especially if Lyla didn't recover. The jury would need to see the site.

Drummond held the shirt under the dog's nose. "Zuke."

Evan arched her brows, and Drummond said, "It's Dutch. He was trained in the Netherlands."

Trigger took off, nose near the ground, zigzagging until he picked up the scent. Once he had the trail, his ears pointed and his tail stiffened, wagging back and forth in rapid motion. The dog trotted down the perimeter path on the back side of the cemetery and then, midway, veered toward the middle. For a few minutes, he weaved through the headstones and across the scraggly grass. As Evans spotted a small building to the left, Trigger stopped, then circled back. He seemed excited, making little whimpering noises, as he tried different directions but kept coming back. Evans stood still, hoping this would be the crime scene.

Finally, Trigger stopped and lay down next to a large statue of a soldier, surrounded by small headstones.

"Good boy." Drummond offered the dog a treat. "This is where the scent is strongest and the trail ends."

"Thank you. And you, Trigger." She didn't know if it was appropriate to pet the working animal. "You guys don't have to stay. I can search on my own."

"You're sure?"

"Yeah. It's a small area and I need to take photos too."

"Then we'll clear out. Good luck with your case."

"Thanks."

Evans took photos of the base of the statue, then photographed the surrounding area. Nothing popped for her through the lens. No dropped items, no fresh blood. If Lyla had bled openly here, the dog would have picked it up and followed the scent of dripping blood to wherever she'd been loaded into a car.

Time to get on eye level. Evans was glad she'd worn black slacks. But then she always wore black slacks to work, with pastel jackets over matching sleeveless blouses. Today she had on a black overcoat as well and didn't relish making contact with the cold wet grass and dirt. She squatted and duckwalked around for as long as she could stand it, then dropped to her knees. She could have asked for a technician, but the victim wasn't even dead and she'd already used resources on the search dog.

Crawling around the twelve-foot-square area, she picked up a hairpin that looked as old as the graves, a faded blue button, and an old roach from a marijuana joint. The joint looked freshest but she bagged them all. At one point, two college guys wandered by and stopped to ask if she was okay. She flashed her badge and asked what they knew about graveyard hazings. They shook their heads and moved on.

After an hour, daylight was fading fast and her knees felt frozen. Finally, she stood and decided she'd done enough. The fastest way to her car was to cut across the cemetery. As she hustled along, Evans kept her eyes on the ground. The attackers could have come this way with Lyla.

Just as she reached the perimeter path, she spotted a white scrap of paper on a tuft of long grass. Even though it was damp and blurred, close scrutiny revealed it was a receipt from the Gap in the amount of $34.95. The last four digits of a credit card number showed too. Had Taylor dropped it out of her purse or pocket as she and her partner carried Lyla to the car? Evans bagged it, then kept moving. She had just enough time to race home, shower, and throw on a dress—something she rarely did—and make it to the restaurant by six.

That evening, as Evans watched Ben take off his jacket and weapon in her bedroom, the gritty day disappeared and excitement pulsed through her. Ben was six-three with a gorgeous face and a shaved head she found unexpectedly sexy.

"Are you going to remove that dress or do I have to peel it off you?" His deep voice added to her fire.

"Peel it, please." She put her arms around his waist and they kissed deeply. For a second, her mind flashed to a moment when she and Jackson had almost kissed. Evans wondered what that would be like.

Later, as she watched him get dressed, Evans knew it was time. "Ben, I have to tell you something. I may regret this, but it seems only fair."

"It sounds serious." He sat on the edge of the bed and met her eyes.

"Yes and no." She pulled the sheet over her nakedness, suddenly self-conscious. "I like you very much and I want this relationship to continue, but I have unresolved feelings for Jackson. I'm trying to get past them, and you're helping." She gave him her most charming smile.

"I knew that." He leaned in and kissed her deeply. "That mama's boy doesn't stand a chance."

CHAPTER 29

Tuesday, January 10, 5:40 p.m.

As Jackson climbed from his car, Katie came running out of her aunt's house. He hugged his daughter tightly, inhaling her special scent, a fragrance he could never describe with words but that he'd know if he were blind and she were only one of twenty people in a room. It had filled him with joy since she was a baby in his arms. He loved this girl more than everyone else in the world together and all he could think was, *Thank god they didn't take her instead of Renee.*

Katie hugged him just as tightly. After a long moment, he finally pulled back. "How are you holding up?"

"Not good. Aunt Jan and I have been watching movies to distract ourselves but it's not helping. Have you heard anything?" Her voice had a new control and she sounded more like an adult and less like a panicked teenager.

Jackson realized the last of her innocence was gone and it broke his heart to give her more bad news. "Ivan paid another ransom this afternoon, but the courier got away with the cash. We're hoping he'll let your mom go now. And we know she's alive because Ivan talked to her this morning."

Her lower lip trembled. "How long has it been since he got the money?"

A smart question. "Only a few hours. No need to worry yet." Jackson turned her toward the car. "Let's grab some dinner. I have to get back to work soon."

"Let me tell Aunt Jan the news. She's worried too."

Jackson knew he should go in and deal with Renee's sister in person but the day had already pushed him to his limit. Seeing Dakota's mauled body this morning, then learning that Renee was still out there, possibly suffering a similar death, had put him on emotional overload. It was all he could do to keep it together for his daughter. "Give her a hug for me. I need to make a call."

He climbed into the car and called the department's spokeswoman. Matthews didn't answer so Jackson left her a message: "It's time to send photos of Renee to the media and ask the public for help locating her. Give no details except that she disappeared Saturday afternoon and is being held against her will. Ask people to call our tip line." He held back on releasing information about Dakota's death. He would give that info to Sophie first. She had earned it on previous cases. He wouldn't be surprised to learn that Sophie knew Dakota. They were both journalists and a similar age.

Katie climbed in, buckled up, and glanced at her cell phone. "I've looked at my phone a hundred times today, hoping I'd see a text or a missed call from Mom."

"We'll hear from her soon. Why don't you call in our order?"

Jackson drove to Tasty Thai, one of their favorite nearby restaurants. It was nearly full, but they found a small table and took a seat. Coming here had always been fun for them and it had seemed like a good way to cheer Katie up. Now it felt wrong. He was glad they'd ordered in advance.

Their favorite waiter, a middle-aged guy who practiced his comedy routine at work, stepped up to the table. "You both look so serious. Did somebody die?"

Katie burst into tears.

"I'm so sorry. I'll leave now." The waiter took off, but came back in a few minutes with a black coffee and a Diet Sprite. He set them down without a word.

"Do you want to leave?" Jackson asked his daughter. "We can take our food to the car. Or skip this altogether." He felt stupid for trying to have a normal dinner.

"I'm fine." Katie gave him a brave smile. "It's almost over, right?"

"I think so."

They talked about picking up Katie's assignments from school, then Jackson said, "We found your mom's car in front of Serenity Lane. She must have driven there to check in. She was going to get sober again."

"Good to know." Katie gave him a tight smile. "I know she's not the most responsible mother but we've had a lot of fun together and I love her. I can't imagine my life without her."

"You don't have to."

The waiter brought plates of spring rolls, pot stickers, and a stir-fry to share—an indulgent dinner for both of them. But that was why they came here.

"I'm starving." Jackson grabbed a spring roll.

"Me too." Katie laughed a little. "I can hear Mom nagging us for eating these." She mocked her mother's voice: "*Those rolls are nothing but deep-fried grease and starch.*"

They joked about Renee's other little quirks while they ate and it felt therapeutic, almost like warding off danger. They wouldn't be able to laugh about her if she wasn't coming back, would they?

When the meal was over, Katie glanced at her silent phone. "Will the kidnapper call and say where to pick her up? Or will Mom call us?"

"I wish I knew." Jackson reached over and held Katie's hand. "We're putting her picture on the late news tonight and the task force is out there talking to their informants. One way or another, we'll find her."

"I trust you."

A stab of worry penetrated his full belly. What if he failed Katie? What if she lost her mother and her faith in him at the same time?

"I'd better get back to work." Jackson dug out his wallet, left cash on the table, and stood to leave. "Derrick is home for a few days if you want to come home to our house."

"I think Aunt Jan needs me. Uncle Steve is on a business trip and I don't want her to be alone."

"Then I'll take you back there." He started to apologize for having to work late, then stopped. She'd heard it a hundred times.

On the drive to Dakota's condo, Jackson called Kera and left a message, updating her about Renee's situation. If he hadn't just come back from a vacation with her, he would feel guilty about not seeing enough of his girlfriend either. Sometimes he considered going over to the DA's office to become an investigator with regular hours so he could have more time with his family. But that wasn't who he was. He loved his job and was proud of the work he did. So many victims and their families had closure because he never gave up.

He pulled into the tree-lined parking lot and stared at the bright new condos. When he'd been here the night before looking for Dakota, he hadn't noticed the expensive touches, such as the stone patios and multiple skylights in every unit. He dug

Dakota's purse out of his carryall and found her keys. Had she come here at all after leaving the TV station?

Moving slowly up the stairs to unit 10, he searched for anything unusual, a drop of blood, a cigarette butt, a fresh scuff mark. Nothing but icy dew drops on the stone steps. Jackson glanced through her key set, looking for a house key. He held the clicker out of the way, assuming it was for Dakota's car, then noticed what looked like a second large car key. Did Dakota own a second vehicle? He'd have to ask Schak which key had worked on her car. Jackson selected a small silver key with a perforated wide end and stuck it into the lock. It turned and the door swung open.

Out of habit, he reached for his weapon, then stepped in. Stillness penetrated the space, the scent of new fabric filled the room, emanating from the cushions covering the couch and the overstuffed chairs. Artwork hung from every freshly painted wall and each corner and nook held an ornamental vase or metal statue. The spacious living room had been turned into a home decor showroom.

Nothing was out of place, so no struggle had occurred here. Jackson moved toward the dining room, where a laptop was open on the table. Eager as he was to access it, he turned into the hall and checked both bedrooms with a quick glance to ensure there were no intruders or obvious signs of a crime.

He paused in the smaller room, pulled on gloves, and looked around. A Precor elliptical workout machine took up much of the space and had a forty-inch flat-panel TV mounted on the wall in front it. A floor-to-ceiling cabinet held sports equipment, including skis, tennis rackets, and a lacrosse stick. Its cherry-wood twin held full-length coats, ski jackets, several pairs of fashion boots, and designer scarves. Renaldi had not exaggerated when he'd said Dakota was a shopaholic. Her father must have given her a credit card because she sure hadn't paid for all this on a TV reporter's salary in Eugene, Oregon.

In the main bedroom he found a closet stuffed with clothes and sacks of new, unworn clothes on the floor, but nothing else worth noting. The bathroom also contained little of interest, except a prescription bottle of Celexa, which he thought was an antidepressant.

He hurried back to the dining room and sat down at the computer. It was a Mac, and Dakota used Entourage for her e-mail. Jackson clicked open the purple icon and the screen filled with subject lines. He noted the number in the bottom left corner: 582 e-mails in her in-box. Almost all had been opened and the dates went back three years. Dakota apparently didn't delete e-mails and the volume seemed low. He suspected her load at the news station was much higher. He opened the latest two, which still had bold subject heads and had come in that day.

The first was from a friend named Serena who lamented they hadn't seen each other lately and wanted to get together for lunch. The second was from a credit card company, warning that she'd overspent her limit and they'd suspended her card. The e-mail didn't include balance information, so Jackson called the phone number listed and gave his name and badge number. "I'm in Dakota Anderson's apartment now, investigating her death. I'd like to have access to her account statements."

"I'll have a supervisor call you back."

"You can verify my credentials with the Eugene Police Department." He gave the department's number and his cell phone number, then returned to scanning e-mails.

Many were from political groups asking for money. Others were from Travelocity, offering great deals on trips to a variety of island destinations, and some were from social media sites, asking her to join. Jackson was surprised that so few were personal, then remembered the younger generation preferred to text each other, consolidating phone calls and e-mails into a single instant communication form. He thought he would eventually spend more time reading Dakota's e-mails, but for now he had to move on.

Scanning the folders on her computer desktop, he clicked open Photos and found a collection of more folders. They had names such as College Friends, Coworkers, Trips, Family, Vacations, and News Features. Because Dakota had e-mails from Travelocity, he clicked open Trips and found another list of folders, each marked with a date. The newest was from October, only a few months ago.

Most of the photos were of the same group of attractive people, all in their late twenties or early thirties, enjoying a variety of leisure activities such as jet skiing, scuba diving, and sunset beach parties. Many of the photos were taken on a large boat and Jackson noticed the same seven people appeared in most of the pictures. Four men and three women, including Dakota, who was in a few group shots. While he sent one of the group files to his e-mail at work, his cell phone rang.

"This is Amanda Peterson, customer service manager at Pacific Ridge Bank. I've verified your ID, so how can I help you?"

"Two main things. Tell me how much she owed on her account and send me PDFs of her last four credit card statements."

"I'm not sure about sending her statements but her current balance is $28,562."

CHAPTER 30

Tuesday, January 10, 5:36 p.m.

After the meeting, River opened her laptop and stared at Noah Tremel's mug shot. Pale and gaunt with a crooked nose, he looked thirty-five, but his file said twenty-seven. She was surprised it had taken this long to get his name. First the medical examiner had failed to send photos of his corpse, then the vice detectives in the Eugene Police Department hadn't prioritized identifying him until she'd called several times. *Let it go.* It had only been twenty-four hours since they'd found his drowned body. Everything happened when it happened and now was the right time. She had his name and data and would soon be on her way to visit his live-in girlfriend. Tremel's file listed a string of drug busts, burglaries, and one assault. He'd never had a gun at any of his arrests though.

Later, while she was buying a burrito from a street vendor, her personal phone rang in her briefcase and she struggled to answer it in time. She received so few personal calls she didn't bother to keep the phone handy the way she did her work phone.

"This is River."

"This is Jared Koberman. I'm calling about your ad for a remodeler."

"Oh, good. What kind of experience do you have?" He was only the second person to call, and the first guy had sounded old and confused.

"I've built houses from the foundation up. I'm also a good cabinetmaker and I've put down plenty of floors."

River liked the sound of this man. Friendly, confident. Maybe even sexy. "Can you replace windows?"

"Of course."

"This project could take months. Are you available for steady, long-term work?"

"I *crave* steady, long-term work."

His tone made her laugh. "I'd like you to come out and take a look at the place."

"Tell me when and where."

She gave him her e-mail instead and said, "Send me your résumé and I'll get back to you with a time. I'm in the middle of something important." She also needed time to run a background check.

"I look forward to meeting you."

"Likewise." She hung up, relieved to be moving forward on her remodel. It would be nice to have someone in the house occasionally too. She hoped Jared was as pleasant as he sounded.

River arrived at the apartment complex early and parked on the street. The building had three levels, and in the dark, much of its grime was out of sight. But the location on Fourth and Adams told her all she needed to know. Low-rent, drugs, gangs, and single mothers. She pitied the children growing up here. But people had pitied her as a child and she'd turned out fine. She checked her work phone in case she'd missed a call. She kept hoping Agent Torres, who was staying with Anderson now, would notify her that Renee had been released and that part was over. Then she could focus her energy on finding the bastard who'd taken Renee and put her and her family through hell. This case could still be in the early stages, but she'd learned to be patient.

Two cars went by in rapid succession, but both were too small and fast to be a law enforcement vehicle. After another minute, a dark sedan parked behind her and Detective Quince got out. River joined him on the sidewalk, where rain was starting to splatter.

"Another Kings member lives in this complex," Quince said, pointing to a unit on the bottom left, where a light was on. "Or used to. We'll stop there next."

They trotted up the steps to the second floor and stopped at apartment 6. The exterior light was burned out and a TV blared inside. River knocked on the door, and Quince put his hand on his hip near his gun. Footsteps padded toward them and a young woman's voice called out, "Who is it?"

"Open up, Trina. I've got information about Noah."

"Who is it?" An edge of panic.

"FBI." She grabbed the door handle and turned before the woman could lock it. "This is important."

The door yanked open and the woman yelled, "Where the hell is Noah?" She looked barely old enough to vote, six months pregnant, and mad as hell. When she saw the two of them standing there in long dark coats, Quince with his badge showing on his belt, she clamped her mouth closed.

River stepped toward her and Trina backed up. A toddler with a bottle waddled up and laid her face on Trina's lower legs.

Oh christ. The poor kid's dad was dead and his mother's life was about to get harder than it already was.

"I'm Agent River and this is Detective Quince. Let's go sit down."

Trina didn't move but her chest began to heave. "Where's Noah?"

"I'm sorry but we have bad news."

"Oh fuck!" Trina looked like she wanted to throw something at them. "What happened? He promised me he was out of the gang life."

"Let's sit down."

Trina scooped up the little girl, hugged her tightly, and sank into a dirty green couch.

River grabbed a dining chair from the kitchen and sat in front of her. She wanted to face Trina and didn't trust the couch or the padded chairs. Detective Quince stayed standing near the door.

"I'm sorry to tell you but Noah is dead. He drowned."

"What the fuck?" Confusion filled Trina's face before tears filled her eyes. "Drowned where?"

River hated this part of the job and she'd had to do it twice in the last twenty-four hours. "In the Willamette. He was using the river for a getaway. He picked up ransom money for a kidnapped woman."

"A kidnapping?" She started rocking and crying and the little girl struggled to get away. Trina let her go and she crawled to the other end of the couch.

"Yes. We believe he helped kidnap a woman named Renee Jackson. Do you know her?"

"No. This is too fucked up. He hasn't been involved with the Kings in a year or so."

"Did he talk about making a big score recently?"

"Just that he was going to get us out of this ghetto soon." She glanced around at the battered walls and stained beige carpet.

"Who has Noah been hanging out with lately?"

"No one new. Just a guy from work."

"What guy?"

"James Branson. They work together at Jiffy Lube." Trina cried as she talked and was hard to understand.

River took long slow breaths to keep her emotions detached, like she was watching this scene instead of living it. It was cheating, but it was also survival. She'd learned the trick while coming to grips with the details of what her father had done to those women. "Is James a Westside member?"

"No. Neither was Noah. He was out of the gang and trying to be a good daddy to his baby girl." Trina abruptly stopped crying and her eyes narrowed. "Who is Renee Jackson?"

Good question, River thought. "She's the fiancée of a wealthy man. And her kidnapper demanded a lot of money."

"How old is she?"

Odd question. "I'm not sure. Maybe forty. Why?"

"Just wondering if Noah was cheating on me."

She was jealous? "Renee is still missing and we need to find her. Do you have any idea where she might be?"

"No. Why would I?"

"You know Noah. Where would he hide someone if he had to?"

Trina shook her head. "I don't even believe this."

River prepared to accept that they'd learn nothing here but she had to try. "Who else would be involved in this? Who would Noah trust to pull off such a crime?"

"He used to run drugs to Portland with Bartolo Diaz, but Tolo got out too, and he's the only Westside King that Noah still respected."

River made a note of the two names. "Where can I find Bartolo Diaz?"

"He used to hang out at Max's, but now he's working for some guy who builds fences."

"Does the fence builder's business have a name?"

"I don't know."

One last long shot. "Do you know Daniel Talbot? Or Jacob Renaldi?"

"I've heard of Jacob. He sold Bartolo a dog."

CHAPTER 31

Tuesday, January 10, 4:17 p.m.

Sophie Speranza uploaded her story to the shared server and sent her editor an e-mail, letting him know it was done. She'd spent most of the day working on what she hoped was her last feature about a young woman who'd been falsely charged with killing her newborn child. After a mistrial and an acquittal, she expected the woman to sue the Springfield Police Department. Sophie was glad she would not be assigned that article. The newspaper now had her working the crime/court beat almost exclusively and she loved it. Yet after months on the same story she was ready to let it go.

Especially now that she'd learned Renee Jackson had been kidnapped. She'd seen Dakota's broadcast the night before and called immediately, but her friend hadn't called back yet. She'd met Dakota Anderson in journalism school at the University of Oregon, and since they were both still in Eugene, working for news media, they'd stayed in touch.

Sophie looked at her cell phone to see if she'd missed a text or call. *Damn.* No one had gotten back to her. Not Dakota or Detective Jackson or even the police department's spokesperson. As Sophie checked her contact list for someone else who might know Dakota, her phone rang. Jasmine's sweet face was on the screen. She'd finally captured a smiling photo of her beautiful but often solemn lover.

"Hey. So good to hear from you. My phone has been a dead zone all day." Sophie kept her voice low. Her cubicle had no privacy and she and Jasmine were keeping their relationship private for fear of jeopardizing Jasmine's job.

"Do you have time for a quick dinner?" Jasmine asked. "I'm starving but I have to work late so there's no point in going home."

"Would love to. Where do you want to meet?"

"Lucky Noodle in half an hour?"

"Sounds good." Sophie clicked off her computer. "Why are you working late? Did you get called out to a scene?"

"I'll tell you when I see you."

Sophie's pulse quickened. She loved getting inside information. "See you soon."

She grabbed her oversize red shoulder bag as her editor, Carl Hoogstad, shuffled up to the open space in the half wall she called her office. Age had not been kind to him and the hair straggling down his neck did not make up for what he'd lost on top.

"What did you find out about the kidnapping? Should we hold a spot for your story?" He blocked her exit with his round body.

"I don't have anything yet." She started to apologize, then caught herself. Her stories were the most widely read after the sports pages and she could only do so much in an eight-hour day. Especially now that half the staff had been laid off. "I will though. I'm meeting with a source now."

"Let the night editor know by seven if you can."

"I will." She stepped toward him and he moved out of her doorway.

"Good job on the Swartout wrap-up, by the way. I can't believe she got off."

"I can't believe she spent a year in jail for a crime she didn't commit. There was never a baby."

"She confessed."

"She's mentally ill and the police pressured her." Sophie had kept her opinion quiet while writing the stories, but now that the case was over there was no reason to hold back. "The second jury deliberated less than two hours. They didn't have a case."

"I'm glad it was Springfield's money wasted and not Eugene's."

"Me too. See you later." She headed for the stairs before he could find a reason to keep her late.

Sophie slid into a booth in a dark corner and ordered a cup of green tea. The short walk from the parking lot across the street had chilled her to the bone. God, she hated winter in Eugene. After growing up in Santa Fe, she'd never gotten used to months of cold gray days. She hadn't planned to stay after getting her education, but the *Willamette News* had offered her a job and there was so much else to like about Eugene, Oregon. Great theater and art exhibits in addition to liberal attitudes. She felt accepted here as a bisexual. Still, her job was probably short-lived. The newspaper was no longer losing money after cutting half its staff and benefits, but it wasn't profitable either. She'd come to believe that a daily newspaper was not a sustainable business model. They printed yesterday's news on paper and delivered it to people's houses, often in gas-consuming vehicles. How long could it last? Soon, they would be online only and probably get by with about twenty employees.

The waitress brought her tea and laid down menus. Sophie didn't even pick one up. She would order the fire-eater's salad with rare beef like she always did. In each restaurant she frequented, she only ate her favorite thing on the menu.

While she waited for Jasmine, Sophie checked her home e-mail on her iPad. A brief note from her mother, who was still teaching in China. Her parents had sold their home and trotted off to the other side of the world just a few months after she'd announced she was dating a woman. She didn't know for sure the two things were connected, but she couldn't help but think so.

Jasmine rushed in, a little late as usual, her cheeks pink against her smooth pale skin. Tall and lean, Jasmine was older than her, with dark hair and eyes, making Sophie feel a bit like a kid with her small frame, short red hair, and freckles. But Sophie had never lacked for attention, either from men or women. Some people were naturally drawn to her energy. Jasmine slid in and squeezed her hand. It was the most affection she would show in public.

"Your hands are as cold as mine and I've been outside all day." Jasmine peeled off her leather coat, weariness evident in her struggle.

"A crime scene?"

"Yes. And I'll tell you about it after we order. I don't have much time. I need to get back to the crime lab and finish logging in evidence." Her voice was hushed and heavy.

Sophie repressed her compulsion to ask questions and let Jasmine study the menu. After the waitress took their orders, Jasmine leaned over and whispered, "Dakota Anderson is dead. She was killed last night, most likely by a dog, in Wayne Morse Park."

"Oh my god." Sophie stared at Jasmine, her mouth open. "I can't believe she's dead. I've been calling her all day." Grief and guilt jumbled together, making Sophie afraid to speak.

"You knew her?"

She swallowed back her distress. "We met in J-school and saw each other at media functions. I liked her. She was never afraid to say what she thought." Sophie was surprised at how quickly she thought of Dakota in the past tense. Was she getting jaded?

"I heard she went on the air last night and asked the public to help pay her stepmother's ransom."

"I watched the broadcast. I've never seen her so upset."

"If she had been killed any other way, I would assume her death was related to the kidnapping." Jasmine shook her head. "Today was awful. Taking samples from her wounds was one of the worst things I've ever had to do."

"I'm sorry. Maybe you should treat yourself to a glass of wine."

"Not yet. I still have to work."

Sophie had to ask. "Whose dog? What are the circumstances?"

"We don't know. It happened in the middle of the night and there are no witnesses."

"That is so bizarre. Who's working the case?"

"Jackson and Schakowski. They're on the kidnapping too, so Lammers must think the cases are related."

They talked about possible scenarios until their food came, then ate in silence for a few minutes. Finally, Jasmine said, "You can't run this story until the department gives a statement. Except for the woman who found her body, no one but law enforcement knows she's dead."

"Her father must know."

"Yes, but I'm sure he's focused on finding his fiancée, so the story isn't out there yet. You have to wait."

Sophie made a face. "Okay. I'll start making calls though. I'm sure KRSL will start investigating soon too."

Jasmine pushed her bowl of pasta and shrimp aside. "I'll take the rest with me. I'm too upset to eat and I have to get going."

"Do you want to come over tonight?"

"Yes, but I'd better not. I'll need sleep. I suspect tomorrow will be long and stressful too."

"Still overworked because of funding cuts?"

"Of course." Jasmine pulled on her coat. "And Joe was at the hospital today photographing an assault victim, so he was no help."

"What assault?" Sophie was surprised she'd missed it.

"A young woman named Lyla Murray. She was attacked Saturday night and dumped at the hospital. She's still in critical condition. That's all I know."

"Who's handling the case?"

"Lara Evans. She sent Joe to photograph the victim's bruises."

"I'll give her a call. She's been friendlier to me lately. Maybe she'll tell me something about Dakota's death."

Jasmine squeezed her hand in a painful warning. "Do not ask her about Dakota. This can't come back to me."

"I know." Sophie dug out her credit card, now eager to make some calls.

Jasmine laid cash on the table and patted Sophie's leg. "I really could use a hug but it'll have to wait."

Sophie gave her a quick kiss on the cheek. "Thanks for telling me. Your tips have led to some of the best writing I've ever done."

Jasmine winked and left without saying anything. Sophie looked forward to the day they could be more open about their deepening affection for each other. But she feared Jasmine might never become that kind of person, even if she didn't work for the Public Safety Department.

The table next to her was seated with a noisy group of women, so Sophie moved to the bar counter. The sun had set and she wasn't ready to embrace the cold, dark walk to her car yet. She dialed Detective Evans, left a message, then called the hospital. All they would tell her was that Lyla Murray was in the ICU.

Sophie dug out her iPad, looked Lyla up on Facebook, and discovered she was a UO student. Sophie scanned through Lyla's friends to see if she knew any of them, but she'd been out of college for three years and didn't expect to get lucky.

Her phone rang and she was surprised to see Detective Evans had called back. "Hey. Thanks for returning my call. What can you tell me about Lyla Murray's assault?"

"I think she was the victim of a hazing." Evans hesitated for a long moment. "I'm telling you because Lyla is not the first. I hope by going public with the story, someone who's no longer connected to the sorority will come forward."

"Which sorority?"

"It's a private house and no one will admit they're a club, let alone tell me the name. I think I know who one of the assailants is, but without Lyla's testimony we may not be able to convict her."

"You don't think she'll live?"

"She's coded twice and had two surgeries. Even if she survives, she might not tell me anything. No one in the house will talk about the initiation."

Feeling hyped, Sophie scribbled notes as Evans talked. If there were other women who'd been injured, this could be an important story. She flashed back to her own high school tormentors. Hazing was part of the bully culture in schools and she hated everything about it. "I'll get the story into tomorrow's paper. They were holding a space for me anyway."

"Will you ask victims to contact you or the police department?"

"Of course. Where is the sorority house located?"

Evans gave her the address and Sophie thought she might have been to a party there once. But the university area had many old houses rented by groups of students. "Thanks. I'll call you if I hear from anyone. Whatever I can do to help make hazing a thing of the past. It's a heinous practice."

"This was a particularly vicious assault. I've got to go. Bye." Evans hung up quickly, as if something had diverted her attention. Or maybe she didn't want her peers to know she'd talked to a reporter.

Sophie called the paper and let them know she was coming back in to submit a late story for the morning's edition. It wasn't quite as attention grabbing as a kidnapping/dog mauling, but she'd find out more about that development soon. She would call Mr. Anderson if she had to.

CHAPTER 32

Tuesday, January 10, 7:45 p.m.

While Jackson searched Dakota's filing cabinet for more banking information, his phone rang.

"This is River. We just found a connection between Jacob Renaldi and Bartolo Diaz, a Westside King. I called the task force members with the update and put out an attempt-to-locate with your department, so we're looking for Diaz already." She sounded calm as ever. "I'm heading to your department now to interview Renaldi, if you'd like to join me."

"I'll be there in twenty minutes. I'm at Dakota's place now."

"Have you found anything?"

"No signs of a struggle or threatening e-mails, but she owes nearly thirty thousand on a credit card."

Agent River whistled. "That's sizable. But not totally unexpected for a rich kid just out of college. I wonder if her father knows."

"I'll ask him. Meet you at the department."

After parking his car, Jackson walked over to Full City for a cup of coffee, his legs heavier with every step. It was too late to be drinking caffeine but he didn't care. He needed to be sharp for the interrogation and his brain was dragging. Still, he kept working the case over, and what he came back to was motive for Renaldi. Everything pointed to him: his connection to Dakota, his connection to Talbot, and his ownership of attack dogs. But why kill Dakota, except to silence her? The kidnapping had to have been motivated by money. Talbot wanted his lost investment back from Anderson. What had his e-mail said? That he was down eighty thousand? The extra twenty in the first ransom could have been Renaldi's cut for assisting. But why was the second demand only for twenty thousand? Was Talbot settling for what he thought he could still get of Anderson?

A full moon lighted his way as he trudged up the wide steps to the city hall buildings. The night had dropped to a bitter cold but at least it wasn't raining. Warming up was always faster than drying out. He entered the department, nodded at the desk clerk, and used his ID to open the door leading from the small lobby into the winding corridors of the department. He couldn't wait for the move to the new building. This one had grown claustrophobic. He started to head for the conference room to wait for River, then decided to check on his suspect. Renaldi had been in the interrogation room for about six hours. But that was common and desk officers had been checking on him and giving him bathroom breaks.

He unlocked the metal door and stepped in. Renaldi was on the floor on his side, not moving. *Oh crap!* Jackson rushed over and knelt down, pressing his fingers against the man's throat. He had a pulse. Thank goodness. What the hell had happened? He grabbed his cell phone from his pocket and dialed 911.

"Detective Jackson here. I need a paramedic at the Eugene Police Department. A suspect is unconscious but still breathing. I just entered the room and don't know what happened, so don't ask questions. Just send an ambulance to city hall. Park on High Street and come up the back side."

He clicked off and stared at Renaldi. A stroke or heart attack? He seemed too young and physically fit for either, but anything was possible. Jackson gently pressed a thumb against Renaldi's eyelid and pushed it open. The white of his eyeball was nearly all that showed, with only a curve of the iris peeking out from under the flap of skin. A seizure? Jackson wanted to rush to the front area and ask why no one had checked on his suspect but he couldn't leave until medical help arrived. He felt useless, with no idea of what to do except watch and make sure Renaldi didn't stop breathing.

Jackson leaned against the wall and dialed the front desk to alert them to what was happening. If this guy didn't make it, they might never know how or why Dakota died. If he lived, Renaldi would probably sue the department—and him personally.

* * *

River waited for Quince to park so they could walk upstairs together. She didn't have ID clearance for the EPD's locked doors. She admired Quince for coming back to the department to watch the interrogation, even though she'd told him to call it a night. Most law enforcement officers were like that. They didn't watch the clock and wait for quitting time. They kept going until the urgency was over or someone with fresh stamina relieved them. The wail of a siren filled the underground parking lot as Quince jogged toward her. Red lights flashed in the sloped entrance.

"What the hell?" River tried to visualize where the ambulance had parked.

"Lammers probably snapped and finally killed someone." Quince grinned and motioned for her to follow him up the stairs.

As they entered the building, paramedics rushed down the hall in front of them. Had a cop had a heart attack? River and Quince both hurried after the men in light-blue shirts. Her legs still burned from her wild bicycle chase that afternoon.

River saw Jackson come out of the interrogation room and felt a sense of relief. The medics left the gurney in the hall and entered the small space.

"What's happening?" River called out.

"Renaldi passed out. I think he had a seizure." Jackson rubbed his temples, stress and bad lighting making him look older than she remembered.

"But he's okay?"

"He's breathing but that's all I know."

"Did you get a chance to question him?" Quince asked.

"He was on the floor when I came in."

The three had to press themselves against the wall to let the paramedics pass with Renaldi on the gurney.

"What now?" River's body screamed that it was time to go home but she wasn't quitting until Jackson did.

"Do we have an address for Bartolo Diaz?" Jackson asked

Quince answered, "His last known location is two years old, but it's not far from here. I'll go with you if you want to pick him up."

"Let's do it." Jackson squared his shoulders.

"Should I follow or wait here?" She was ready to get out of the narrow hallway.

"Neither," Jackson said. "He's probably not there and we don't need three people to find that out. Go home. If we get him, we'll call."

"I'll hang out at my office for a while and see what happens."

"We'll let you know."

Moments after River sat down at her desk, Jackson called to say Diaz was no longer at the known address. They agreed to call it a night and River left the federal building, feeling relieved. *Not quite*, she reminded herself. She made a mental note to call the prison soon and find out what she could about Darien Ozlo, the inmate who'd threatened her. Did he know she was in Eugene?

Despite how badly she wanted to go home and soak in her hot tub, she found herself driving toward the teen shelter. She'd missed the night before and wanted to make up for it. For her, it was only an hour delay in what would be another night of not sleeping well. But for Saul and June and the other kids, it meant going to sleep knowing that somebody thought they were worth the time.

CHAPTER 33

Wednesday, January 11, 2:55 a.m.

Jackson woke with a horrible pain in his lower gut. He climbed from bed and hobbled his way to the bathroom. The pink urine made his heart pound. *Crap.* He hadn't seen that since before the surgery to remove the fibrosis around his kidneys. He took two naproxen and tried to remember when his next CAT scan was. Was it this Thursday? Or next week? What day was it anyway? Deciding it didn't matter at the moment, he headed back to bed. The pain was less intense now that his bladder was empty. Maybe the blood was just a fluke. His last scan had shown the fibrosis shrinking. But he couldn't worry about it right now. Renee was still missing and Dakota Anderson needed him to find her killer. Her death had not been an accident. He climbed back into bed, noting the light in his brother's room was still on.

Four hours later, Jackson left the house, thermos of coffee in hand. A small intestinal ache was still with him but he ignored it. He drove to Renee's sister's, had breakfast with Katie and Jan, and updated them on the case. His announcement that they had the names of the two couriers and would soon find Renee gave the women little comfort. Neither understood why the kidnapper hadn't let Renee go after getting the money yesterday. Neither did Jackson, and nothing he said sounded convincing. Without actually speaking the words out loud, they both expressed the sense that Renee might be dead. Jan was stoic but Katie seemed distraught, and Jackson had no idea how to comfort her. On his way out, he asked Jan to find a counselor that might help. On the drive to the department, he checked in with River, who hadn't heard from the kidnapper.

His hope of finding Renee faded and he tried to remember the last time he'd talked to her. Had he been kind? He hoped so. The ache in his heart began to drown the pain in his gut. His next stop was at the department and he hoped it would be brief. He had to update Sergeant Lammers and he dreaded telling her about Renaldi's collapse. Her office door was slightly ajar, as always, and he knocked as he spoke her name.

"It's a good damn thing you're here," Lammers said, waving him in. "I don't appreciate hearing about your cases from the gossip mill, as I did first thing this morning. What the hell is going on?"

Jackson straightened his shoulders. Where to start? "We brought in Dakota Anderson's boyfriend yesterday for questioning. Jacob Renaldi breeds and sells what he calls protection dogs. He also works for Evergreen Construction, which is owned by Daniel Talbot, a suspect in the kidnapping. And he was the last person to contact Dakota by phone. So he's a very viable suspect for both crimes."

"How did he end up in the hospital?" Lammers tapped her pen on the desk.

"He had a seizure while he was alone in the interrogation room." Jackson had called the hospital and extracted some basic information. "I left him in custody because it seemed imperative until we could get a court order to search his place. I notified the desk officer and asked him to check on Renaldi and to bring him food and water."

"Which officer?"

Jackson hated to point fingers but there was no way to protect him. "Chad Rogen."

"Did you know the suspect was an epileptic?"

"Not at the time. I learned it this morning when I called the hospital. Renaldi is doing fine, an officer is watching his room, and Quince is on his way to question him again."

"I want him released immediately after questioning. We'll be lucky if he doesn't sue us. And if he does, it's on you." Lammers jabbed a finger at him. "This is your case and you are responsible for him while he's in your custody."

"I understand." But he didn't really. What would that mean for his job? "I asked the hospital to hold Renaldi as long as they can. We haven't searched his home yet."

"What are you waiting for?"

"A signed subpoena. The DA's office is working on it and I haven't heard from them." Jackson felt overwhelmed. He'd stayed up late to update his case notes and prioritize their tasks, then realized they hadn't even begun to look at phone and bank records. "I could use another detective or two. We still need to comb through the files and question Westside gang members."

"I can pull Evans off her assault case for a few days. What are you and your people doing this morning?"

"I'm headed to Dakota's autopsy, Quince is questioning Renaldi again, and Schak is trying to locate Bartolo Diaz."

"Who the hell is Diaz?"

"He's a known associate of Noah Tremel, the gang member who died in the river with the first ransom. We learned that Diaz bought a dog from Renaldi, so we think he might be involved and may even have been the courier for the second money drop."

"I know we're understaffed but every lawsuit takes even more money out of the budget. No more screw-ups." Lammers' voice softened. "Send me your notes. I may have some time to work this case with you."

Surprised, Jackson mumbled "thank you" and stood to leave.

The county performed autopsies in a small bright room in the basement of the old North McKenzie Hospital next to the University of Oregon. Giant stainless steel drawers lined the wall to the right and a built-in counter ran along the back, cluttered with microscopes and various cutting and measuring tools. Jackson closed the door, nodded at the three men in the room, and started to suit up. He didn't recognize the short man with a thin gray mustache who looked like he hadn't had a good meal in a long time.

Rudolph Konrad, the pathologist, who clearly ate well, introduced the stranger. "This is Sam Larson. He's with county animal control."

"Detective Wade Jackson." They both wore gloves and didn't shake hands. "Thanks for being here."

"It's an unusual situation." Larson looked over at the body on the small raised table. Dakota was still covered with a white plastic sheet.

"Let's get started." Rich Gunderson, the medical examiner, stepped up to the table and pulled the sheet back. Jackson remembered what he'd said at Dakota's crime scene about getting laid off. Would the county really cut out the ME's office? The pathologist, who performed the actual autopsies, would be overwhelmed if he also had to attend death scenes, process the bodies, and send out all blood and tissue samples.

"The first thing to note is her tattoos," Gunderson said. "She has one on each upper arm. The right arm says *Kerry* in a cursive script and has a small heart under it, and the left arm says *Nadine* in a similar script and has a small shamrock under it." He looked at Jackson. "Any thoughts?"

Jackson stayed at the end of the table near the corpse's feet. "They're most likely the names of her mother and stepmother, who both died."

"Poor girl." Gunderson pointed to her ankle. "She also has a small pink and silver tiara."

Jackson glanced down at the pretty, but unusual, tattoo. "Symbolic of Daddy's little princess?"

"Good possibility."

From there the pathologist took over, starting at her toes and examining her skin closely. He used a magnifier at times and made small comments, his voice deep and deadpan. His seriousness contrasted with his round face and boyish looks.

Jackson avoided looking at Dakota's body. She was ten years older than his daughter but still a young woman, and his mind kept imagining Katie on the table and how it would feel for him. The anguish Anderson must be experiencing. Jackson knew he had to go see him as soon as he had the chance.

Konrad worked his way up to Dakota's genitals, probed her gently, and took fluid samples. "She likely had sex within hours of her death."

Jackson knew that and hoped someday, when it was his time to go, a pathologist would say that about him. He tuned out for a moment, wondering if the assistant DA had a warrant for Renaldi's place yet. He was eager to search it, yet he dreaded dealing with the dogs.

He became aware that Konrad was talking to him. "She has scars on the inside of her wrists," he repeated. "Most likely a suicide attempt. They're quite faint now, possibly incurred as long as ten years ago."

After her biological mother died? Jackson hadn't known Dakota had been that troubled. According to Anderson, she'd been an exceptional college student and was a successful TV journalist with a bright future. His next thought was for his own daughter. How would she cope if Renee died? Pain surged through his body and he didn't know if it was physical or emotional. He forced himself to focus on the autopsy.

Larson, the animal specialist, leaned over Dakota's head and studied her wounds. "Definitely a dog," he said. "Her tissue has been crushed and torn by dull teeth, rather than punctured or lacerated like a cougar mauling." He looked shaken.

"Can you take measurements for comparison to particular dog teeth?" Jackson asked.

Larson looked at him with raised eyebrows. "This is not a single bite. She's been chewed to death. We'll have more luck finding her tissue in the dog's teeth."

The room was silent. Jackson felt a little queasy.

"I took plenty of tissue samples," Gunderson finally said. "Maybe the state lab will isolate the dog's DNA from the saliva it left in the wounds."

"She might have saliva on her clothing as well," Jackson added.

"I'll send it all out this morning."

Jackson's phone rang in his pocket. "Excuse me." He hurried from the room, grateful for the chance to escape.

Out in the hall, he looked at the screen. Jim Trang, the ADA. "Jackson here. What have you got for me?"

"A signed warrant to search Jacob Renaldi's home and property. It's limited to items that might be connected to Dakota Anderson's death. No computer or bank records."

"It's a start. What about the dogs?"

"I have a subpoena to collect saliva samples and teeth impressions."

"Finally. Now we just need someone who knows how to do that. I'm still waiting to hear back from the state police."

"I made some calls," Trang said. "There's a national laboratory in Ashland that specializes in animal forensics. They're sending someone up today."

"Excellent. I owe you." Jackson glanced over at the door to the autopsy room. He couldn't make himself go back inside. Searching Renaldi's place was more important. "I'll head out now and pick up the warrant on the way."

A new surge of optimism flooded him. They might get a breakthrough—or maybe even find Renee on the property somewhere.

CHAPTER 34

Wednesday, January 11, 5:47 a.m.

Evans put on running pants and a lightweight jacket with pit zips. After a kickboxing workout, she was headed out for a short run. She'd done five miles the night before but her weight was still up a pound, so she would do double runs until it came off. She tucked her cell phone, spare house key, and pepper spray into a pocket and left her duplex in west Eugene.

Starting slow, she let her legs warm up and her body find a rhythm. Soon she was pounding down the bike path, hoping the sun would break over the mountain. The cold and darkness didn't bother her as long as she kept moving fast enough to make her heart pound. She'd grown up in Alaska and was used to real winter, which was the worst time to slack off on exercise because she tended to eat more carbs. Like the damn bread on her pastrami sandwich last night, after eating that egg roll on campus. But she loved to exercise, so it tended to balance out.

For the first two miles, she mulled over Lyla's case. Like most of the crimes her unit investigated, this one wasn't a puzzle. She'd found the perpetrator in short order, but the real task was proving it. Sometimes it took months to gather enough evidence and testimony to press charges, and that aspect of the job was tedious. She loved the hunt, the first few days of an investigation when she was tracking her prey. Like all the other victims, Lyla deserved justice and Evans would be patient and do whatever it took, even if it meant interviewing twenty annoying college girls. Maybe she'd get lucky and Joe would be able to match one of Taylor Harris' sports weapons to the bruises on Lyla's body. Or better yet, maybe Lyla would wake up and name her attackers.

Evans wondered what Jackson would be doing on the job this morning. Whatever it was, she wished she could join him. She loved working his cases and going out on suspect calls with him. He'd been her mentor for a year and she'd learned so much. She'd also fallen stupidly in love for the first time in her life. When they started working together, he was going through a divorce and she'd let herself fantasize about having sex with him. It seemed harmless enough until she realized she was thinking about a future with him. But the feelings had all been in her head, not Jackson's. Then he'd met Kera, a tall gorgeous, wounded woman, and he'd fallen hard for her.

After that, Evans had started dating again and tried to let go of her feelings for Jackson, but it obviously hadn't happened yet. She was grateful for her relationship with Ben, the first man she'd been excited about since she'd met Jackson. But she worried she would always have feelings for Jackson. It was like that for some people, even after they married someone else and lived a happy life together. Maybe she needed to transfer out of the Violent Crimes Unit.

Evans arrived at the department early, determined to find some-thing new to bolster her case against Taylor Harris. She wanted to call Joe and ask about the bruises but it was too soon. Hers was not the only crime he had to process. She called Mrs. Murray at the hospital and learned that Lyla was still unconscious, but the bleeding in her brain had stopped and they were going to let her wake up from her coma…if she could. Evans asked Karen Murray to call her the minute Lyla was able to speak.

After an hour of running background checks and combing through Facebook pages, she'd learned nothing relevant. None of the women in the sorority had criminal histories, except one for minor in possession of alcohol, and of course they were all Facebook friends. Yet no one had disclosed anything specific about their house, its rules, or its initiation. She stood, thinking she'd make another trip to the sorority, and her cell phone rang. She glanced at the screen. Sophie Speranza. Did the reporter have something for her already?

"Hey, Sophie. Did you get your story into the paper last night?" Evans hadn't looked. She got her news online and the *Willamette News* was slow to post in the morning.

"I did, and a woman just called me. Anna Compton. She wants to meet with both of us right now before she goes to work."

"Where?"

"The Keystone Cafe on Fifth."

"I'm on my way."

Evans didn't get far before running into Sergeant Lammers in the hall.

"I need an update. Come into my office." Lammers' scowl was deeper than usual.

"I only have a minute."

"It'll only take a minute."

Evans followed her into her office and closed the door, thinking it would be nice to have a private office. But she'd rather be in the field. "I'm making progress. In fact, I'm almost certain Taylor Harris, one of the victim's roommates, assaulted her. Taylor texted and arranged a meeting with Lyla right before the attack."

"How did the search dog work out? Worth the department's money?"

"I think so. We found the crime scene and I took photos. I also found a receipt that I need to match to a credit card. And I turned in several potential weapons from Taylor's room. Joe is comparing them to her bruises, using high-tech photography."

"Good. Because I need you to work the kidnapping/homicide case. The media has been calling nonstop about what we're doing to find the kidnap victim, and now Dakota Anderson's death by a dog attack is out there too. We have to get this under control and Jackson needs help. He left a suspect in the interrogation room for six hours yesterday and the man had a seizure."

Evans cringed, then regretted it. She had to get better at keeping her cop face on all the time. "We've all done that. Sometimes longer. We count on the desk officer and the rest of the office staff to check on them."

"Don't make excuses for him." Lammers gave her a brief rundown on the kidnapping/homicide case, then said, "Now check in with Jackson and help him close out this mess."

Evans started to mention her interview, then changed her mind. "I'm on it." She bolted out of the sergeant's office, fully intending to follow orders—right after she talked to Sophie's witness and stopped to see Joe at the crime lab.

Anna Compton was bone thin and dressed in baggy purple scrubs. Her short hair radiated a similar color. Across from her at the table sat the reporter with bright-red hair, a red handbag, and a pale-pink shirt. They were quite the rainbow, and Evans felt a little drab in her sage blazer. She slid into the booth next to Sophie.

"Sorry I'm late. I had to meet with my boss right after you called." She looked at Anna. "I'm Detective Lara Evans. Thanks for coming forward."

A group of male college students came into the small restaurant, and the young woman tensed like a deer ready to run. "I don't have much time. I have to be at the nursing home soon."

"You work as a CNA?" Evans wanted her witness to relax a little.

"Yes. After four years in college and forty thousand in debt, this is my future." She seemed more sad than bitter.

"What did you major in?"

"History."

No wonder, Evans thought. She had no words of support or advice.

A waitress came to the table and Evans said, "Just black coffee, please." The other two women already had mugs and Sophie was picking at a bagel.

It was time to get some answers. "Did you live in the house at 1985 Potter?"

"Yes, for my last two years at the university. I moved out two years ago."

"I need to document this interview." Evans pulled out her recorder, heard no objections, and pressed the button. "What's the name of the sorority?"

"They don't think of it as a sorority, but it's called the Kappa Non Gratas. They take pride in their non-approved status, but the name is a secret, so no one ever uses it."

"Were you initiated when you moved in?"

"Yes." Anna looked down.

"Please describe that for me."

"I promised myself and my house sisters that I would never tell a soul." She twisted her napkin into a tight roll. "But it's gone too far. I can't believe that girl is in the hospital."

"Do you know what happened to Lyla Murray?"

"No. I'm sorry. But I can imagine."

"What did they do to you in your initiation?" Evans wanted names but it seemed wise to work up to it.

"There were two phases. First they made me sit naked while everyone in the house critiqued my body. It was bizarre and humiliating." Anna didn't make eye contact while she talked. "For the next part, only the house leader and her second in command participated." She paused and sipped her coffee. "They took turns beating my ass with a paddle."

"This took place in the house?"

"Yes."

"How long did it last?"

"I don't remember. It seemed like forever at the time."

"Did you have bruises or welts?"

"Both. I carried an extra sweater around for two days to sit on in my classes."

"I'd need to know the names of the women who assaulted you."

"Ashley Harris and Jennifer Warzinsky."

Taylor's older sister. Evans made a note of the names. She'd question them as soon as she had a chance. "Did Taylor Harris live in the house at the time?"

"Yes. She was a freshman."

"Do you know if she participated in any beatings?"

"Not that I know of. She wasn't house leader until this year."

"Did you participate in any hazings?"

Anna bit her lip and glanced away. When she looked back, tears rolled down her face. "I never hit anyone physically, but I helped humiliate other girls who joined the house."

"Will you testify to this in court?"

"Yes, but there's no point. I let them beat me. I signed a consent form."

That startled Evans and she wondered if Lyla had signed anything. Would such a document hold up in court? Would a prosecutor even take the case if Lyla wouldn't or couldn't testify?

"Can you help me understand why you would let them do that? What was so special about joining that club?"

"I wanted to have friends I could count on and to hang out with pretty, popular girls. Most of all, I needed a stable place to live while I finished college. My first couple years were awful. I moved three times, worked too many hours, and almost flunked out." Anna pulled on her jacket. "I have to go."

"How did you get in? I mean, how does the house choose members?"

"By invitation. You have to know someone to get accepted." She slid out of the booth. "I don't know who hazed Lyla or why they hurt her so bad. I'm not in touch with anyone there. Maybe it just got out of control, but it's time to make it stop."

Sophie, who'd been quietly making notes, reached for Anna's arm. "Can I call you with some follow-up questions?"

"There's not much else to say." The young woman rushed from the restaurant. Through the window, they watched her unlock her bike and ride away.

Fifteen minutes later, feeling charged, Evans jogged upstairs to the second floor of the crime lab. She'd left Joe a message and hoped to find him here. He wasn't in his office but Jasmine Parker said to look in the big bay, so she headed back down.

The row of large processing rooms had overhead, garage-style doors accessible from the parking lot, but they could also be accessed from a hallway along the back. She stopped at the second door, knocked briefly, and entered the room. Except for the high ceiling, it looked much like a garage, only with unusual tools. Joe was taking fingerprints from the door of a new silver Honda.

"Hey, Joe. How's it going? Working on a stolen vehicle?"

He laughed. "Not a chance. We don't have time for that." He glanced over. "Sorry, but I don't have good news on your case. I wasn't able to match the victim's bruises to any of the weapons you brought in."

"Crap."

"But I think I know what they used." He cocked his head. "I wish I could show you but the images are on my computer. I think it might be a golf club. In close-up, the bruises have an inner edge that looks curved but I haven't had a chance to do an actual comparison."

She hadn't seen clubs in Taylor's room. Had the other hazer supplied the weapons? Evans tried to let Joe off the hook. "You must be swamped."

"We all are. I was going to call you, then I got orders to help process everything from the kidnapping/murder case ASAP."

"Is that Renee Jackson's car?"

"No. That one is next door and already processed. This is Dakota Anderson's. She was killed the next day and is somehow connected."

"She's the daughter of Renee's fiancé, Ivan Anderson. He's the one who got the ransom demand." Evans felt a tug of adrenaline that she'd been assigned such a bizarre, high-priority case. "They think Dakota was killed by a dog."

"I heard the Westside Kings might be involved."

"That's the theory. I'd better run. I've been assigned to the case now too. Let me know about your golf club theory when you have time."

Jackson called on the drive to the department. "Evans, I need your help on Dakota Anderson's death. Have you got some time today?"

"Sure. Lammers told me you'd call. What do you need me to do?"

"Dig through Dakota's computer and credit card records. Her laptop is in an evidence bag in my desk drawer and the paperwork is in a box under my desk. I haven't had time to go through it all yet."

"Anything in particular I'm looking for?"

"I want to know how much debt she had, but more important, I'm curious about a group of photos. The same people, including Dakota, are in several vacation pictures. See if you can identify her friends on Facebook or other social sites."

"I'm on it."

"And bring it all to the task force meeting at the FBI office this afternoon at two thirty."

"See you then."

CHAPTER 35

Wednesday, January 11, 1:43 a.m.

The sound of beeping worked its way into an already weird dream. River sat up in bed, realizing it was her work phone. She grabbed it from the nightstand and answered without looking at the screen. "I'm awake. What is it?"

"It's Torres. Anderson is trying to drink himself to death. I poured out what was left of the alcohol but he tried to get in his car and drive to buy more. So I took his keys. Then he started on his wine collection. I'm worried he'll drink himself into a coma."

Just what they needed. "Tell him he's a suspect in his fiancée's kidnapping, slap some cuffs on him, and question him until he passes out."

"Copy that. I considered cuffing him but I wanted to run it by you first."

"Sorry you have to deal with this. If we don't hear from the kidnapper today, we'll stop babysitting Anderson. But we won't quit looking for his fiancée until we find her."

"I feel sorry for the guy. He's taking his daughter's death really hard and he's given up hope of getting Renee back."

"When he's sober, try to talk him into getting help. A rehab center or grief counselor, something." River had seen her share of counselors over the years. Some were a waste of time, but her last counselor had helped her let go of a lot of guilt.

River woke several hours later and couldn't go back to sleep. After her morning yoga, she had leftover lasagna for breakfast, made a cup of chai tea, and opened her laptop to review her case notes. There was something about this case they hadn't seen yet. Some reason Renee was still a hostage after the kidnapper received the money. The *courier* had the cash, River corrected. Maybe he had never delivered it to the ringleader. Or maybe the leader had killed Renee to keep her from identifying him. She could be buried in the woods and never surface.

River read through everything, ruminating over the details. The disparity in the amount of the two ransom demands bothered her. Had one of the couriers taken over the scheme? A gang member with lower expectations of what constituted a windfall? Or had Diaz tried to kidnap Dakota and for some reason ended up unleashing his dog on her instead? River realized she didn't know enough about Dakota's death. She started to call Jackson to set up a task force meeting when her phone rang. *Agent Fouts.*

"Hey, partner. I could use some good news."

"I located Bartolo Diaz. An informant called back this morning and said the guy lives in an apartment off Centennial."

"Where's that?"

"It's the corridor that runs by Autzen Stadium and connects Eugene and Springfield."

"I thought that was Martin Luther King." River was confused now.

"Sorry. It used to be called Centennial and us old-timers will always think of it that way."

"What's the address? I'll meet you there."

"I don't have a street number but my CI says it's the front building in a big complex between Kinsrow and Chevy Chase. Apartment fifty-eight. We'll find it."

A half hour later, she spotted Fouts parked on a side street, leaning against his car and smoking a cigarette. She thought he'd quit. River made a left turn, pulled into the complex parking lot, and eased into a reserved space. They wouldn't be here long. She climbed out of her car, zipped her leather jacket, and embraced the cold. She preferred blue-sky cold, but gray-damp cold was good too. Any day that didn't induce sweat was fine with her.

As Fouts trotted over, she scanned the building, looking at apartment numbers.

"I hope this is the right complex," Fouts said. "I'm going on the word of a CI who's a couple sandwiches short of a picnic."

River smiled. "Not to worry. We're not going in with flash bang."

"Maybe we should." Fouts scanned the building too. "I see fifty-eight on the second floor near the end."

"Let's do it."

"I hope we don't have to shoot his dog."

"You can always use pepper spray and hope for the best."

Fouts snorted. "I'll do what I have to."

At the top of the stairs, they knocked on the brown door and waited. Pounded again. No answer.

"What now?" Fouts sounded annoyed. "Do we have an ATL on this guy?"

"I called it in last night." River pounded again. "FBI! Open up!"

The door to the apartment on the right opened instead and a thirty-something woman wearing a bathrobe leaned out. Yawning, she said, "You're wasting your time. And keeping me from sleeping. Some people work nights, you know."

"We're looking for Bartolo Diaz. Have you seen him?" River stepped back to get a better look at her.

"Like I said, you're wasting your time. He packed up and hit the road yesterday afternoon. I saw him stuffing all his crap and that big dog into his little car."

River pushed off her disappointment and pressed forward. "What time was that?"

"About five, I think. I was getting ready for work."

Fouts asked, "What's your name?"

"Chrissy Stuck."

"Did you talk to him? Ask him where he was going?" Fouts' voice was low but his tone had a surprising menace.

"I told the prick I wanted the two hundred bucks he owed me." Chrissy lit the cigarette she was holding. "To my surprise, he paid me. Then Tolo said he was leaving town. Going somewhere for a fresh start."

River took back the questioning. "Did he say where he was going?"

"No. Why are you looking for him? Did he rob a bank?"

"Why do you ask that?"

"Cuz he paid me. He owed me that money for months. And I know he doesn't have a job, so he must have made a score." Chrissy shivered. "Shit, it's cold out here. I'm going back in."

"Just a few more questions," River said. "We can go inside if you want."

The neighbor shook her head. "You're not coming in here. Just make it fast. I was at the club until four this morning and I need to go back to bed."

"What kind of car does Bartolo drive?"

"A silver Toyota."

"Except for yesterday afternoon, have you seen him over the last four days? Has he been home?" River wanted to know who'd been guarding Renee, if anyone.

"He had been gone since the weekend. Then I saw him yesterday. That's all I know."

"Any idea where he'd go? Does he have friends or family in other states that you know about?"

"No clue." Chrissy shrugged. "We weren't that chatty. I loaned him rent money once because I felt sorry for him. He looked for work all the time and nobody would hire him because of his record." She pulled her robe tighter. "I'm going in." She stepped back inside and closed the door before River could respond.

"He's a thug. Law enforcement somewhere will pick him up." Fouts nodded at Diaz's door. "Should we go in and take a look?"

"Let's get the manager. If we find something, we need to be able to use it in court."

"What if Renee Jackson is in there?"

"I doubt it. This place is too busy, too public. But if we can't get the manager here promptly, we'll bust it down."

"Your call." Fouts looked disappointed.

They found a manager home in the corner apartment on the first floor. He let them into Diaz's unit, then started swearing. "I knew he had a damn dog in here."

"Could you wait outside?" River pushed the door closed after him.

The apartment was half empty, as if someone hadn't finished moving in. A couch but no TV. A mattress but no bed frame. A few empty beer cans and a sack of trash in the dining room, but no table.

And no Renee Jackson.

Her task force hadn't found her in any of the construction sites they'd checked either. Unease crept into River's bones and she couldn't make peace with it. If all the kidnappers were dead, gone, or in the hospital—who the hell had Renee?

CHAPTER 36

Wednesday, January 11, 10:15 a.m.

Jackson got out of his car, buttoned his overcoat, and wondered when they'd see the sun again. The gray, frigid days wore on him the way a virus did, making him feel sluggish and irritable. He tried to shake it off. They finally had a warrant to search their main suspect's home, and with any luck, they'd find Renee in a back bedroom. But he couldn't make himself believe it. He hadn't believed it yesterday when they'd picked up Renaldi—or he would have gone in without permission. Dogs or not. Doubt nagged at him. Had he left Renee here in captivity overnight because he feared the dogs?

Gravel crunched behind him and he turned to see Schak pull in. The barking from the kennels started again. God, he hated the noise. Cold fingers of dread squeezed his already tender abdomen. Jackson tried to reassure himself. Several animal control experts would be here soon, and the forensic specialist from

Ashland was on his way. He just hoped that only the one dog—a massive creature—was loose in the house. After seeing what it had done to Dakota, he wouldn't hesitate to shoot it.

Schak joined him at the edge of the walkway. Thin, wild grass grew on either side of the path and circled around the cedar-siding house. He knew from their last visit that a tall metal fence hid the kennels from view.

"Ready?" Jackson asked.

"As a sinner on judgment day."

Knowing Schak was also a little nervous didn't make him feel any better. "I'll try to pick the lock but we also have Sergeant Bruckner and a few SWAT guys on their way out with the door knocker." Jackson didn't care about damaging Renaldi's front door with a battering ram, but he would save his coworkers the trouble if he could.

He had no luck with the lock and wasn't surprised. Someone who bred protection dogs could be expected to have a secure home. Possibly even an alarm. They would deal with that when they came to it. He'd also called Quince, who was at the hospital with Renaldi, and asked him to persuade the suspect to give him the key. That hadn't worked either.

"While we wait, let's go out back and see how many animals we're dealing with." Schak stepped off the small porch. "It'll give the experts a head start."

Jackson would have preferred to skip it, but he was a police officer. Show no fear. "What's your best guess?" Trying to sound casual.

"From the barking, I think around twenty."

"At least."

They came to the tall fence. Schak shouldered up against it and held out his interlocked hands for Jackson to step into. Good grief. The last time he'd done anything like this had been at fifteen when he'd helped his brother Derrick over the back fence of his girlfriend's house. Jackson grabbed the top of the fence, pushed off Schak's boost, and reached over for the latch on the other side. As the gate swung open, he dropped down.

Schak went through first, Sig Sauer drawn and ready. Jackson kept his weapon at his side but had his taser in his other hand, ready to fire. They passed a small greenhouse and came to the first row of kennels. A carport-like roof covered the row of cages and each dog had six-by-twelve feet of bark dust to move around in. The carport didn't keep the wind off the dogs and Jackson had a tiny flash of sympathy for any creature spending January outside.

A similar structure lined the other side of the narrow property. The barking became a raucous roar, but it only came from some of the animals. Other dogs were silent, which was just as creepy.

He and Schak moved down the middle, each tallying a kennel. Jackson counted fifteen dogs of various breeds and ages: German shepherds, Doberman pinschers, and several mastiff mixed breeds. He turned to look at the dogs on the other side and noted they were all some breed of pit bull.

"Twelve over here," Schak said.

Jackson noticed empty pens at the end. "Fifteen on this side. The animal control guys will have their hands full. This could take all day."

They both turned to the back of the property, where they saw outbuildings and two fenced areas, one of which contained an adult-size stuffed dummy.

"The training ground."

"Could Dakota have been killed here?" Schak started toward the large fenced area.

"It's possible, but unlikely." Jackson followed. "Let's check the buildings. Just in case they're holding Renee here."

The structures were locked, but they pounded and heard no response. Jackson moved to the back of one and found a small window. Without light from the inside and little sunlight, he couldn't see enough to know. "Renee!"

No response.

"We'll get the door knocker out here too when SWAT shows up," Schak said.

"I think I hear a car now."

They strode past the barking dogs and through the metal gate. The county's animal control truck was parked in the gravel lot and two men got out. Jackson had met Sam Larson at the autopsy. The other guy was bigger, younger, and darker skinned. He introduced himself. "David Estes, veterinarian for the county. Another private vet is coming to help with tranquilizing the animals."

"Thanks. And good luck." Jackson glanced down the driveway, hoping to see the SWAT unit. "The first animal we need to process is probably in the house where we left it yesterday. And we can't get in without a battering ram, but it's on the way."

Schak added, "We've got twenty-seven dogs out back, plus the one we know of in the house."

"Holy moly. This will take some time." The vet looked worried.

A few minutes later, the SWAT unit rolled up in a dark box truck. It wasn't the oversize purple vehicle they called Barney, but Jackson had only asked for the battering ram. Bruckner didn't like the equipment to go out without him and he probably got a kick out of using it. SWAT members were the only personnel in the department required to maintain their physical training. There had to be some payoff for all that work and knocking down doors was good clean fun.

Two men climbed from the truck and Bruckner approached with a grin. "So we just go in? No people inside to warn?"

"Just a big, and possibly vicious, dog. The animal may have killed a woman recently."

"In that case, after we pop the door we'll let you guys go in." Bruckner chuckled and headed for the back of the rig.

Why wasn't the dog in the house barking? Its silence bothered Jackson.

Bruckner and his partner hauled out a four-foot-long, heavy metal cylinder and trotted toward the door. Schak drew his weapon, and Jackson turned to the animal control officer. "Do you have a tranquilizer I can shoot at the dog?"

"Let me do it. I'm experienced." Sam Larson grabbed something from his truck and returned to the house.

At the door, Bruckner yelled, "Stand clear. We're coming in." On the count of three, he and his partner swung the ram into the door. On impact, a piston fired to maximize the blow.

The door stood its ground.

"Damn!" Bruckner tapped two fingers around the door. "It's solid metal and there must be reinforced locks up and down the frame."

"Let's hit it again. It'll weaken," his SWAT partner urged.

"Here goes."

They rammed it again. The door gave a little but didn't open or fall.

A vehicle barreled into the driveway and screeched to a halt. They all turned to see Jacob Renaldi jump from the passenger's side of a truck. A younger man was behind the wheel, but stayed put.

"What the hell? You can't break down my door."

Schak aimed his taser at him, while Jackson said, "We have a warrant. Give us your keys and we'll spare the door."

"I'm not letting you in. My door is reinforced for a reason."

"We are going in," Jackson countered. "Even if we have to cut a hole in the wall. Just give us the keys. We need access to the kennels too."

"No." Renaldi crossed his arms. "I'm already going to sue you for risking my life. I'll just add this to my list of grievances."

"You're under arrest for obstruction of justice. Put your hands in the air and get on your knees." Jackson and Schak both stepped forward.

For a second, Jackson worried about what an electric current would do to someone with epilepsy. He didn't want to find out. Just as he started to warn Schak to put the taser away, Renaldi spun, like a person getting ready to run or reach for a weapon. Schak zapped him with the taser prongs, one landing in his back, the other in his right butt cheek. Renaldi jerked and moaned but didn't go down.

"No more. I've got him," Jackson called. He rushed in before the suspect could recover, cuffed him, and pushed him to the ground.

Quince drove up while Jackson retrieved a set of keys from Renaldi's pockets. The driver watched but didn't interfere.

"He left the hospital against medical advice," Quince said, climbing from his car. "And Lammers said all I could do was follow him here."

"It's fine. We needed his keys anyway." Jackson stood and started for the house. "Keep an eye on him while we search his place. And call 911 and get a paramedic out here just in case."

"Covering my ass?" Schak grinned.

As he got close, he noticed the door had three locks. But he never got a chance to match the keys to the deadbolts. Bruckner hit the door again with the ram. It sprung loose with a metal-popping screech and hit the floor with a thud. Jackson pulled up his weapon. "Do you see the dog?"

Larson, the animal control guy, stepped through the open space and stood on the downed door, tranquilizer gun ready.

The crowd outside the door inched forward and peered inside.

Out of nowhere, the mastiff-rottweiler charged Larson, leaping from six feet away. Larson fired the tranquilizer dart, hitting the animal in the neck midair. But momentum was still with the dog, and the two-hundred-pound beast knocked Larson down and sunk its teeth into his throat before it blacked out. Jackson's fingers had itched to pull the trigger, but Larson was right there and no one had a safe shot.

For a moment they froze, weapons aimed at the interior, watching for signs of movement, of another attack dog.

The house was silent, the only noise the barking dogs beyond its walls.

Jackson spun and yelled at Quince in the yard, "Get an ambulance out here ASAP."

He turned back to see Schak and Bruckner rolling the dog off the animal-control guy.

Larson sat up. "I think I'm okay." His voice was distorted and blood ran from the bite wound.

"Secure the house," Jackson commanded. He stepped outside and yelled to the veterinarian who had stayed back. "Get a first-aid kit in here."

Jackson pressed Larson's shoulder and forced him to lie back down, then held his hand over the wound. His brain told him Larson would live, but after seeing Dakota's ravaged face and neck, Jackson couldn't take it for granted. He stayed with Larson until the vet taped a large piece of gauze over the wound and assured him the bite wasn't deep or lethal.

Bruckner and his partner came out of the hallway. "The house is clear. Do you need us to stay and help search?"

"No. But thanks. Get back to your patrols." The SWAT guys had been pulled off their regular duties—or day off—to assist him.

"Start with the back bedroom," Bruckner said. "I think you'll find it interesting." He and his partner left without further explanation.

Jackson's first thought was Renee, but they would have brought her out. He hurried across the spacious living room and turned down the hallway. At the end, he stepped through the open door into a good-size room, partially filled with computers, scanners, and a high-end, freestanding printer. The blinds were fastened closed and a sense of secrecy loomed. Schak, who was leaning over a table looking at documents, turned and said, "He creates phony IDs."

CHAPTER 37

Wednesday, January 11, 2:15 p.m.

River ordered coffee and pastries to be delivered from Full City, then called Agent Torres. "How's Anderson?"

"Better. He slept for a while this morning and now he's sitting in his office staring out the window. I think he's sober, unless he has a stash I didn't find last night."

"No word from the kidnapper I assume?" She knew there was no point in asking. Torres would have called her.

"Not unless Anderson is keeping it from me."

River had sent the tech people home to Portland the night before. The burner phones were impossible to trace and the kidnapper had gone silent. "The task force is meeting here in a few minutes if you want to join us."

"As much as I'd like to get out of here, I hate leaving Anderson alone."

"You're a good man, Torres, but we're not babysitters. Does he have family you can call?"

"I left a message with his sister in Los Angeles but I don't know if she's coming."

"Try her again, then head this way. You can go home and get some rest afterward."

River hung up and headed for the conference room. A vague guilt tried to work its way into her head. Long ago, when they'd found body parts in the basement and taken River's father away, an FBI agent had been present in their home for nearly a week. Not the same agent; they'd taken turns with the overnight shift, but their presence had been comforting to her and her mother. But this was Eugene and they only had ten on staff, several of whom had been preoccupied with searching construction sites for Renee. River decided she would go see Anderson after the meeting.

While she waited for the group to arrive, she updated the board with what little she knew about Bartolo Diaz. Fouts was first to come in and she asked him what he thought about terminating the post at Anderson's.

He shrugged. "Anderson's part is over. We either find Renee or we don't."

"Harsh, but true."

Two more agents came in, followed by a pretty woman River didn't know. She held out her hand. "Detective Lara Evans. Sergeant Lammers asked me to join the task force."

"Agent River. Welcome. We could use a fresh perspective."

Evans took a seat and River tried to guess her age. Thirty? She seemed young to be a detective.

River looked at Gilson. "How are we coming on searching the construction sites?"

"We only have two left. They started with the most-remote places and worked their way in. And the site with the underground safe room was empty, so we're not optimistic."

A few minutes later, Jackson, Schakowski, and Quince came in. She noticed they were silent and their mouths had the same grim expression.

"What happened at Renaldi's?"

"We didn't find Renee." Jackson slumped into a chair next to Evans and she reached over, touched his hand, and quickly pulled back.

Just a friendly gesture, River wondered, *or was there more going on?*

Jackson continued, "As if that weren't bad enough, the animal control officer was bitten by one of the dogs, and we tasered Renaldi, who has a history of epileptic seizures. The citizens review board will probably ask for my resignation."

"Fuck 'em," Schak said. "They have no idea what our job is like."

River empathized, but none of it was relevant to the investigation. "Did you find anything connecting Renaldi to either Renee's kidnapping or Dakota's death?"

Jackson shook his head, seeming weary. "We found a fake ID business, so we booked Renaldi into jail, but there was nothing linking him to either crime."

"We still haven't searched his computer though," Schak added. "And now that we discovered his illegal-ID business, we can get a subpoena for his bank records."

"I doubt if you'll find any of the kidnapping money there." River tapped Diaz's name on the board. "Bartolo Diaz left his apartment yesterday afternoon and took all his personal things with him. That was after paying his neighbor the money he owed and telling her he needed a fresh start." River turned to the board and made a note. "He's driving a silver Toyota and we have a state-wide lookout for him."

"How is Diaz connected?" Evans asked.

River hoped they wouldn't have to brief her on everything. "He's a known gang associate of Noah Tremel, the first ransom courier, and Diaz also bought a dog from Jacob Renaldi. So he knows all the players. Our working theory is that he picked up the second ransom, slipped away from a team of FBI agents, and left town with twenty grand last night." She backtracked a bit. "Or he might have given Renaldi, or Talbot, a cut first. We don't know. Did you find any cash?"

"A couple thousand in an envelope in a false-bottom drawer," Jackson said. "We picked it up as evidence if you want to compare it to the serial numbers in the ransom money."

"We didn't have time to record the numbers." River would send Renaldi's cash to headquarters anyway, along with the glove and a few other items. She decided to bring it up again. "Any thoughts on the white glove found in Renee's car?" She turned to Schak. "Anything like it at Renaldi's?"

"We found some panties and a scarf that could be Dakota's, but Renaldi admits she was there on many occasions." Schak shrugged. "No gloves."

Jackson suddenly sat up straighter. "I remember a robbery I worked about six months ago. A convenience store on Royal Avenue. After the perp left, the clerk found a playing card on the floor. A jack of spades. Someone had dropped it; either the robber or the customer before him." Jackson grimaced. "I never solved the crime. It was a one-off, unlike most robberies, which are part of a string. The perp usually just keeps hitting stores or banks until he makes a mistake or someone identifies him."

"What are you saying?" River wanted him to spell it out.

"It's probably irrelevant, but someone mentioned *calling card* at the last meeting and it made me think about that card on the floor." Jackson sounded unsure but he continued. "If a gang like the Westside Kings is involved, maybe the crimes are part of an initiation. And they leave a calling card as part of the—" Jackson paused, then finally said, "risk."

"I'm intrigued." River wrote *initiation* on the board. "But gangs aren't usually that sophisticated in their crimes or initiations. They prefer an old-fashioned beat down." She turned back to the group. "Any other crimes fit this pattern?"

No one had anything new, but Quince had something to add. "Both Tremel and Diaz are supposedly ex-gang members. At least according to Tremel's girlfriend, Noah Tremel has been out of the gang life for a year. And she thought Diaz was too. So they may be working independently of the gang."

"But still thugs," Schak added. "Worse if they're kidnapping people."

After a silent moment—during which they mentally assessed whether kidnapping for ransom was really worse than home invasions and forcing women into prostitution—Detective Evans spoke up. "I've been looking through Dakota's computer and paperwork for a few hours. She had nearly seventy thousand in debt from four credit cards and was getting notices from collection agencies."

Schak whistled. "Holy shit. How does a single young woman run up that kind of debt?"

A dark feeling crept up River's spine. "That kind of financial trouble could motivate someone to look for a big score."

Jackson looked distressed. "Would Dakota do that to her own father?"

* * *

The thought made Jackson ill. He'd seen teenagers assault their own parents and drug addicts steal their single-mother's grocery money, but this was different. Putting her father through that anguish—not to mention taking his life's savings—was selfish beyond description. And it was all too close to home. Dakota was practically Katie's stepsister. Jackson was shamefully pleased that Dakota would not be able to influence his daughter.

Evans turned and stared at him. "You'd met Dakota before this, right?"

"Yes, once, for a family dinner. She seemed smart. And normal."

"Well, she's not." Evans jerked back, as if she'd just had a revelation. "I just realized Dakota's silver Honda matches the description of the car seen leaving the hospital in the assault case I'm working. The witness finally called me an hour ago. A woman was stripped and beaten in the university graveyard, then dumped at the hospital with internal injuries. She's still in a coma."

"Silver Toyotas and Hondas are the most common car on the road," Schak said. "And the gangbangers love 'em."

Evans jumped up and began to pace. "Jackson, you searched Dakota's place. Does she own golf clubs?"

He remembered the clubs in the trunk of her car. "Yes, why?"

"Joe at the crime lab says the victim's bruises could have been made by a golf club. I want to bring in her set for comparison."

River held up her hands. "How is any of this connected to Renee Jackson? Who still happens to be missing. She has to be our priority."

Scenarios were finally coming together for Jackson. "If Dakota orchestrated the kidnapping, that opens up new places to look for Renee."

"Wait a minute." Schak shook his head. "If Dakota is the kidnapper, who killed her and why? Or was her death an accident?"

"Renaldi and the gang boys were probably helping Dakota," Jackson suggested. "Then Renaldi turned on her when the money ended up in the river."

"Then one of the bangers must have orchestrated the second money drop," Schak said.

"Or maybe it was someone else." Evans' eyes sparked with excitement as she grabbed her laptop and opened it. "I looked at those photos you mentioned, Jackson. And I recognized one or two of the people." Evans clicked open a digital folder. "This older guy on the left is Austin Hartwell. He owns the sorority house connected to my assault case." Evans turned the monitor toward Jackson and pointed to a picture of a pretty blonde. "This woman looks so much like my suspect, Taylor Harris, I think it must be her sister, Ashley. She used to be the house leader. Clearly, Ashley and Hartwell are both good friends of Dakota's, and they even take vacations together."

"We need to talk to Anderson again." Jackson stood, feeling charged. This case was about to break wide open. "Agent River, I think you should come with me."

Evans' face fell and Jackson backtracked. "Good work, Evans. Your insight has been critical. But the kidnapping is River's case and she has a rapport with Anderson."

"I understand. I'd like to search Dakota's place again and bring in her golf clubs. I have a case to solve too."

"They're in the trunk of her car." Jackson turned to Schak and Quince. "Find out what you can about Austin Hartwell and the others in the photos. Be on standby."

As River started to adjourn the meeting, her cell phone rang. She took the call, so it had to be important. After a brief minute, she hung up and said, "Daniel Talbot left his office today and purposely lost our tail. We have to consider that he may be on his way to either release or silence Renee."

CHAPTER 38

Jackson followed Agent River across town and south toward Anderson's home. He couldn't stop thinking about Talbot suddenly going AWOL. All the talk about gangs and Dakota and a sorority house now seemed like wild speculation. The kidnapper was likely the man Anderson had believed guilty from the beginning. A man who'd lost a lot of money because of Anderson's financial advice. But would Talbot let Renee go? She'd been a hostage for nearly four days.

A gray sky loomed over the city and threatened rain. Once they'd passed the downtown area with all the transients and aimless teenagers, the sidewalks were empty. Even few cyclists were on the road today. Agent River drove like a woman in a hurry and Jackson pressed to keep up. They could have gone together, but no one in law enforcement wanted to be without their own vehicle if a scenario suddenly changed direction.

River waited in Anderson's driveway. When Jackson reached her, she said, "I wanted to warn you that Anderson's been drinking heavily for the last few days. Agent Torres reported him to be hungover, but sober, a few hours ago, but that could have changed by now."

"So this could be a waste of time." Inwardly, Jackson raged at Anderson for drinking, for leading Renee back into the disease.

"Maybe. I'm also hoping you'll help look out for him if we don't get Renee back."

Jackson didn't respond. Anderson was not his family, and he had all the responsibility he could handle. "Let's go see what he says about Dakota."

Anderson was in his study, looking at photos on his computer. His eyes were dull and watery and his skin seemed loose on his face. He looked ten years older than he had when Jackson had met him a few months ago.

Looking up, Anderson said, "You're both here. That can't be good."

"We don't have any news," Jackson said. "Just questions. We need you to tell us the truth, even if it's painful."

River pulled up a chair and sat next to Anderson. Jackson stayed standing. "Did you know Dakota was nearly seventy thousand in debt?"

Anderson blinked and swallowed. "I didn't know it was that bad. I knew she'd gotten into trouble with credit cards again but we were working something out."

"What does that mean?"

"She agreed to cut up the cards and see a debt counselor and I was going to help her pay the collection agencies."

Agent River sat quietly, watching Anderson, so Jackson continued. "Was Dakota ever involved with a gang?"

Anderson closed his eyes. When he opened them, they shimmered with tears. "She dated a gang member her first year in college. He went to jail for a while and she broke it off."

"Was it Noah Tremel?"

"I don't remember. What does this have to do with Renee?"

"Both couriers who picked up the ransom were members, or ex-members, of the Westside Kings. Why would they target Renee?"

"I don't know what you're saying. Daniel Talbot kidnapped Renee." Anderson sounded desperate. "Why haven't you arrested him?"

"Why would Talbot hire gang members to pick up the cash for him?"

"I don't know. That's your job."

Jackson knew it was time to confront him but he still wanted to ease into it. He realized how devastating the accusation would be for a father to hear. "Dakota had suicide scars on her wrists. Why did she try to kill herself?"

"Her mother had died of cancer and she'd been depressed even before that. I told you."

"Has she ever seen a counselor for any emotional problems?" Jackson recalled the Celexa in her medicine cabinet.

"Off and on. But she lost two mothers; who could blame her? I tried to be that person in her life but I failed." Tears rolled down Anderson's face. "Dakota was always looking for someone or something to cling to. In high school, it was a group of gamers and one friend in particular. Then her first year at the university, she dated that gangster and I was so worried. But thankfully it didn't last. Finally, she found a private sorority and they were like family to her. Dakota settled down and got serious about her education."

Maybe Evans was right about the sorority connection, Jackson thought, but he didn't know how it would help find Renee. It was time to say it. "We think Dakota may have orchestrated the kidnapping to get the money she needed to pay off her debt."

"No." Anderson's whole body shook with denial. "She would never do that. I know she wasn't close to Renee but that's unthinkable."

* * *

River decided to step in. "It may not have been Dakota's idea. Maybe her ex-boyfriend Noah approached her. I'm sure he promised her that Renee would be safe and no one would get hurt. She probably thought they would both walk away with a pile of cash and the whole thing would be over in a couple of days."

"Dakota wouldn't have gone along," Anderson argued. "She would never commit a crime just for the money. Not as long as I was able to help her."

"She had a compulsive shopping habit," Jackson said, still standing.

"So? Lots of people have vices." Anderson's voice rose a notch. "Dakota had a void to fill but she wasn't a criminal."

River kept her voice gentle. "Of course she wasn't. But Renee is still missing and we need your help."

"If you think Dakota kidnapped Renee, you must know what happened to Dakota. Tell me whose dog killed her." Anderson started to stand.

River put a hand on his arm. "We need your help. If Dakota was involved in the kidnapping, where would they keep Renee?"

"She wasn't." Anderson folded his arms across his chest.

River sensed him shutting down. "Can you visualize Renee somewhere?"

A moment of silence.

I know where she is.

River heard Anderson's thought. It was weak and filled with pain as it eased into her head. She took a slow breath. "Tell us where Dakota would hide Renee. You want her back, don't you?"

"Of course. But I can't help you and I resent your insinuation that my daughter was a kidnapper." Anderson pushed to his feet, looking a little unsteady. "You're just blaming her because she's dead and can't defend herself against the charges."

River suddenly knew how this would play out. "I'm sorry for your pain and I hope you'll get some counseling. If you think of anything that can help, call me." She stood and stared at Jackson, willing him to go along.

He started to speak, then closed his mouth and stood too. "Take care of yourself." Jackson touched Anderson's elbow and walked out. River followed.

Out in the driveway, she said softly, "We wait and watch. I'll go left and you go right."

"You really think he knows?"

"Yes. Let's go."

They jumped in their vehicles and backed out. River drove two blocks, backed her car into an empty driveway, and slumped down in the seat. She hoped Anderson wasn't intoxicated, but with Renee still in captivity after four days and possibly alone for the last twenty-four hours, they had no choice but to see what happened.

CHAPTER 39

Pain gnawed at Renee's stomach and she felt queasy from dehydration. The little sink in the bathroom didn't work and no one had brought her water in a long time. She lay on the bed, listening for the sound of footsteps in the hall or a car driving up outside. The last time she'd had contact with her kidnapper had been yesterday around noon, or so she thought. He'd silently given her a sandwich and a glass of water and left again. His face hidden by a ski mask, she had no idea who he was, but he dressed like a gang member and smelled like dog. She thought she'd heard whimpering noises at one point too.

She was pretty sure the same man had been feeding her from the beginning, but then yesterday, she'd heard a car leave. And never come back. Another night had passed and she'd slept off and on, waking from hunger and worry. Now most of another day had passed and no one had brought her food or water. It was the longest she'd ever gone without sustenance or human contact.

Now she'd been abandoned. It was very possible she would die here in this room, slowly starving. Renee sat up and moved to the floor again. Yesterday, she'd rubbed the tape that bound her wrists against the corner joint on the bed frame for an hour, then had given up in despair. But she had to try again. She couldn't lie here and wait to die.

After a few minutes, she knew it was pointless and began to sob. But her despair was again driven out by determination. Now that she knew her captor was no longer out there, she had nothing to fear. These walls were probably made of sheetrock and she might be able to kick a hole in the interior one.

She picked a spot, brought her knee up and smashed her heel into the wall with all her might. The pain made her eyes water but she'd made a little crack. Renee brought her foot up again and the sound of a car caught her attention. Thank god, someone was here. Tears of relief flowed freely as she scrambled to decide her next move. Sit here and wait to see who came through? Or press herself to the wall and shove him as he opened the door?

The footsteps sounded different this time. Quicker and lighter. Was it someone to save her?

He called out her name and her pulse accelerated. A rescuer was looking for her!

Renee rushed to the door. "I'm in here." Her throat was so dry she could barely project any sound. She pounded on the door and soon footsteps were in the hall.

She stepped back and the door opened. At the sight of the mask, her heart sank. He wasn't here to rescue her.

Silently, he took out a pocketknife. Renee cried out but he reached for her bindings as if to cut them.

What now?

The sound of another car outside. The man spun around, surprised. When he turned back, he had a gun.

* * *

Ten minutes later, Anderson's car rolled by. Jackson waited for a count of three and pulled out behind him, driving slowly. The poor son of a bitch. Jackson empathized with Anderson's desire to protect his daughter's reputation, even beyond her death, but it enraged him that Anderson was willing to risk Renee's life for it.

In the distance, Anderson's sedan slowed at the intersection, so Jackson pulled off and waited. He must not believe Renee was in danger, Jackson reasoned. Or else he knew she was already dead and planned to move or bury her body so Dakota wouldn't be blamed for the kidnapping. Or maybe Anderson had no idea of what he would find or how he would react. But it was obvious he'd decided to keep his knowledge from the police.

The Lexus turned right and Jackson pulled out and followed. They were headed out of town on Willamette, toward Spencer Butte. Jackson wondered how far he would go to protect his own daughter if she got into trouble. Would he break the law or lie to police officers? Especially if he believed no harm could come of it? Jackson didn't know and he hoped he never had to find out.

When they passed Braeburn, Anderson picked up speed. Jackson finally had to pass the little car in front of him to stay with the Lexus. He glanced in the rearview mirror and didn't see River's vehicle. Had she gone the wrong direction? It didn't matter. He could call and let her know their location. Should he contact Schak too for more backup? It seemed premature. They didn't know where Anderson was headed and it seemed inevitable that Renee had been abandoned and would be alone or dead. Dakota, the ringleader, was dead, and one of the couriers had drowned during the money exchange. The other courier had left town and Renaldi was in jail. Who was left?

Talbot? Was that why he'd ditched his FBI tail earlier today? Jackson shook his head. Either Dakota or Talbot had planned the kidnapping, not both. If they had been working together, they would have demanded a lot more money. He called Schak. "Hey, partner. Where are you?"

"At my desk, checking out Hartwell, who seems pretty wealthy. What's up?"

"River and I are following Anderson. We think he might be headed to where Renee is being held."

"You think he kidnapped his own girlfriend?"

"No, but we convinced him his daughter did. Now he might be trying to find out for sure, while still protecting Dakota."

"You mean he plans to bring Renee home and say the kidnapper dropped her off and everything is fine?"

"Something like that. He's probably not rational right now."

"What do you need from me?"

"Nothing yet. I just wanted to check in and get you on standby. We're headed up Willamette and just passed Spencer Butte. If you don't hear from me in thirty minutes, head this way."

"Will do. Be safe."

"I'm more worried about finding my ex-wife dead in a basement."

"I hope not."

They hung up and Jackson got another call. River. "Are you still with me?"

"I was stuck behind a school bus for a few minutes. Still on Willamette?"

"Yes and I see Anderson turning off. There's a sign on the left. It's faded but it says Harper House."

"What is that?"

"I think it may have been a bed-and-breakfast once. I'm turning now." Jackson clicked off. He needed to be on full alert.

The asphalt driveway turned to packed gravel after a short distance and curved up through a wooded hillside. Jackson pressed the gas. At this point, it didn't matter if Anderson saw him. If Renee was out here, he would find her.

At the top of the hill, the driveway widened into a parking lot. Next to Anderson's Lexus sat a new SUV. So they were not alone. As he pulled in, Jackson called Schak, didn't get an answer, and left a location and request for backup. Anderson had climbed out of his car and was staring at the large A-frame building nestled in the fir trees.

Jackson joined him, his hand on his gun. "Do you own this property?"

"My business partner and I do." Anderson's voice was soft and calm, like a man in dream walk. "We had planned to reopen it, but then the recession hit and money dried up. Then we ran into problems with the kitchen and county building codes, so we put it on the market and couldn't sell it. So it sits here, running up property taxes."

"Whose car is that?"

"I don't know. I didn't expect anyone but maybe Renee to be here."

"Please get back in your car. This could be dangerous." Jackson wanted to hear the sound of River's vehicle behind him.

"I'm going in to get her." Anderson started up the brick path.

Jackson grabbed him by the shoulder. "Get back in your car and drive away. Now!"

A door banged open and Jackson looked toward the building. Someone stepped out. The person wore a dark, puffy down-filled jacket, jeans, and a knit cap. Another gang member. With a gun aimed at him.

Jackson pulled up his Sig Sauer. "Drop your weapon!"

The perp started to run toward him.

"Drop it!"

The perpetrator staggered on, making a strange noise, weapon held out.

Jackson had no choice. He fired twice in rapid succession.

The gunman dropped to the ground. Weapon still drawn, Jackson moved toward the fallen body. Doubt and dread slammed him like a rolling boulder. Something was wrong! He charged up the path. The perp's face had one side pressed against the red brick. The profile he could see was suddenly very familiar.

No!

Jackson dropped to his knees and rolled the still body to its back. No!

Dear god, he'd killed the mother of his child.

CHAPTER 40

As she pulled into the parking area, two shots rang out. River saw the perp go down. She cut the engine and leaped from her car, Glock drawn. Instinctively, she scanned the scene in all directions as she ran toward Jackson. Anderson sat in his car, like a man in a trance, and a figure darted out from behind the A-frame building, then bolted into the trees. What the hell was going on?

"Jackson! Are you okay?" Her heart pounded as she ran. Where was Renee?

Jackson knelt next to a small figure in dark clothes. Similar clothes to what the second courier had worn. River stared at the bleeding body. A woman! She glanced at Jackson and saw no blood on him, but the expression on his face scared her. "What happened?"

"I shot Renee. She had a gun." The hollow voice of a man in shock.

River stared at the lifeless woman. Her hands had been duct-taped to the gun. Oh christ. A cruel set up. But this wasn't over. "Call for backup. We have a runner."

Jackson's eyes focused and he reached for his cell phone.

"I'm going after him." She squeezed Jackson's shoulder. "It's not your fault."

River pushed to her feet and pounded toward the woods. Her legs were still sore from yesterday's bicycle chase and running had never come naturally to her. She felt heavy and awkward and out of shape. Still, she pushed as hard as she could, jacket flapping in the cold. She passed the back of the A-frame and ran along the edge of a grassy courtyard. Ahead, the stand of trees thickened. As best she could tell, the perp had gone into the woods just ahead to the left, where the courtyard ended. She spotted a trail and raced toward it.

As she left the clearing, the trees closed around her and blocked out the sun. River focused on the path and kept running. She listened for the sound of footsteps but could only hear her own labored breath. The path narrowed and wet branches slapped her arms as she pounded down the muddy trail. Where did this lead?

A sense of doom and pointlessness clenched her overworked heart. She wasn't a woodsy person and the perp had a head start. She told herself to let him go, to wait for a search team. His car was in the parking lot and they would soon have his ID.

But she kept running, following the curves and dips as the path climbed the hillside. The terrain grew steeper and she became aware that it dropped off dramatically on her left. Ferns grew thick on the forest floor. Where did this lead? To the butte? If so, once the perp made it to the top, several new paths leading down would be open to him. If he made it to the other side, he could hitchhike back to Eugene…or to Cottage Grove. If he was resourceful, he could elude them and leave the state. If he was rich, he could leave the country.

River pressed on.

A minute later, she heard a startled cry. Had he slipped and fallen?

She rounded a rock-walled curve and saw a glimpse of maroon coloring below the path to her left. She slowed and approached with caution, pulling her weapon up with both hands. The man had fallen to a narrow ledge about twelve feet below the path. Beyond the ledge was a steep drop-off. He struggled to climb to his feet but cried out and collapsed on his knees. Hearing her winded breath, the perp looked up. Did he seem familiar? Maybe one of the men in Dakota's vacation photos? As far as she could tell, he didn't have a gun. "Show me your hands."

He laughed, a short dry sound, and held them out. "I think you're pretty safe up there. But my ankle might be broken. How are you going to get me out of here?"

River had never had a suspect in this situation before. A surge of power traveled through her body. Could she make him tell her everything? "Why should I help you? Why not just leave you to die the way you left Renee?"

"Hey, don't misread that. I didn't kidnap Renee. I came out here to set her free."

River didn't believe him but wanted him to keep talking. "Who did kidnap Renee?"

"I thought Dakota might have done it. That's why I came up here to check." Pain made his voice breathy and hard to understand.

"You taped a gun to Renee's hands and sent her out to be shot by the police."

"I needed time to get away, and I didn't want to be blamed for the kidnapping."

"Renee is dead and I'm sure you'll do time for it."

He looked away.

"What's your name?"

"If you don't know, I'm not saying. Anything could still happen. This isn't over."

"You're right; it's not. When I walk away, you'll be here alone. In a few hours, it'll be freezing as well as dark. If you're lucky, you'll die quickly. But it could take days. And you sound like you're in pain." River couldn't believe what she was saying. Was this how her father had felt when he killed those women? To have the power of life and death?

No. She wasn't like him. She wanted to set things right.

"You won't leave me." The perp didn't sound that sure.

He *was* right though. She wouldn't leave him to die, even if he had killed two women. "Why did you sic the dog on Dakota?"

The man on the ledge was silent.

River turned and walked away. How much time did she have before backup arrived? What could she learn? And would it hold up in court? Either way, she had to know. She kept walking, noticing that her daylight was fading fast.

"Hey, you can't leave me here." His voice was faint but filled with panic.

River stopped but kept her feet moving in place for a moment.

"Don't leave me. I'll tell you everything."

River turned around and sauntered back. "Who are you?"

"Austin Hartwell."

"Why did you kill Dakota?"

"She broke the rules." He moaned in pain.

"What rules?"

"The club rules. No crimes for personal gain. No one gets hurt."

"A crime club?" *Good glory.* "No one gets hurt? But you killed Dakota and Renee."

"None of that was ever supposed to happen. Dakota got herself into trouble and fucked up everything."

River heard footsteps climbing the hill. Her time was up. "We're right here," she called out. "And we need a rescue team." Hartwell would probably recant everything, but now that she knew the basics, they could find the other club members. Once their leader was charged with murder, someone would talk.

CHAPTER 41

Wednesday, January 11, 8:15 p.m.

Lead filled his legs as Jackson trudged up the sidewalk to Jan's house. How could he tell Katie he'd killed her mother? How could he make her understand when he didn't understand himself? River and Schak had both offered to break the news to his daughter, but he had to be the one.

The porch light flickered on and the door opened. Katie stood in the frame, looking hopeful. "Did you find her?"

"Yes and no. Let's go inside. Your aunt Jan needs to hear this too."

"What do you mean? You're scaring me." Katie grabbed his arm as he pushed through the door.

Jan rushed into the living room, already in her pajamas. "Tell me you found her."

"We did, but it didn't go well. Let's sit down." Jackson wanted to get this over with more than anything he'd ever faced. Yet he had to go slow, so Katie would know what it was like to be there. She had to understand and forgive him. He hated himself enough for both of them.

Katie clutched her shirt in her hands. "Don't tell me she's dead."

Jackson plunged in. "She was being held in an empty bed-and-breakfast near Spencer Butte. When I arrived, there was a car I didn't recognize, so I assumed the kidnapper was there. And he was." Sharp stabbing pains drilled into Jackson's gut. He couldn't bear to see his daughter's face when he said it. Why hadn't he let someone else do this?

Katie and Jan both sat on the edge of the couch, waiting, hands twisting in their laps.

"Someone came out of the house. They had a gun and they were dressed like the gang member who picked up the ransom yesterday. I yelled for them to drop the gun." His breath was suddenly shallow and Jackson felt light-headed. "The person ran toward me instead. Holding a gun. I had no choice but to shoot. That's my training. That's how I stay alive."

The house was silent and neither woman seemed to move or breathe.

"I fired two shots and the person with the gun went down. But when I went over, I saw that it was a woman."

Katie sucked in her breath so sharply it had to hurt. Jackson felt the pain too.

Just say it. "Her hands had been duct-taped to the gun. The kidnapper sent her out to distract us so he could get away." Jackson knew Hartwell wasn't actually the kidnapper but that didn't matter right now.

"You shot Mom?"

Like a knife in his heart. "I didn't know it was her. I'm so sorry." Hot tears filled his eyes and he fought the tide of emotion. Katie needed him to be strong.

Jan lurched forward and hugged him. "Oh, you poor man." She cried and squeezed until he thought he might pass out.

Katie just sobbed, shoulders heaving. A silent deluge of grief. Jackson freed himself from Jan and sat next to his daughter. "You have to forgive me. It's not my fault." Yet he knew he would never forgive himself.

After a long moment, she leaned her head on his shoulder and he finally let his tears flow.

* * *

Wednesday, January 11, 7:05 p.m.

"Maybe you should leave us alone for a few minutes." Evans needed Mrs. Murray to step outside. The hospital had called earlier to tell Evans that Lyla was awake, but so far, all the young woman would say was that she didn't remember much.

Karen Murray had a new worry line on her forehead, but she patted her daughter's hand and said, "Tell her what happened."

After the mother left, Evans tried again. "I understand it was an initiation and you don't want your friends to go to jail, but—"

"They're not my friends." Lyla's voice was soft but angry.

"I agree. They're not. And my concern is that the practice will continue until someone dies or is crippled for life. Do you want that to happen to another young woman?"

Lyla closed her eyes. "No."

"Then tell me their names. Tell me why they beat you so badly."

Lyla was silent.

"We know who they are. Taylor Harris and Dakota Anderson. And we will prosecute even without your help. But if Taylor knows you're willing to testify, we can probably reach a plea agreement and save everyone the pain and expense of a trial."

"Why just Taylor?"

Of course—she didn't know. "Dakota Anderson is dead."

After a long moment, Lyla suddenly cried out, "It wasn't supposed to be like that."

"What was it supposed to be like? Do the initiations have rules?" Evans wanted this woman to open up and help her understand. "Tell me everything."

* * *

Lyla didn't really know what the initiation was supposed to be like because the other women in the house hadn't talked about it. But she knew they'd all been through it and had not only survived, but thrived, in the Potter house. And she'd wanted to join so badly. Even though she'd told the detective she didn't remember anything, the details of that night were burned in her brain. And they came flooding back to her.

She'd downed a can of Moonshot, hoping the caffeine would give her courage and the alcohol would make her a little numb. She'd waited until the last minute to leave, then hurried out into the chilly night. From her tiny apartment she walked five blocks toward campus, noticing other students and wondering how each of them survived the pressure. The endless reading, studying, and memorizing. Biking to work in the cold to wash dishes for a paycheck that barely covered the rent. Could she survive three more years of it? Probably not without the help of the house she was about to join. The upper-class girls had cheat sheets, class notes, and old term papers to work from. And some had family money to share. All of it would help get her through. She wasn't as smart or as confident as her mother thought and failure was not an option. Her mother expected a return on her investment.

Lyla crossed Eighteenth Avenue and entered the cemetery across from Mac Court. She'd passed by it a hundred times and until tonight hadn't given much thought to its purpose and reason for being on campus. Tonight, the bones of the dead seemed to hum in the ground below, but not in a comforting way. Goose bumps formed on her arms and the laughter in the distance seemed to mock her. Only a fool would put up with everything she'd endured this week. A fool, or a terrified teenager a thousand miles from home.

She hurried through the headstones, using her miniature flashlight to find the statue. Her instructions were to be there at eight, strip naked, sit, and wait for the assault. But it was near freezing, and for a moment, she couldn't make herself take off her clothes. What if they didn't show up for an hour? They'd promised that tonight would be painful but fast.

Unlike the hour Monday when she'd sat naked under bright lights while her *sisters* wrote nasty comments all over her body with a black felt pen. This time she would endure a solitary hazing, *customized* for her. Lyla suspected someone had read an essay she wrote about her fear of cemeteries and decided this was the perfect spot. The dead didn't scare her anymore though. What frightened her were the living, laughing women who were about to hurt and humiliate her.

Lyla peeled off her jacket, an old zip-up fleece she didn't care about, and set it on the ground. She pulled off her jeans next and folded them on top of the jacket. Before yanking off her shirt, she looked around, not seeing another soul in the graveyard. Even in the dark, she could see the outlines of students across the street, passing the old basketball court. But in the cover of trees, they couldn't see her. Lyla stuffed her bra and panties into her jacket pockets and dropped down on the pile of clothes. Keeping her socks on, she pulled her legs up to her chest and wrapped her arms around them, protecting herself from the frigid air as much as she could.

She dreaded the assault that was coming, yet she wanted it now rather than later. Was that the point of making her sit naked in the freezing night air? To force her to look forward to the beating? To actually begin to crave it as an end to the cold, dread, and humiliation?

After a long stretch that seemed like fifteen minutes, her teeth began to clatter and her back ached from tensing against the temperature. Should she give up and go home? What if she did? Would she be rejected or have to endure something worse tomorrow?

Leaves crackled behind her and she braced herself, afraid to even turn. A split second later, something putrid and gooey hit her in the back. Dog shit, she suspected. Lyla clamped her teeth together. It would wash off, she told herself, easier than the damn black marker had. Taylor suddenly stood in front of her. She drew back her arm and slung a handful of dirt into Lyla's chest. But it wasn't just dirt. Wiggly worms dripped and crawled down her body. Lyla shuddered and picked them off her stomach, not wanting them anywhere near her private parts.

Another woman named Dakota, who no longer lived in the house, doused her with cold water. The shock of it pushed her over the edge. Lyla jumped to her feet, anger burning in her chest. She was torn between the impulse to run and the need to strike back. But her rising was their cue.

The assault began.

Taylor grabbed her by the elbows and pulled her arms together behind her back, while Dakota rushed forward and struck her with a golf club. The first blow landed under her left breast and the pain hurt more than anything she'd ever experienced. Lyla saw stars and felt like she couldn't breathe. Another blow nailed her rib cage, and in the searing pain, Lyla thought she heard a crack. She tried to stay upright but the pain pushed her to her knees.

"Get up, you little cunt, or we'll make this worse."

Taylor grabbed her by the ear and twisted, pulling her up at the same time. Lyla was on her feet but she felt foggy and unable to think straight. Someone began to beat her back with what felt like a bat. Then a blow landed on the back of her head. The pain was a fireball of explosion. Blood rushed out of her brain, she felt her eyes roll back in their sockets, and she dropped to her knees again. Before she passed out, Lyla's last thought was *If I die, I hope my mother gets her tuition back.*

But what she said to the detective was, "If you promise she'll only get probation or something, I'll tell you what I know."

The detective looked annoyed. "Let me make a call."

CHAPTER 42

Friday, January 13, 2:30 p.m.

Jackson pushed away his last-minute doubts, squared his shoulders, and walked into Sergeant Lammers' office. "Sorry I'm late. I just had a long interrogation session."

"I hope it was connected to the kidnapping case." His boss signaled him to sit down.

"Indirectly. Ashley Harris confessed to vandalizing the Elks Lodge last summer. It was her initiation ticket into the crime club founded by Austin Hartwell."

"The crime club?" Lammers pulled off her glasses and gave him a look.

"A group of bored, rich young people who mostly party and vacation together. But to belong, they have to commit a crime every once in a while, just to prove they're sporting." Jackson couldn't hide his disgust.

"For fuck's sake."

"They have rules though. No one can get hurt, they can't use the crime for personal gain, and they have to leave some kind of calling card." Agent River had given him just enough information to pry the details out of Ashley. He'd also used the assault charge against her sister, Taylor, as leverage. Jackson continued, "But once you've committed a crime, it gets easier, and Dakota Anderson finally kidnapped her future stepmother for the money. She'd run up nearly seventy thousand in credit card debt and we assume she was feeling desperate."

"How does a young person run up that kind of debt?" Lammers shook her head. "Never mind. Tell me how and why Dakota died."

"Our theory is that Austin Hartwell saw her televised plea for help with the ransom and decided she was a wildcard and a risk to the rest of the club. We think he waited for her outside her apartment, lured her out to the dog park, then commanded his Presa Canario to kill her. A dog he bought from Renaldi, by the way. The two are friends and that's how Dakota met Renaldi." Jackson slumped a little, knowing the real work on the case was just beginning. "Hartwell isn't talking and he's hired Roger Barnsworth to represent him."

"Can we connect Hartwell's dog to her death?"

"The lab found nonhuman saliva on Dakota's necklace and we're still waiting for the state lab to compare the dog's DNA to the saliva. But the county's animal expert pulled seeds from the dog's fur that match seeds found at the crime scene and on Dakota. So it's starting to add up."

"Will Harris testify that Hartwell knew about the other crimes?"

"Yes. The DA offered her a probation plea deal, so she's given us all the names and crimes she knows about."

"Good work, Jackson. This was a fucked-up case."

"I had a lot of help. And we caught a break showing up at the hostage location when Hartwell was with Renee." Jackson didn't feel lucky. He wished they'd been ten minutes late. Renee might still be dead, but at least it wouldn't be his doing.

"It's not your fault," Lammers said, as if she could read his mind. "It was a clean shooting. Tragic yes, but not a mistake."

"It's hard for me to see it that way." Jackson took a deep breath. "I have to resign. I don't think I can carry a gun anymore." His CAT scan the day before hadn't looked good either, and they wanted to increase his meds for a while.

Lammers gave him a long hard look. "I understand how you feel, but I want you to give it more time. I don't accept your resignation, but I will put you on paid leave of absence."

A wave of relief rolled over him. "Thank you. My daughter wants me to be home with her for a while."

"Do what you have to do, then come back. This town needs you."

He turned to leave. At times he hated this job, but he wondered if he could live without it.

ABOUT THE AUTHOR

Photograph by Gwen Rhoads, 2011

L.J. Sellers is a native of Eugene, Oregon, the setting of her thrillers. She's an award-winning journalist and bestselling novelist, as well as a cyclist, social networker, and thrill-seeking fanatic. A long-standing fan of police procedurals, she counts John Sandford, Michael Connelly, Ridley Pearson, and Lawrence Sanders among her favorites. Her own novels, featuring Detective Jackson, include *The Sex Club*, *Secrets to Die For*, *Thrilled to Death*, *Passions of the Dead*, *Dying for Justice*, *Liars, Cheaters & Thieves*, and *Rules of Crime*. In addition, she's penned three standalone thrillers: *The Baby Thief*, *The Gauntlet Assassin*, and *The Suicide Effect*. When not plotting crime, she's also been known to perform standup comedy and occasionally jump out of airplanes.